PRAISE FOR STINA LINDENBLATT

Tell Me When

TELL ME WHEN is a heartbreaking and emotional story. Be prepared to do nothing else but read once you start this book! —*Fresh Fiction*

"I felt that even though the subject matter is a little over used, Tell Me When did it in a way that was rawer, darker and more realistic and that made it feel fresh and unique."—*Bookish Treasures*

"If you're looking for an exciting read, filled with secrets, mystery, danger, and realism, this story is a perfect match! I give, Tell Me When, by Stina Lindenblatt, 4 Intense, Powerful, Healing, and 'Falling in Love' filled Stars!"—*A bookish Escape*

"I. LOVED. THIS. BOOK!!!!"—*Seeking Book Boyfriends*

"If you are looking for well written story that will take you on a ride of highs and lows of our human emotional states and of the good and the bad of what life is willing to offer, then I highly suggest you read this fantastic story!"—*Biblio Belles Book Blog*

Let Me Know

"I love Stina's writing style. It's very emotive, and flows beautifully. I felt connected to the characters from very early on and cried several times at the pain these characters go through"—*Reading Realm Blog*

"Overall, I think Ms Lindenblatt did a phenomenal job writing this series. From the intriguing plot, interesting and unique characters, to the overall well written storyline, this series is a must read"—*Tyhada Reads*

"This was an amazing read, I could not out this down. The author really wrote this one so beautifully. Let me say that the author's writing bought out so many emotions from me, I just loved it"—*Lustful Literature*

This One Moment

"A thrill ride that kept me on the edge of my seat, *This One Moment* is hot, intense, and filled with emotion—contemporary romance at its finest. Nolan stole my heart from page one, and Hailey was a heroine with whom I could truly identify. I was in reader heaven!"—*New York Times* bestselling author Rachel Harris

"A well-written story that kept me entertained from start to finish."—*Harlequin Junkie*

"I loved this book; this is romance at its best, this is that perfect ending we all read romance for, this is an absolutely beautifully told love story."—*Guilty Pleasures Book Reviews*

"Very satisfying . . . Stina Lindenblatt is a new author to me and a very good one I may add. . . . I will sure keep an eye on her in the future. She is really worth it!"—*Collector of Book Boyfriends & Girlfriends*

"The story is amazing and the suspense is thrilling."—*Just One More Chapter*

"Filled with emotion, intensity, a lot of sexual tension and the perfect amount of heat."—*About That Story*

My Song for You

"Romantic angst powers this fast-paced novel, and readers will return to the series to learn more about the enigmatic side characters whose own stories are waiting to be told."—*Publishers Weekly*

"The author has an amazing and deep connection with her characters. . . . I loved every single page."—*Extreme Damage Blog*

"From the first to the last page—greatness unfolded."—*Ellie Is Uhm . . . A Bookworm*

"Filled with romance, misunderstandings, lies and a whole lot of heat . . . [*My Song for You*] has everything to satisfy the romance itch in all of us."—*Twin Spin*

"Six stars—Stina Lindenblatt has a skill to write heroes with some depth like few can."—*Collectors of Book Boyfriends & Girlfriends*

"Oooh, a secret baby story with a twist . . . and I liked that twist. I also really liked that this was somewhat of a friends-to-lovers story. . . A really good, entertaining read and I enjoyed it a lot. I'd definitely recommend it."—*Smitten with Reading*

I Need You Tonight

"Ms. Lindenblatt has penned another remarkable read for this series. . . . Full of exquisite heat and passion, and the ending brought happy tears to my eyes. . . . I would highly recommend *I Need You Tonight*."—*Book Magic*

"*I Need You Tonight* is one of those books that you go into thinking one thing and end up getting your mind blown because you were not expecting the emotion that this made you feel. Honestly, this had to have been the best book of the series because of that."—*Life of a Crazy Mom*

"[Stina Lindenblatt's] writing shows superb talent and care for both the storyline and her characters. This is not a book you want to pass the chance at reading."—*Ellie Is Uhm . . . A Bookworm*

"There are so many, many things that I loved about this story. . . . I hadn't realized I'd been missing and I was craving the Pushing Limits boys until this one came along. And it came with a bang!" —*Collectors of Book Boyfriends & Girlfriends*

ALSO BY STINA LINDENBLATT

CONTEMPORARY ROMANCES

Carson Brothers Series

One More Chance

One More Secret

Pushing Limits Series

This One Moment

My Song For You

I Need You Tonight

Lost in You Series

Tell Me When

Let Me Know

ROMANTIC COMEDY NOVELS

By The Bay Series

Decidedly Off Limits

Decidedly with Baby

Decidedly with Love

Decidedly with Mistletoe

Decidedly by Chance

Decidedly with Luck

Decidedly with Wishes

Visit stinalindenblattauthor.com for more books

LET ME KNOW

LOST IN YOU DUET, BOOK 2

STINA LINDENBLATT

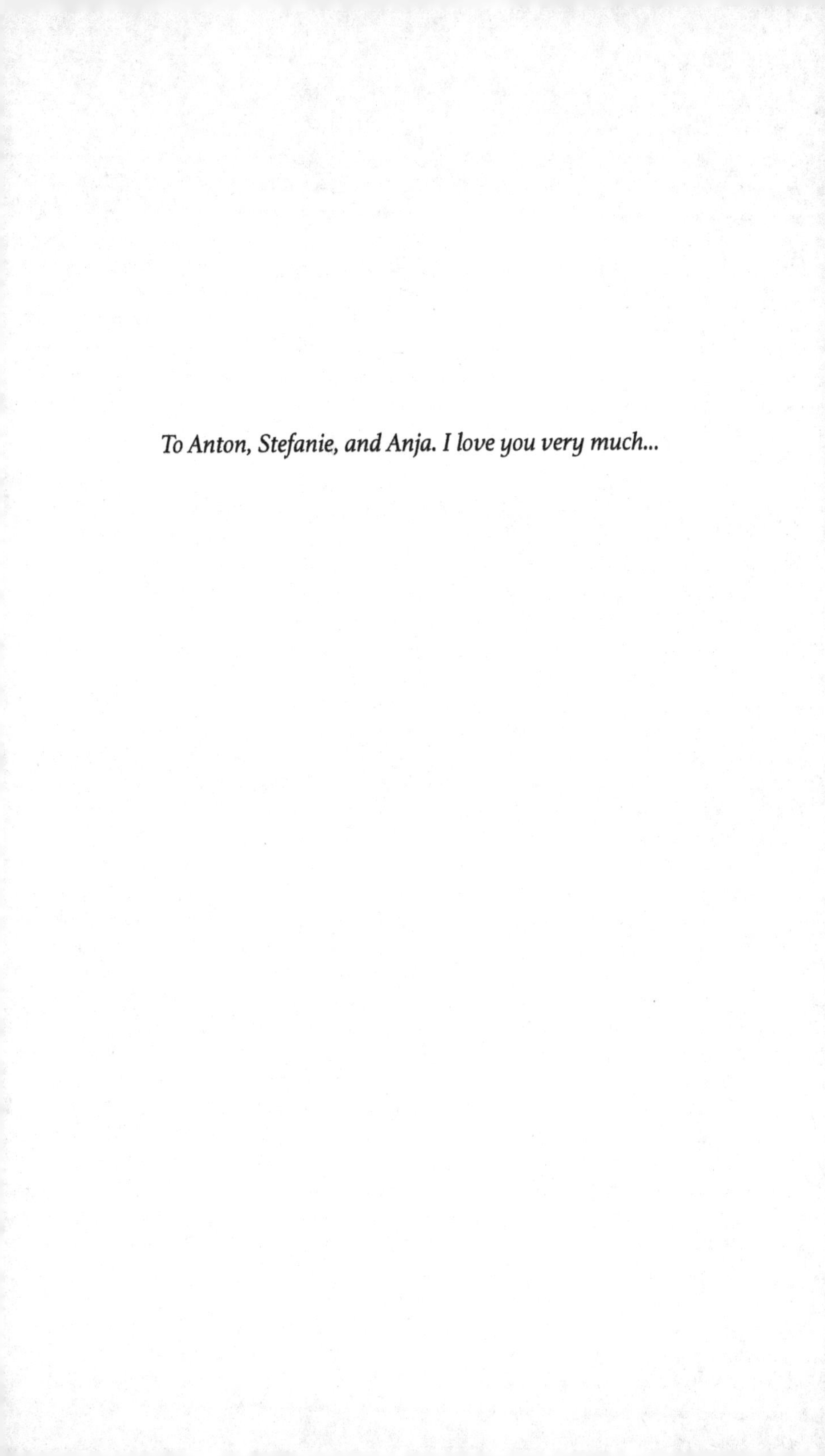

To Anton, Stefanie, and Anja. I love you very much...

LET ME KNOW

1

___

AMBER

I used to think there was no better place than home. I was
wrong. There's no better place than lying beside Marcus,
naked, with nowhere to go for the next...

I roll over and check his alarm clock on the pile of textbooks by
his bed, then groan. The midmorning sunlight pours through the
slats in the blinds and nudges me further awake.

"Mornin', Kitten," a husky voice says behind me. Marcus plants
a soft kiss on my right shoulder, the location of my lotus flower
tattoo.

I shift around and burrow my face in his neck. My lips touch
the soft skin and I breathe in his faint spicy scent. The smell I
associate with feeling safe.

His injured arm rests on my waist. My version of heaven.

"Emma's gonna be here in twenty minutes," I murmur, my lips
still on his neck.

He strokes my back, brushing the hideous scars as if they don't
exist. "You don't have to go. Stay. We can drive down together." His
voice drops to a sexy rumble, which is exactly why I can't stay.

"Maybe if you weren't taking your finals over the next few days."
I give him a quick kiss. "But you have to study, and you can't do that

I

if you keep trying to"—another kiss—"convince me you study better in bed." I look pointedly at his ethics and engineering textbook lying haphazardly on the floor and peer up at him again. "I'm not sure how having sex with me will help you do well on your exams."

I'm still surprised we're even able to have sex since he's recovering from the gunshot wound. And even though he's tried to convince me otherwise, I'm pretty sure "regular sex with your girlfriend" was not on his discharge orders.

Marcus flops back on the pillows. His eyes sparkle with life as his lips curve into a half smile. "Hey, if you can get an A on your math final..."

I punch him lightly on his good arm. "I didn't get that 'cause I was having sex with you. I got it because Brittany helped me study, and my math teacher's a saint."

After studying with Marcus for most of the semester so I'd pass math, I'd walked out of the final in order to be with him in the hospital after his stepfather shot him. My professor contacted me the next day and after confirming my story, he offered to let me make up the exam the following afternoon.

"Anyway," I continue, "as much as I'm gonna miss you and your math jokes, Emma and I need to spend time together before you join me." I drape my arm over his hips and snuggle close while pretending I don't have to drag myself away from him anytime soon. While pretending the next few days won't be tough for Emma and her family, and for me and mine.

It will be our first Christmas without Trent and Michael.

Marcus rolls onto his side again, and his injured arm, currently free of its sling, squeezes my waist. I'm so attuned to everything about him, I can't help but notice his jaw muscle twitch. The movement is small, easy to miss by most. I trace my finger along the healing flesh, wishing my touch could whisk away his pain.

"Are you sure about me joining you?"

I lean over and kiss his jaw. "You're not backing out of this." *I need you with me.* My lips trail along his unshaven jaw, his one-day growth teasing me as much as I'm teasing him. My mouth finds his and I tenderly kiss him, letting him know without words how much I need him. He's not just my boyfriend—he's one of my best friends. And one of the few people who understands what I've been through.

His lips part and I deepen the kiss, consuming him, tasting his very soul. My mind goes blank as to what I'm supposed to do this morning. As far as I'm concerned, the only place I need to be is here, kissing Marcus.

A muffled bang outside his room intrudes on our moment. With a level of willpower I didn't realize I possessed, I reluctantly pull away. This time Marcus doesn't protest.

I scoot off the bed and slip on my panties and his red T-shirt from the floor. The T-shirt I claimed for my own once I started staying here on a regular basis. The last thing I want is for Chase to accidentally see me naked while I walk to the bathroom.

Marcus pulls on his boxers and jeans. I help him secure his sling, fussing over him like he's a child. He doesn't seem to care. If anything, he enjoys it. From what I've learned about his childhood, he didn't get much of that from his own mother. Until recently, he thought he was unworthy of someone's love.

With a quick kiss on his cheek, I prove to him once again that he is worthy—something he still struggles to believe.

Chase is in the living room setting up an...oversized carpeted tree? Everything about it is carpeted, including the green branches.

"You bought a scratching post?" I ask, taking in the array of cat toys scattered on the floor.

Chase doesn't seem to notice that I'm standing here in nothing but Marcus's T-shirt, which barely skims the top of my thighs. He gives us his usual goofy grin. "I wasn't sure if Smoky had one, and this one looks cool."

Marcus laughs. "Dude, don't you think you went a little overboard, 'specially since Amber is *my* girlfriend?"

The smile wipes off Chase's face. "I've always wanted a cat." He glances around at the cat toys and shrugs. "Sorry, guess I did get a little carried away."

I give him a one-armed hug. "Well, I think it's sweet. And I'm sure Smoky will love it."

Marcus rolls his eyes. "Great. How am I supposed to compete with that?"

I pull away from Chase. "Smoky already likes you."

Marcus ensnares me in his good arm and kisses the top of my head. The arm captured in the sling is pressed between us, but that doesn't seem to bother him. "I wasn't talking about Smoky. I was referring to you."

Chase chuckles. "I think Amber has proved that she likes you. Or at least that's the impression I got last night."

My face heats up several degrees at the implication behind those words. Marcus grabs a pillow from the couch and hurls it at his best friend. Chase ducks and the pillow lands on the floor with a soft thud.

Chase is still chuckling as I hurry into the bathroom.

Marcus doesn't follow me this time, which is just as well. If he did, I wouldn't be ready to leave when Emma shows up.

A few body parts that remember our steamier showers together tingle at the memory. It's amazing what that man can do, even with an injured shoulder.

The buzzer shrieks as I enter the living room, showered and ready to go. Chase answers it and Emma's voice crackles through the intercom. He lets her into the building, then heads to the bathroom.

As soon as the door clicks shut, Marcus pulls me into his good arm and we make up for the several days we'll be apart. The kisses are sweet and tender. Anything more and I won't be able to leave.

Chase turns on the shower, and the stream of water hammering the bathtub covers any sound escaping my lips as I tease Marcus with a few sexy noises I know drive him wild. His free arm slides down to the curve of my spine and pulls me closer.

A loud knock startles us from our kiss. Marcus murmurs a curse against my lips and removes his hand from my back. I instantly miss the warmth of that hand and wish we could have another hour alone before I have to leave. Even if it's just to curl up on the couch and discuss our favorite TV shows or our plans for the day.

He lets Emma in. Like me, her long blond hair is pulled up in a ponytail. She's wearing a soft-pink ski jacket that I suspect she bought in a pricier store than Marcus and I would ever shop in. Even her slim-fitting jeans proclaim "I love to shop."

She hands me a brown paper bag with Five Point Café printed on it. "Here's your special order." The corners of her mouth creep up as she holds in her laugh. She knows it's not for me, as much as I love their chicken noodle soup.

"I got something to help you remember me while I'm away," I tell Marcus.

He takes the bag from me. Not a hint of curiosity marks his face. Laughter crinkles around his eyes. "You're the best. You know that, right?"

"Hey, you ready?" Emma asks. Although she might be talking about the trip, I know what she's really asking—am I ready to spend Christmas without Trent and Michael?

I give Marcus a quick kiss on the cheek. "See you in two days."

With his gaze still on me, he says to Emma, "Drive carefully. You've got something that's important to me."

Emma giggles. "Yes, Mom."

I could have driven home myself, but Emma and I have plenty of catching up to do, which we haven't been able to start on since I took the first steps toward repairing our friendship two weeks ago. Schoolwork came first for both of us. Emma can't risk her basketball scholarship, and I'm programmed to want perfect grades.

Marcus escorts us downstairs and helps load my suitcase into Emma's trunk. In the side mirror, I watch his building grow smaller as Emma and I drive away. The vanilla-scented air freshener tries to push away the memory of his spicy scent, but I refuse to let it go.

"Reporters have been calling my parents about the psycho's trial," Emma says.

I take several deep breaths. I'm not looking forward to that part.

After my ordeal last spring, Mom kept the reporters at bay while I recovered in the hospital from my injuries. I've never been comfortable talking to them—or talking in public, period—even when I used to play varsity basketball. After what I went through with Paul, there was no way I could tell the media what happened. Not if it meant the horrific details of what I went through would be splashed across the page for all to see. Fortunately the cops kept quiet on certain details that were being saved for the trial.

But soon everything will become common knowledge. Every word Paul and I say on the stand could wind up front-page news.

"I'm sorry," I tell her.

Emma shoots me a puzzled glance. "For what?"

"For everything. For what Paul did and for the reporters."

"I don't know why you're apologizing. You didn't do anything, Amber. You've gotta stop apologizing for what everybody else does."

The corner of her lips curl into a smirk though her eyes hold an edge of sadness. "When we were younger, Trent quickly figured out your habit of taking the blame for everything. Your brother knew it, too. You made it too easy for them. You're not responsible for what that psychopath did to them or to you, and you're not responsible for the reporters. All they want is a story."

"Have your parents talked to them?"

Emma nods. "They issued a statement that we're looking forward to closure in Trent's..." I can practically hear her throat close up. "In Trent's murder. And the trial can't come soon enough for us."

Wish I could share those sentiments. I'm freaking over the trial and having to speak in front of everyone, and how everyone I know will find out details I'd rather keep secret. The only person I want there with me, other than my mom and grandma, is Marcus. I don't want Emma and her family to hear everything Paul did to me, beyond what's already public knowledge from the original news stories and the details I did share with her. Marcus knows. They don't.

"Have they contacted you?" she asks.

"All questions have to be directed to the DA," I say, sounding like a spokesperson from the DA's office.

"How come?"

"They don't want me accidentally saying anything they're saving for the trial, you know, to prove Paul's guilt."

Emma pulls her gaze from the road and narrows her eyes at me. The stark coldness in them causes me to shiver. "Why do you call that sick psychopath by his name?"

I look away, unable to take the pain in her eyes. "Because before I knew what he was, he was my friend."

"And after everything he did to you?"

I shrug, the movement mechanical. "Habits are hard to break, I guess." Even when he turned into the monster everyone knows him as, there were still moments when I thought my old friend would return, and he would realize how much he was hurting me. It was in those rare moments when he did show compassion, doing things for me that under other circumstances would be considered sweet. Like bringing me my favorite magazines to read.

Emma nods slowly as if reasoning her way through everything I said. "You mean like Stockholm Syndrome?"

"Yeah, something like that."

We spend the rest of the trip singing along to the pop station as we drive on Interstate 80. Already I miss the classic rock station Marcus and I love listening to. That Trent loved listening to. Emma, not so much.

"Things between you and Marcus seem to be going well," Emma says as we turn off the interstate and head down the main road toward our hometown. Considering her brother was my boyfriend, whom I loved, I'm surprised at how casual she sounds. There's no pain in her voice, only curiosity.

A grin sneaks onto my face, despite my attempts to prevent it. Thinking about Marcus always has that effect on me. "They are. What about you and Liam?"

Her grin matches mine. "I like him. A lot. He knows how to make me smile. Something I'd almost forgotten how to do."

Because of me.

"Hey, can we stop at the mall first?" she asks. "I need to buy Liam a birthday present so I can mail it to him before the weekend."

"Yeah, okay." As long as we don't bump into anyone I know.

Once we reach the mall parking lot, we drive up and down packed rows of cars, searching for an empty spot. We eventually find one in another time zone.

Emma scoots out of the car. I remain seated, frozen on the warm car seat for a minute, until I realize I can't stay here forever. I can't keep hiding.

The biggest benefit of living in Chicago is that most people have long since forgotten about the stalking and kidnapping. I'm not Amber, the victim. I'm a nameless face in the crowd, like everyone else. In Chicago, I can escape the sympathetic looks that were all too common after the firefighter found me in Paul's burning building.

To the rest of the country, I was the nameless teen. To everyone in Crossfields, I was Amber, the girl who had been raped and tortured. The girl no one knew what to make of. The girl who was stared at or whispered about like some kind of freak show.

And this trip appears to be no exception.

As Emma and I walk through the mall, I feel all eyes on me, staring through my winter coat and long-sleeved T-shirt. Stripping me down to my dark secrets.

Emma steers me to the adult store, located in a wing that sees the fewest shoppers. A female mannequin stands in the window, wearing a white transparent baby-doll outfit with sheer white stockings reaching midthigh.

"This is where you're getting Liam a present?" I ask, voice part squeak, part awe.

Emma grins, a light blush hitting her cheeks. "More like a joke present. I bought his real gift in Chicago last week."

My gaze darts to the store again and my heart flutters in my chest, like a thousand butterflies searching for a way to break free. "I'll wait for you here." The last thing I want is to have a flashback because I spot a red slip, like the one a Victoria's Secret model might wear.

Emma tugs on my arm. "You have to come." Her voice is as squeaky as mine was a moment ago. "I can't go in there alone. I'll feel stupid."

I look between her and the store, digging my teeth into my lip. I owe her for being a crappy best friend after what happened with Paul, and I owe her for what Paul did to Trent. "Okay."

We walk into the store, with Emma practically dragging me in, and draw up short as our virgin voyage takes us into the land of erotic clothing and triple-X movies. My face heats up and feels as hot as Emma's appears, her blush now a supercharged red.

Emma giggles nervously as we walk down the aisle, beyond the sexy clothing and movies. She gives them a cursory glance. I focus on her and nothing else.

We end up at the rear of the store, at a wall containing everything from the mild to the shocking: multicolored condoms, edible body lotions, vibrators, sex toys. None of which I have a clue how to use. And I'm not about to read the directions to find out.

Emma removes a package containing small balls. She reads the description and her eyes go as wide as her mouth. She shoves it back onto the display rack, almost missing it in her haste, and moves on.

"One of the girls on the team made a sex video for her

boyfriend for Christmas." Her voice is low even though I'm the only person within hearing range.

"Seriously?" I didn't say it loud, but it feels as though the word bounced around the store at full volume. I look around to make sure no one's listening, not that they would know what we're talking about. No one's paying us any attention.

"I couldn't do that. What if it ends up on YouTube? She could get kicked off the team."

"Did you tell her that?"

"Yeah, but she trusts her boyfriend."

"But what if they break up?"

"I don't know. I've met him and he's nice, but it's still risky."

I laugh shortly. "Does that mean I don't have to worry about you showing up on YouTube, other than for something to do with basketball?"

"Definitely." She returns to searching through the items hanging on the wall. I select a bottle of strawberry-flavored body lotion, which seems a safe enough gift, and read the instructions.

"What about these?" Emma holds up a pair of pink fur-lined handcuffs.

My wrists and shoulders hurt, and my hands feel like they're floating in the air. I'm sitting, propped against a cold wall, the same temperature as the concrete floor. The cool air wraps itself around me and I shiver.

My breathing comes in fast, lungs fighting to draw in more air, which currently is evading them. The store blurs. I close my eyes and reach for something to steady me. My hand lands on something fairly solid. *It's only a memory. It can't hurt me. Paul can't hurt me.*

"Can I help y'all?" a male voice says with a faint Texas drawl. Whatever my hand is pressed against moves.

My eyelids snap open, and I peer into the deep blue eyes of a good-looking blond man. His jeans, light-denim-blue shirt, facial growth, and Stetson spell cowboy. His name tag spells store employee.

I pull my hand from his muscled chest.

"No, we're fine." I will my face to not heat up, which of course is already too late. I look at the bottle in my hand. "I was wondering what flavor to get."

An easy smile spreads on his face. "Strawberry's the most popular choice, though chocolate's up there too."

"I'll take strawberry." Marcus once told me he loves the smell of my hair, the result of my strawberry-scented shampoo.

Emma grabs a bottle of chocolate-flavored lotion. "This should be good enough," she says, eyeing the nearby merchandise.

"You sure?" the guy asks. "I've got some sex toys that are bound to get your boyfriends hot and bothered." He doesn't say it in a sleazy way. His tone is professional with a hint of teasing.

"Maybe next time." My gaze falls on a display of whips I hadn't noticed until now. My muscles tense at the memory of thin leather slicing across my back more times than I care to remember.

"Many people find whips result in an intense sexual release." He reaches for one and whacks it lightly against his palm. I flinch at the sound of it slapping his flesh.

All I want is for my fight-or-flight instinct to kick in so I can run, but my legs refuse to read the memo. My head feels foggy, not part of this world. I'm not having an out-of-body experience, and I'm not having an "in" body one, either. I'm neither here nor there—and I hate this feeling.

Em calls my name. It sounds distant. Foreign. And I'm unable to respond.

2

MARCUS

I slap my math book shut. The force of it is hard enough that I wouldn't be surprised if my eighty-year-old neighbor heard it through the thin walls and over the sound of her soap opera. If it weren't for that fuckhead, Frank, I'd already be finished with my exams and on the way to Crossfields with Amber. No thanks to him, I wasted several days in the hospital, recovering from being shot, and now I have to take four exams in two days. It was that or dwell on them over the Christmas break.

The only thing I want to dwell on is how great I feel when I hold Amber in my arms. I can almost smell the sweet strawberry scent that lingers on her, almost taste her tempting lips on mine. She's the one person who can make me feel whole. The one person in my fucked-up world who understands me.

I shove my chair away from my desk and retrieve my backpack from the floor, barely missing the stack of books next to it. As I stride out of my room, the buzzer for the building's main entrance screeches.

I push the intercom button. "Yeah?"

"This is Officer Mitchell from the Chicago Police. I need to speak to Marcus Reid."

My heart bounces a few extra times against my ribs for good measure. He's probably here about Frank, but no matter how many times I tell myself that, it doesn't stop the irritating feeling scraping inside my gut. The feeling I always get when dealing with cops. A situation that occurred all the time in my old neighborhood.

"Okay, I'll buzz you up." I push the button below the intercom. Even though I'm on my way out, no way am I discussing Frank where other tenants can overhear.

A few minutes later a sharp knock at the door drags me away from my less than pleasant thoughts about my stepfather. I open the door to reveal a uniformed officer with buzzed hair, and a build that can snap a drug user in half without any real exertion.

He flashes his credentials. "Marcus Reid?"

My eighty-year-old neighbor shuffles past, her hair as white as the dingy walls. Her old-woman scent of mothballs and lavender claws at my nostrils. I do my best not to scrunch up my nose and give her another reason to make my life miserable—beyond increasing the TV volume while I'm studying.

She eyes the cop as if he were her favorite actor from *Law & Order*. Then her gaze lands on me and her expression changes. To her, I'm nothing more than a worthless piece of shit. That much is obvious.

Fighting back the temptation to tell her where to go, I open the door wider and move aside to let the cop in. He steps inside the doorway but doesn't go much farther.

I close the door, blocking the woman's pinched expression. It's nothing I haven't already witnessed on her.

"I can't stay long," I point out. "I have two exams this afternoon."

"This won't take long," the cop says. "It's about Frank Wilson. He's been released on bail, and he and your mother denied the allegations that he raped your brother and sexually assaulted you. Is there anyone else who can substantiate your claims?"

His words are like nails hammered into my flesh, the shame of what my stepfather did to me digging deep. I'd rather let the memory die. I'd rather not admit to this man what Frank did to me, just like every fucking time I've had to tell the cops the same fucking details.

"You mean other than my dead brother?" I shake my head even though I do know someone. "I seriously doubt Ryan and I were his only victims. We moved away from home over three and a half years ago. Frank didn't become an outstanding member of society during that time. If he had, he wouldn't have tried to rape me the night Ryan was shot."

Giving no indication of what he's thinking, the officer glances at his notepad. "You're twenty, right?"

I nod. What the hell does that have to do with anything?

"You were sixteen when you left home?"

I nod again. "Once Ryan turned eighteen, he moved away and took me with him."

"Even though you were underage?"

"He knew if he left me with Frank, I would be his next victim. I would've rather died than have Frank rape me like he did my brother."

"Why didn't you and your brother contact the authorities?" His tone lacks any hint of compassion, but it's not judgmental, either. He's doing his job and beyond that, he doesn't care. Just like the cops in my old neighborhood.

I push away the anger snaking its way in, and I repeat what I've already told the cops. "Because what would they have done? Take us away, split us up, and put us in another hellhole? Ryan didn't want that, so he made me promise not to say anything to anyone. And yes, I might have been underage, but I can guarantee no one filed a police report. It's not like our mom and stepdad were worried and wanted us back."

The cop jots a brief note in his book.

"So what now?" I ask.

"Now you keep away from Mr. Wilson and we wait for the courts to decide how to proceed."

Fuck. "You're not looking into the possibility of other victims?"

"We've asked around, but until someone steps forward, there's nothing we can do."

My fingers curl into a fist, ready to slam into something, most likely the wall. Nothing has changed. No one cares about victims. Not when they come from my old shitty neighborhood. It's easier to ignore the problem than deal with it.

Before I can say anything, the apartment door opens, almost slamming into the cop. He steps away from the doorway, hand on gun.

Eyebrows drawn together, Chase looks between the officer and me. "Is this a bad time?"

"No," I tell him. "We're talking about Frank, and how everything Ryan and I went through means nothing. Like last time, when he killed Ryan."

Chase glares at the cop. "You mean that shithead gets to walk again?"

The cop doesn't so much as flinch at Chase's thorn-filled tone. "Mr. Wilson wasn't charged for the murder of Ryan Reid. It was ruled self-defense." Some self-defense. I'd gone home to talk to my mom last summer, and Frank had surprised me by being there. Unfortunately, dear old Mom wasn't there. Frank had pressed himself against my back and held his gun to my head—his way of convincing me to have sex with him. If Ryan hadn't picked that moment to show up, thanks to Chase telling him where I'd gone, I would have been the one who died. No way would I have let Frank rape me. He would have had to kill me first. But instead of killing me, he killed Ryan when my brother tried to protect me.

"For someone who goes around abusing and shooting his stepsons," Chase says, "the shithead sure gets a lot of get-out-of-jail passes."

Wariness creeps into the cop's eyes but his posture remains

rigid, cool. "There are no records that Marcus and Ryan were abused. Now if they had complained to someone, we would have a record of it and things would be different."

"Marcus and Ryan aren't the complaining type." Chase's tone is verging on a new territory for him. Dangerous.

"Other than a couple of hospital reports, none of which raised any alarms at the time, there's nothing to substantiate Marcus's claims." The cop nods at me when he says the last part.

"Broken bones and the need for stitches doesn't raise any alarms?" Chase steps forward. The cop holds his ground.

Worried Chase will do something we'll both regret, I place my hand on his shoulder. "Not when Ryan and I told the hospital we got them skateboarding," I say, mostly for Chase's benefit. We didn't have a choice. We knew the consequence if we didn't lie.

Chase huffs. I can't tell if it's because Ryan and I kept silent about what happened or because he had, too. He hadn't wanted to keep quiet about the beatings, but I hadn't given him much choice. He was young, and we were best friends. He knew once we were removed from our house, he and I would never see each other again. And that was asking a lot for a pair of eight-year-olds.

The cop gives me his card in case there's anything else I can add; otherwise, the DA will contact me when Frank goes to trial. At least, for now, the asswipe isn't getting away with shooting me. They haven't patted him on the back and walked away. Yet.

And not for the first, second, or hundredth time, I kick myself for letting Ryan's and my pride and fear and shame keep me from telling the truth about what Frank did to us for all those years. Our silence came at a cost. A cost that Alejandro—and possibly other boys—has had to pay. The only reason I even know about Alejandro is because the night I was shot, I had gone looking for him, thinking he was getting tight with a gang. It would have explained why he had been acting weird lately. Not once had I realized the truth: My stepfather had slithered his way into my fourteen-year-old friend's life and was doing to Alejandro what he had done to me—or maybe even worse. The night I was shot, I found them together, and in my attempts to protect Alejandro, I fought Frank. Being the coward that he is, Frank shot at me. But unlike my brother, I was able to duck out of the way. I was only wounded. And unlike my brother, I'm not willing to let Frank get away with what he's been doing, and I'm not willing to let him get off on self-defense, again.

At the thought of Frank's trial, my mind shifts to Amber and her upcoming ordeal. The Frank situation pisses me off, but she's my bigger priority. Although she hasn't said anything yet, it's easy to see she's scared. And even though she's seeing a therapist to help her deal with everything she's gone through, I want to be there for her and help her move on.

For us both to move on.

Together.

"What was that all about?" Chase asks once the cop is gone.

"He came to tell me that, big surprise, Frank's denying he raped Ryan or touched me. And since there's no proof, he's going to get away with it."

Chase frowns. "What kind of proof are they looking for? Videos? Fuck, this is ridiculous."

"I know, but without witnesses, their hands are tied."

Chase's expression turns thoughtful; then his frown deepens. "You and Ryan aren't the shithead's only victims, are you?"

"No, there's someone else. But he won't tell the cops. I think he's scared." I don't blame him. Alejandro's fourteen, and only a year older than when Frank first sexually assaulted me. He doesn't want anyone finding out what Frank did. Prior to Amber, I spent the past six years screwing any hot girl willing to spread her legs for me, to prove to myself I wasn't Frank. To prove to myself I wasn't messed up like Ryan—except, I was equally messed up. It took Amber for me to realize that.

"You need to convince him to talk." Chase releases a long, deep breath. From his stiff stance, it's obviously not enough to ease the tension building in him. "Look, I never knew about what Frank was doing to you and your brother, not until you told me. But I knew something was up with you. I've known for years. You've been set on self-destruct for quite some time. At least you were until Amber came along. But if you don't convince the other guy to step forward, he could wind up like you and Ryan, except a lot worse."

"I thought your major was mechanical engineering."

A puzzled expression crosses Chase's face. "It is."

"Then why do you sound like a fucking psych major?"

He laughs, erasing the last of the tension. "I guess that's from hanging out with Jordan."

A smile quirks on one side of my mouth. "So, what's going on with you two anyway?"

He backs away, walking toward his room. "Nothing. We're just friends." Jordan might have started off as Amber's closest friend when they began college last semester, but she and Chase have been spending a lot of time together lately, beyond when the four of us hang out as a group. Either those two are in denial about their feelings for each other, or they're lying to me and Amber.

"Whatever." I check my watch. "I've gotta get outta here unless I want to be late for my exam." I leave the apartment and head for the stairs. Before I get far, the eighty-year-old from next door emerges from the elevator.

"What did the police officer want?" she asks, eyeing me as though I'm a dangerous criminal, except she's the one who looks ready to attack me with her overstuffed purse and rolled-up newspaper.

I don't bother with a reply. Why can't she be one of those sweet grandma types you see on TV?

"We don't tolerate your kind in the building," she calls after me, her voice paper thin from years of use yet loud enough to be heard halfway down the hallway.

Sighing, I turn. "And what kind is that?"

Her gaze sweeps over my body, taking in my scuffed military

boots, jeans torn at the knees, and the ski jacket I bought at a thrift store three years ago. It's not ratty or anything. When I got it, it looked as though the previous owner had worn it maybe a handful of times.

She slits her eyes. "Trouble. That's your kind. Trouble and heading nowhere in life."

I could tell her she's wrong. She's describing my parents, not me. I'm going to be an engineer one day, which would have made my brother proud. I plan to make the most of my life, something he never had the chance to do.

I could say all that, but I don't. Walking backward, I call out, "I guess there's nothing else to say, then."

3

AMBER

"Amber?" Emma's voice breaks through the fog in my head.

I blink, then snap out of my frozen state. Both the salesclerk and Emma are watching me, waiting for my answer.

"Sorry, what did you say?" I ask, wrapping my arms around me to hide my slight trembling.

Her pale eyebrows draw together. "Are you okay?"

"I'm good. I zoned out, that's all." Something I've been doing a lot since last spring. I shrug as if it's no big deal, and inventory what happened so I can tell my therapist.

I remove my wallet from my purse, hinting that I want to pay for the body lotion and leave. The sooner we get out of here the better. The only place I want to be right now, other than in Marcus's arms, is at Grandma's. More than anything, I want to see Smoky.

"Are you sure?" Emma asks.

"Yeah, I just need to get out of here." I don't want to explain beyond that. Emma has seen the scars on my back. She doesn't know Paul whipped me until I finally stopped screaming. I told her the scars were from the broken glass when I tried to escape.

Emma and I pay for our purchases, then weave through the

crowded mall, stopping every so often to visit Emma's favorite stores.

"There's a book I want to look for," she says, carrying several bags from various clothing stores she'd practically lived in when Crossfields was our home. "Everyone on the basketball team has been talking about it, so I figured I'd get it."

"Okay." Marcus isn't due here for two more days. Until then, I'll need something to keep my mind off how much I miss him. I hustle to the romance section in the store we end up in and scan the tightly packed bookshelves. Anything to keep my mind preoccupied for a few minutes, to keep it from heading to Marcus again.

My phone buzzes in my purse as I reach for a book. As if reading my thoughts from over two hundred miles away, Marcus has sent me a text.

> Marcus: Love you. Will call after exams finished.

> Me: Love you back. Good luck!

"Here." Emma hands me a book with a black-and-white picture of a couple on the cover. All you can see of them is the waistband of their jeans, their otherwise naked bodies pressed together.

Instantly my thoughts go to Marcus and I inwardly groan. It's going to be a very long two days.

"This is the book." Emma points to it. "The guy's a hot guitarist and everyone's in love with him."

I grin. "Didn't realize you have a thing for musicians."

"I don't, normally. They're too moody."

I hand it to her and remove a copy from the shelf for myself.

"I thought you moved away," a high-pitched voice says behind me, and what feels like a nest of spiders scurrying over my body puts me on alert. *Melissa.*

Against all instincts, I twist around to find my former classmate glaring at me. Nice to know things haven't changed. She hated me even before Paul stepped into my life. His actions only intensified her venom.

"Back off, Mel." Emma steps between us.

"I can't believe you're defending her after she killed your brother." If Melissa were a dog, I'd have her pegged as a snarling pit bull.

"You know she didn't kill Trent. She wasn't the one responsible for the car accident. And she was as much a victim as he was."

"Yet he's dead, and she isn't."

Yep, nothing has changed. Like when I was released from the hospital last spring and allowed to return to school, and Melissa "accidentally" knocked me into my locker and I ended up with a concussion. She had planned to humiliate me. My concussion was an early birthday present.

"I would do anything for Trent to be alive." My voice cracks. No matter how many times I say that, it will never bring him back.

She regards me through narrowed eyes. "If you hadn't stolen him from me, he'd still be here."

"Get over yourself." Emma squares her shoulders, aiming for the intimidation she's best known for both on and off the courts when she's pissed. "Trent would never have dated a bitch like you. Amber's the only girl he ever loved. And it doesn't matter how much you try to convince yourself otherwise, he was never interested in you." She turns to me. "Let's go."

Without sparing Melissa another glance, Emma stalks off with me trailing not far behind. From the way Emma's holding her body rigid as she walks, it doesn't take much to realize she's more steamed at her former teammate's words than she needs to be. Especially as they were directed at me.

"What's going on?" I ask as we approach the long line for the cashier. Cheerful Christmas music plays in the background. A contrast to the bored, not-so-cheery expressions on everyone's faces. "You never acted this way when Trent was alive, when she went on and on and on about me stealing him from her."

Emma snorts. "Too bad she never said it to his face. He would have told her where she stood."

"That still doesn't explain why you're angry." I place my hand on her arm to stop her. "She can say all she wants—it won't change anything."

"I don't trust her. You don't know her like I do. She can be malicious." Emma sighs. "Remember when you first started getting those letters from Paul, and then Trent accused you of cheating on him?"

I nod. It was ridiculous and he'd felt bad afterward, after I'd reminded him in ways that left us both breathless that there was no other guy in my life.

"Mel told him she'd seen you with another guy."

"And he believed her because of those letters," I say, filling in the pieces. I don't bother to point out, though, that none of it matters. There's nothing she can do to hurt me again.

4

MARCUS

"**H**ey, babe," Amber says on the other end of the phone line, and I can't stop grinning. "How was your exam?" When we first met last semester, I woke her up from a nightmare and she told me to go to hell. The last thing I expected is that she'd one day call me "babe." The last thing I expected is that I'd love the way it sounds from her lips. Like I belong to Amber and only Amber.

"It's finished. That's all I care about." White puffs of air escape with each word, swept away by the brisk Chicago wind, as I walk from the engineering building to the parking lot. "I have to do a few things first, then hit Haysboro Mall on my way out. I should be at your place in four to five hours." Or less, depending on how long it takes to track down Alejandro.

"I can't wait." Her voice lowers. "My mom won't be home for another five hours..." The implication behind her words is left hanging.

I grin again. "Then I'll be there in four if I can."

Crap, it better not take me long to find Alejandro. This could be my only chance to make love to Amber over the next several days, while we're staying with her mom. I suspect her mom isn't going to let me sleep in the same bed with Amber, even if it's only to keep Amber's nightmares away.

At Alejandro's high school, I park on a side street and stride to the main entrance. The loud buzzer cuts through the air. Several minutes later, students flood from the building, pushing through the doors as if the place were on fire—or because it's the last day of school until the new year.

Alejandro steps through the open doorway, chatting with Juan and another boy who I've seen around the youth center. The new friend is shy. That's all I know about him.

"Hey, Alejandro," I call out when it's obvious he doesn't see me. "What year did the Bulls acquire Artis Gilmore?"

He looks up and a hesitant smile creeps onto his face. "Er, nineteen-seventy-six." He says something to his friends, then makes his way toward me through the mess of students rushing to catch their buses.

"Wanna ride?" I ask.

"Can you give Juan and Matt one, too? They live near me."

I barely keep from groaning out loud. "Sure, no problem."

Alejandro waves his friends over. "Marcus is giving us a ride to my place."

Matt smiles, the movement at the corners of his lips barely noticeable.

Juan bumps fists with me. "In what year did Jordan first retire?"

"Nineteen-ninety-four," I reply.

Alejandro snorts. "Dude, it was nineteen-ninety-three. Thought you were supposed to be smart. What with being in college and all."

This time I do groan. Shit, that was an easy one. "It's not like knowing Bulls trivia is required to be an electrical engineer."

That gets a snicker from Alejandro and Juan. "You said it," Juan says. Matt looks around, either searching for someone or already bored of the basketball talk.

We walk to where I'm parked while I think of ways to ditch Juan and Matt. The only boy who's animated is Juan, and I'm not sure if he's trying to fill the uncomfortable void hanging over us, or if he's clueless about the odd tension suddenly sluicing off his best friend.

I turn to Matt. "Do you play basketball?"

He shakes his head, hands shoved into the pockets of his ski jacket. Unlike Juan and Alejandro's jackets, his is clean and without any obvious wear.

"He's into science," Juan explains. "His dad is a university physics professor. He's really cool. He explained how physics determines which direction a ball will bounce."

Alejandro huffs a laugh and shoves his friend's arm. "Not that you understood any of it."

Juan's face reddens. "Maybe not. But it was still cool."

"And you live near these guys?" I ask Matt. University professors tend not to buy houses in the projects. The school caters to middle-class students, but they're bussed from farther away—and not within walking distance of Alejandro's house. Which means it'll take even longer before I can be with Amber again. Both my cock and my heart grumble in protest.

Matt glances toward the street. "No, but my dad is picking me up later on. He had tests to grade."

"Matt always comes over after school on Wednesdays," Alejandro says. "He's been helping me with math since you got shot."

I cringe. Frank screwed us both up in more ways than one. I used to tutor Alejandro so he wouldn't be kicked off his school's basketball team. He'd been headed in that direction due to his math grades. "Thanks," I say to Matt. "I owe you one."

He shrugs and once more avoids looking at me. He reminds me of a student in my engineering program. He doesn't often make eye contact and is awkward around people, but the guy is a fucking genius. I'm guessing Matt is, too, if his father's a physics professor.

I unlock the car doors and the three scramble inside. A few

snowflakes drift from the dark-gray clouds. Hopefully the heavy snowfall holds off until I get to Crossfields. I'm not missing out on seeing Amber, but I'd rather avoid the fucked-up roads if I can. I don't have chains for the tires.

I park in front of Alejandro's house. Before he can escape the car, I place my hand on his arm. Matt and Juan scoot out of the rear seat. Juan slams the car door and they wait for Alejandro on his side.

"I need to talk to you," I say.

Alejandro doesn't reply. His body turns rigid and he stares out the front window. It's like he's not even here with me, but not in the same way as Amber when she has a flashback. He has shut down, though I suspect it's because he knows what I want to talk about. He's never acted this way until now. Prior to Frank hurting him, he was always outgoing and friendly.

Matt and Juan stand on the sidewalk, waiting for Alejandro to join them. He swallows, his Adam's apple bouncing like a basketball, but he still refuses to look at me.

So not to make the guys any more curious than they already are, I try to appear casual, a relaxed smile on my face. It feels anything but that. "Frank needs to be locked away, but I can't do it on my own. Ryan is dead, and you're the only other person who can tell the cops what Frank did."

I watch for signs that he knows others who are involved, but he doesn't give anything away. He continues watching out the front window. I can't tell if he even notices the darkening sky or the falling snow or the dented bumper ahead of us.

"There's nothing to tell." His voice is lifeless. "I told you he didn't do anything."

"What are you afraid of?" I push down the anger funneling beneath the surface; it fights back. "Did he threaten you? Is that why you won't talk?" I struggle to keep my voice calm. It doesn't work.

Again, nothing.

"He can't hurt you if he's in jail," I say. "He can't hurt anyone." Though I'm sure his jail mates wouldn't have the same qualms when it comes to hurting Frank. Child molesters are at the bottom of the food chain. Where they belong.

Alejandro breaks his gaze from the front window and turns to his friends. They're no longer watching us. Juan is busy talking, hands moving with his words. Matt is listening and nodding, attention focused on the snow-crusted ground.

"I have to go," Alejandro says, voice still flat. He opens the door and escapes the car as if it's about to explode. The same way my insides feel at his stubbornness.

"Shit!" I slam my palm on the steering wheel. As much as I want to shake him, to make him see how nothing's going to change for him until Frank's put away, I know it won't help. I'll have to find another way to get through to him. If I don't, he'll never be free.

Ryan and I kept silent due to the shame we felt at what Frank did to us. Alejandro's silence is no different than ours. We were afraid of what people would think of us, what our friends would think of us. It wasn't only about the risk of being yanked from our home and split up in the foster-care system. It was about the stigma placed on us because a man had sexually abused us. There would be lingering questions in people's minds, wondering if we had enjoyed it. There would have been lingering questions, wondering if we were gay. There would have been lingering questions as to who we were and how to treat us, given what we had gone through.

Silence might have come at a cost, but it was one we had been ready to accept.

Until now.

I watch Alejandro and his friends retreat into the small single-level house. Alejandro doesn't acknowledge me as he shuts the door behind them, and a sinking sensation consumes me.

He'll never forgive me for what I didn't do. I might not have been the one to touch him, but after my silence for all those years, I might as well have been.

And with that realization burning inside me like battery acid, I pull away from the curb and drive toward the mall.

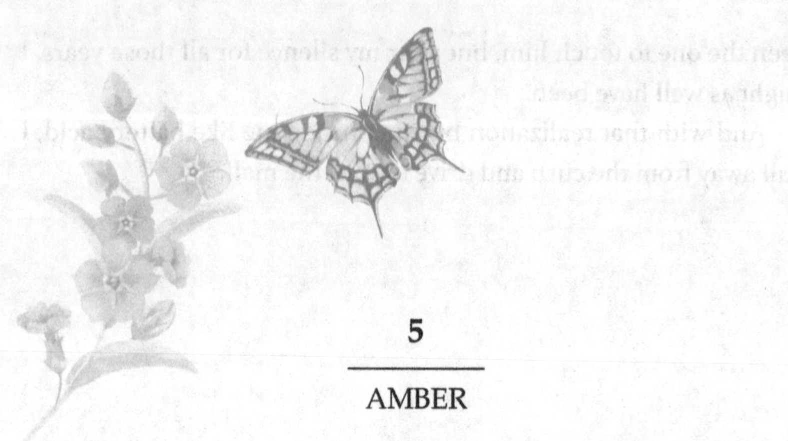

5

AMBER

Leaning against the black granite kitchen counter, I flip the page in the cookbook. I've been flipping pages for the past ten minutes and still haven't figured out what to make. For Marcus. For tonight.

"Jingle Bells" chimes through the house, and a weak smile flickers on my face. Michael and I used to argue which Christmas carol to pick when we reprogrammed the doorbell from the usual boring ding dong. "Jingle Bells" was Michael's favorite.

I push away from the counter. My socks slide over the black-and-white tiles as I walk from the kitchen into the foyer. I open the door and Emma enters the home she hasn't seen in almost a year. She used to believe the place came straight out of a fairy tale, with its Tudor-style design. The complete opposite of the modern furniture and artwork inside.

She smiles even though I can tell the memories of when she and Trent used to hang out here taunt her. The same memories I've had to deal with, too.

"I'm heading to the sports center," she says. "You wanna come? I thought we could toss some hoops."

"Sure. Let me get changed." No way am I missing out on this.

Emma follows me upstairs to my room. "Marcus is coming today, right?"

"Yep. He phoned not long ago and said he had a few things to do in Chicago first." I glance out my bedroom window. White flakes swirl through the air, caught up in the wind. It's light now, but the weather girl promised it'll become heavier in a few hours. "I hope he gets here before the storm."

I slide open my dresser drawer. "I'm making him dinner. Or at least I'm trying to." I remove my long-sleeved T-shirt and basketball shorts. The shorts that at one time I wouldn't wear because of my scarred leg. The scars are still there, but they don't bother me like they once did. "I don't know what to make. All I know is, I want it to be something special."

Emma giggles and flops onto my striped black-and-fuchsia bedding. "You can't cook."

I throw her a disgruntled glare. "Sure, I can."

She laughs harder. "Do you remember how you tried to make a grilled-cheese sandwich and almost burned down the house? And what about when you tried to make Jell-O and it wouldn't set?"

"How was I supposed to know that kiwi prevents Jell-O from setting?"

"It's on the box. Face it, of the three of us, only Trent knew how to..." Her voice fades away. Then she brightens but there's a false glow to it. We're both trying. We're both struggling. We're both grasping for anything to dull the pain.

"I can help," she says. "I bet we can come up with something to keep you from looking incompetent."

I huff. "Thanks for your vote of confidence."

She giggles again and sighs, the wistful note clear and heavy. "You're lucky Marcus is coming. Liam wanted to spend Christmas with me, but being with his family is big for him. They've always been close."

"Your family's close too." While growing up, Michael and I practically lived with Emma and Trent's family, especially during the summers. Often we went camping with them since camping was something Mom wasn't interested in doing. Work always came first.

"They haven't been the same since Trent's death." Emma traces her finger along the wide stripes on my comforter. "It's been hard on them with me gone."

I sit next to her. "Are they going to therapy?"

"I dunno. It's not something we discuss."

"Maybe you should. Before things get worse. My mom's seeing someone." At Emma's confused expression, I clarify. "A therapist. She started drinking again because of what happened. She eventually realized she was screwing her life up and started attending AA again. She said the therapist is helping her cope with everything." And is helping her deal with her own heavy dose of self-blame. I blamed myself for a long time for Trent's and Michael's deaths. She blamed herself for that and for not being able to protect me when Paul stalked me. She also had to deal with tons of guilt for turning her back on me due to a misunderstanding between us after I was found alive. A misunderstanding that drove a king-sized wedge between us, all because she thought I hated her for not protecting me and the ones we loved and lost. But I hadn't hated her. I'd been spending all my time at Grandma's house, taking care of Smoky, who'd also suffered at Paul's hands while we were held captive.

"I just don't know how to bring it up with them," Emma says. " 'Hey Mom and Dad, since you're all messed up, maybe you should consider therapy.' "

I snort. "Maybe not with those words, but it wouldn't hurt to bring it up. You were seeing a counselor, and it helped, right?"

She nods.

"Then tell them that. Do they even know you were going?"

"It's never come up."

"Then it's time to bring it up." I push myself off the bed and hold out my hand to her. "Help me find a recipe. I need to buy groceries after the gym."

It doesn't take us long to locate one that sounds delicious and not too hard to make. I check if Mom has everything I need; then Emma drives us to the sports center. Despite my craving to push myself hard, to punish myself for what happened last spring, I manage to rein it in—like I promised Marcus and my therapist.

We warm up on the treadmill and hit the mats to stretch.

"I wish you were on the team," she says as we hold a pose, stretching our hamstrings.

"I wish I was too." Unfortunately some things weren't meant to be. I can tell she wants to say something, but there's nothing she can that would make me feel better. To make us both feel better.

We head to the basketball courts. Several guys who look as if they could play varsity run up and down one court, playing hard. Sweat soaks through their clothing and drips from their faces. One guy passes the ball to a player who is barely open. The boy next to him reaches out, attempting to block the pass. He fails. The other player catches the ball and sets up for the shot. The ball swooshes through the net.

On the next court, a couple of elementary school kids swing the oversized balls up from between their legs, aiming roughly for the hoop towering above them.

Emma and I exchange glances, and without saying a word, jog to the teens as they charge down the court. The guy with the ball dodges left while passing the ball to a player on his right. The player catches it and performs a lay-up. The ball swishes through the net. He and his teammates high-five each other. The others groan.

"Can we join you?" Emma calls from the sideline.

They check us over. "Not interested." The tall, dark-haired boy wipes sweat from his forehead.

A blond boy jostles him. "Speak for yourself, Dunningham. These two ladies look my speed." From the way he says it, it's obvious he's not referring to the game.

"What speed? You're a virgin. You have no speed."

Blond Boy's face turns the shade of Santa's hat, and he hurls the ball toward Dunningham. It bounces off his shoulder.

"What the fuck was that for?" he grunts.

Emma sashays along the sideline and scoops up an abandoned ball. "Now, boys. Play nice. My friend and I want to play. We'll go easy on you. I promise." She spins the ball on her fingertip.

Something flickers on a few of their faces. It's suddenly dawned on them that Emma and I are tall for girls. Five-foot, eleven inches tall.

"Okay, you're in," a red-haired boy, who's all limbs, says. He points at me. "You're with us. Your friend's with Dunningham's team."

Blond Guy jerks his eyebrows up and down his forehead, already over the proclamation of his virginal status.

"Don't get any ideas," Emma warns, walking past him. "I have a boyfriend, and he's four inches taller than you and about fifty pounds heavier." Not that he has to worry about Liam, who lives in a town about a hundred miles from here.

It doesn't take the boys long to figure out just how good Emma and I are on the court. They challenge us, push us hard, expect us to play at their level. And we do, and so much more.

We play for forty minutes before the guys announce they have to leave. On the way home, Emma and I pick up the few items I still need for dinner.

As I hammer the chicken breasts with the heavy wooden mallet, pretending it's the defense lawyer for the upcoming trial, the phone rings. I rest the mallet on the chicken and grab my cell phone off the kitchen table. I don't recognize the number.

"Hello?" I answer.

"Hello. I'm Roger Tucker with *The Chicago Post*. May I speak with Amber Scott, please?"

Everything inside me clenches. How the hell did he find my number? It's unlisted and I'm selective about who I give it to. "I'm not interested. If you have any questions, you need to inquire with the DA's office." I don't wait for a response. I hang up.

"What was that about?" Emma asks, a knife in one hand and a large tomato in the other.

"It was nothing. Just some dumb reporter wanting to ask questions." Who acted no different than a stalker by tracking down my phone number.

An unexpected chill clutches me. I knock the sensation away. He's doing his job. He's not Paul.

Emma studies the cookbook. "Now you have to dip the flattened breasts in the egg mixture, then coat them with the herbed bread crumbs. Then you sauté them in the frying pan." In the background, Nolan Kincaid sings, "Kiss me, babe, love me, babe, but never leave me, babe."

I dunk a cold chicken breast into the bowl with the egg. The song ends and the radio, jockeys start talking. I'm not paying much attention to their banter—not until one of them says mall shooting.

My head snaps up. Emma's frowning.

"What did they say?" I ask, hoping I misheard him.

"There's been a mall shooting."

"Where?"

She shakes her head. "I don't know. I missed that part."

There must be a million malls in the US, but it doesn't stop me from quickly washing my hands and turning the television on in the family room. Emma joins me. Neither of us can be bothered to sit. We stand here, stunned.

Mom was watching the TV last. It's on the twenty-four-hour news station. A reporter is interviewing a mother bouncing a baby in her arms. Her voice is cracked and choked with tears.

"We were in the luggage store and heard several gunshots from down the mall. Then there was screaming." The mother starts sobbing and the baby grows restless and cries, too.

"Then what happened?" the reporter presses, ignoring the woman's obvious distress.

"Th-then the salesperson hustled everyone into the storage room and we stayed there till we knew it was safe to come out."

"How did you know when it was safe?"

"Someone called the police on their phone and they told us to stay put until security came to get us." The mother switches the baby into her other arm. Large snowflakes blow against them. Neither the little girl nor her mom appear as though they want to be out in the cold, but the woman is an insect caught in a spiderweb—unable to tell the reporter where to go, and walk off.

I want to scream at him to leave her alone. She doesn't need the added stress of him questioning her, not when she's still in shock. But I can scream all I want. He can't hear me, and it doesn't look like he would care even if he could. He's got a story to report, a paycheck to collect.

"How long were you in hiding?" he asks.

"An hour."

"That's a long time. How did you feel knowing there was a shooter in the mall?"

"Scared. I thought we were dead."

"Thank you." The reporter turns to the camera. *"I'm reporting from Haysboro Mall, Chicago, where a shooter went on a rampage three hours ago. So far, eight people are confirmed dead, including the shooter, who shot himself prior to the police department's arrival. Several other people are listed in critical condition. Reports are still coming in as to how many are injured."*

My entire body turns colder than if I had stood in the coming storm, the wind howling around me inside me and out. Storms. *Nothing good ever happens in a storm.* The words play in repeat mode in my head.

"Marcus was going there." My voice is a strained whisper. I want to phone him, to hear his voice, but my body refuses to move, barely able to even breathe.

"Are you sure?" Emma asks.

I nod. "He called this morning and told me he had to go to the mall before heading out."

"But are you sure he went to that mall? He could have gone to a different one."

"That's the mall he mentioned that he was going to." My chest tightens as I say the words, as if by doing that it prevents them from being true.

"Phone him, Amber. There's no point freaking out till you know for sure."

With a shaky breath, I call him on my phone.

"This is Marcus. You know the drill." Voice mail.

"I just heard about the mall shooting. Give me a call when you get this. Okay?" I press End. "He's not answering." I call Chase. He doesn't answer either.

"Chase. It's Amber. Have you heard from Marcus lately? He said he was going to Haysboro Mall before leaving for Crossfields and I just heard about the mall shooting and he's not answering my calls and I don't know what to do." I take a deep breath and hang up.

"*The latest reports indicate his ex-girlfriend works at the mall,*" the male reporter says. "*She's believed to be among the dead. We'll update you once we know more. Back to you, Janice.*"

Janice, the anchor, updates viewers on the current situation and how tragic it is that this happened three days prior to Christmas. But the way she says it, with a slight smile to her tone, you'd think someone won the lottery.

Emma and I watch the news in openmouthed horror. The house could burn down around us and we wouldn't notice.

"*We have an update,*" Janice announces. "*Police confirmed that the suspect, Keith Knight, used to be a mall employee and worked as a security guard. Patrick, are you there?*"

The TV flashes to the reporter from earlier. Snow and wind assault him, trying to push him off his feet as the storm hits Chicago hard. I glance out the window. It's not much better outside.

"Yes, I'm here," he replies. *"The police confirmed a few minutes ago that Keith Knight was indeed a mall employee and that his ex-girlfriend is not among the dead. She has a restraining order filed against him but she works at a different mall."* He doesn't look nonplussed that he's been releasing half-truths just for the sake of having something to talk about and fill airtime, knowing that the country is hanging on to his every word.

"Can the police tell us anything about Keith Knight's motives?"

"They haven't made a statement yet." Patrick moves sideways and stands next to a teenage boy huddled in a winter coat. The boy looks toward the camera in awe. *"We have Simon Lukeman here to shed some light on the situation. Simon works in the food court."* The boy nods. *"Simon, what do you know about what happened?"*

"Keith was fired last week from his job. He never mentioned why, though."

"Did you know him?"

"We talked a few times. He was kind of quiet. Not the kind of guy you expect to go postal."

The garage door rumbles opens. Mom's home. Over an hour early. She strides into the family room and hugs me, something she's started doing again recently. "It's really coming down out there. Grandma phoned and said she's going to stay home. She doesn't want to deal with the roads. They're bad now, and they will only get worse."

She stops talking. "Is something wrong?"

I swallow down the fear that if I say the next words, the truth behind them will become a hundredfold worse. "There's been a mall shooting. At the same mall Marcus was going to before coming here. And I can't get a hold of him." My voice cracks with the last sentence, and the fear I tried to swallow is pushed back up with a small sob.

Mom wraps her arms around me and holds me tight, doing her best to keep me together. She doesn't ask for any details. She doesn't have to. The number of dead and wounded is on the television for everyone to see.

She tightens her hold on me.

The screen flashes to another reporter interviewing several individuals in the mall at the time of the shooting. Mom gasps. The sound is soft, barely heard above the noise on the TV. I only heard it because I'm next to her.

I study the screen to see what she reacted to. All I can see is a tired-looking man standing next to a much older woman. The shooting has taken its toll on everyone. "What is it?"

"It's nothing." Mom steps back, fully recovered. "Let me make some calls and see what I can ascertain. Okay?" She gives me a small painted-on smile that makes the Mona Lisa appear ready to break out in cheer.

"Okay."

She returns fifteen minutes later and shakes her head.

My throat closes, preventing oxygen from reaching my lungs. "What did you find out?"

"The hospitals aren't releasing any information other than to next of kin."

Except Marcus's next of kin doesn't care what happens to him. Never have. Never will. The only reason the surgeon updated me on Marcus's condition after he was shot two weeks ago was because Chase told him Marcus's parents don't give a damn, and I gave a heartfelt speech that convinced the surgeon I was more family to Marcus than his parents ever were.

But that won't work this time.

I drop onto the couch and stare at the TV. I vaguely hear Emma tell me she has to leave, and I'm to call her once I know anything. I nod, the movement robotic, my attention glued to the screen.

6

AMBER

Seven p.m. It's two hours later than Marcus expected to be here and still no word. I've tried his cell phone a few more times, but each time I get his voice mail.

Chase hasn't returned my call, either. What if he was with Marcus when Marcus went to the mall? What if they were hurt or killed? Marcus's mother would never know to call me, and neither would Chase's parents.

A million questions hammer the inside of my skull. My heart was starting to heal after Trent's death, but it won't take much to leave it permanently damaged if something's happened to Marcus.

I stare out the window, watching for his car, hoping that he didn't end up at the mall this afternoon. Hoping he's been delayed due to the weather. Hoping he'll drive up at any second, ready to tell me another lame math joke.

Mom approaches from behind. Her footsteps are quiet, but her reflection in the window gives her away. She doesn't say or do anything. She watches me, at a loss as to how to comfort me. At a loss as to the right words to say. God, why does this keep happening to me? Why is it every time I love someone, they're ripped away? *Please, God...please let him be okay.*

I don't know if that will help. I don't believe in God. Not after Trent and Michael were torn from my life and I barely survived. Not after learning how Marcus's stepfather touched Marcus in a way that is so wrong and raped and murdered Marcus's brother. What kind of God would let those things happen, and to kids no less?

Mom sits next to me and strokes my hair, like she used to when I was sick or scared. Back before she became too wrapped up in her career, back before she struggled with alcoholism. But things have changed, for both of us. Now she's the mom I remember. I lean against her and let her blanket me in her arms, wishing she could simply hug my problems away.

We stay this way for several long minutes, neither of us saying anything. I continue watching out the window; she continues stroking my hair. My cell phone plays a tune, but it's not the one Marcus programmed to let me know when he's calling.

I check the number. Chase. My palms grow clammy. I can't answer it. What if he's calling to tell me Marcus was at the mall and is in critical condition or dead?

But if I don't answer it, I'll never know, a voice in my head reminds me.

"Have you heard from him?" I whisper past the growing lump in my throat.

"No." Chase's voice is no less broken than mine. "I was hoping he was with you."

I sink back into the couch. Mom heads for the kitchen. "He should be here by now. He mentioned he had a few things to do and he had to go to the mall, and he'd be here in a few hours. He should have been here two hours ago."

"You're positive he went to Haysboro? Maybe he went somewhere else."

"He said he was going to that mall. My mom called the nearby hospitals to see if he was admitted, but they're not giving out any information unless you're family. Do you...do you think you can call his mom and see if she knows anything?"

Chase releases a long slow breath, which sounds like wind trapped in a tunnel through the phone. "I could try, I guess, but I'm not promising anything. I'll call you back once I've talked to her, okay?"

"Okay."

He hangs up and I return to staring out the window. It feels like forever before he calls back, when in reality it's been ten minutes.

"What did she say?" I ask.

"Frank answered." Chase's tone, a mix of disgust and defeat, warns me I'm not going to like what he has to tell me.

"Frank? I thought he was in jail."

"He was. He made bail."

And is now free to hurt another boy.

My fist clenches around the phone at the thought of what must be going through Marcus's mind, knowing his stepfather isn't in jail. I can't believe he never told me. "So? What did he say?"

"He said if I'm so desperate to locate Marcus, I should phone the hospitals myself."

Hope kicks at the fear consuming me, but not enough to drive it away. "So that means Marcus wasn't at the mall. Right? He wouldn't have said that if the cops had told him Marcus was among the dead or injured."

"I'm not too sure, Amber. Normally the hospital or cops would contact the family. But since Frank was charged for causing bodily harm to Marcus, maybe they decided not to contact his next of kin."

"Which means if he's dead or unable to tell anyone anything, we'll never know." The reality of the situation weighs down on me further, like a collapsed building pinning me to the ground.

"And maybe he wasn't even at the mall."

"Maybe, but if not, why isn't he already here?" *Because the roads are getting bad.*

Mom walks into the living room as I end the call with Chase. "I take it that wasn't Marcus."

"No. It was his best friend. He hasn't heard anything either."

She gives me a sad smile. This wasn't how we were supposed to spend Christmas. It'll be hard enough as it is with Michael and Trent gone. I'm not sure I have enough strength to get through it if something happened to Marcus, too.

"Do you need anything?" she asks.

I shake my head. Other than being in Marcus's arms, there is nothing I need.

"I'm going to have a shower, then. I put your dinner in the oven to keep it warm." Though from the way she's looking at me, it's clear she knows I can't eat anything until I find out where he is.

I listen to her go upstairs and walk toward the garage door. If I leave now, I'll be gone before she can stop me. I chew my lip, thinking of the consequences. Marcus is the reckless one, not me. At least he was, according to Chase, until recently.

Until he met me.

I've always been the one unwilling to take risks. But this is Marcus. The guy I love, and there is nothing more important to me than making sure he's safe.

I'm about to call the state police first, to see if any accidents have been reported, when the irritating sound of *Jingle Bells* fills the foyer, reminding me once again it's almost Christmas.

I race to the front door and swing it open. Marcus is standing in the doorway.

A smile slides onto his face. "Golden rule of deriving. Never trust any result proved after eleven p.m."

A choked sound escapes me, and I fling myself at him, not even bothering to laugh at his lame math joke like I normally would. Before he can say anything else, my mouth is on his, tasting him, making sure he's not a dream, making sure I'm not asleep on the couch, waiting for him to show up. His lips are cold. I keep kissing them, eager to warm them up.

Marcus doesn't hesitate to kiss me back. His good arm, strong and steady, pulls me closer until we're almost one. The freezing wind pushes into us, but neither of us cares as our tongues continue their desperate dance. If it weren't for his injured shoulder, I'd jump up and wrap my legs around his hips.

He's alive. I can't believe he's alive. All I want is for him to bury himself deep in me and show me how alive he really is, how alive I am. That, and have him distract me from everything I want to forget, everything I'd rather not think about.

But we can't.

Because my mom is in the house. That thought alone is enough to sober me up. I pull away, without an enthusiastic response from either my body or Marcus. But if we don't stop this now, who knows what my mom will walk in on.

Marcus picks up his duffel bag and steps into the house. I shut the door. "Where were you? I thought you had been involved in the mall shooting."

His eyebrows furrow together as he slides his bag to the floor. "What mall shooting?"

"A man entered Haysboro Mall this afternoon and started shooting. Eight people are dead and a lot more are wounded." My voice breaks when I realize how close Marcus came to being part of that statistic. "I tried calling you on your cell but you weren't answering, and Chase had no idea where you were either. He even tried calling your mom, but Frank answered the phone and wouldn't tell him anything." The words are falling so fast, I don't know if he understands anything I'm saying. But that doesn't matter, as long as he's here with me and not in the morgue or alone in a hospital.

"I didn't know," he murmurs, his gaze taking in my face as though he thought he'd never see it again. He wipes the tears from my cheeks with his thumb, his touch full of love. "It must have happened after I left."

I reach up and cover his hand with my mine. "So what happened to you?"

"There was a major accident on the interstate and traffic was rerouted."

My insides clench into a tight ball at how close I came to losing him. Even though he wasn't involved in the shooting or the accident, he could have easily been in either place at the wrong time.

As if sensing my fear, he strokes my cheek. "Don't worry, nothing's going to happen to me. I'm like a cat with nine lives."

That might be so, but he's rapidly going through all nine of them. Who knows how many he has left.

"We need to warm you up," I whisper. *Please don't take any more risks. I'm not sure I can handle it if anything else happens to you.*

Herbed chicken cutlets stuffed with ham and provolone cheese tease the air with their delicious aroma. Mom finished making the dinner Emma and I started prior to getting caught up in the mall-shooting drama.

I stand glued to the spot, torn between leading Marcus to the bathroom and warming him up in the shower, versus tending to dinner.

As much as I want to be the one helping him warm up, it's too risky. Mom won't appreciate my having shower sex with my boyfriend.

As it is, I need to figure a way for us to be together tonight. Mom has prepared the guest room for him, and although she might not have said the words, the look on her face was quite clear—he and I are not sleeping together. I doubt the argument that he helps with my nightmares will hold much weight with her. But after the last couple of hours, the nightmares are going to be unbearable unless I know he's safe with me. Like I'm safe when I'm in his arms.

"Why don't you warm up in the shower?" My gaze drops to his lips.

He leans in. "Are you joining me?" His low voice is a soft brush against my cheek.

A door upstairs opens, then clicks shut.

I step away from him, instantly missing the intimate contact between us. "I'm making dinner."

His lips curve into a beautiful smile that holds much meaning. *Later* is what it's saying. *Later I'll make love to you because you mean everything to me.*

Not wanting to leave him, still amazed he's alive, I thread my fingers with his and lead him upstairs.

"You made it," Mom says, sounding relieved as we reach the top step.

"Yes, ma'am. I got rerouted due to an accident on the interstate."

"Well, I'm glad you arrived safely. Amber, why don't you get Marcus settled."

"Okay, but I'm going to show him where to shower first," I tell her.

She continues past and smiles at me with a subtle reminder that's lost on Marcus but not on me. I'm to help him get settled, nothing more. She no doubt thought we were going upstairs so I could show him my room.

I lead him to the bathroom, and I'm about to leave when he tugs me into the room. I can tell Marcus doesn't notice how large the room is or that the white towels are fluffy. Nor does he notice the coordinating royal blue and white accessories. The only thing he notices is me. His eyes haven't left me since he pulled me into the space.

Before I can make a sound, his mouth crushes mine. Even though Mom expects me to join her in the kitchen, despite what she said, I open my mouth and let him in—and easily get lost in him. I can't tell if he's cold, but I'm getting hotter as our kiss intensifies. I wouldn't be surprised if the mirrors are steamed up even without the hot water turned on.

I guide the zipper of his winter coat down. Marcus watches, a mischievous smile on his lips. Once finished, I ease the coat off his shoulders, taking care with his injured one, and trace my fingertips along the soft fabric of his T-shirt.

"Aren't you supposed to be using your sling?" I ask.

"It's easier driving without it."

I don't have a chance to lecture him on how he's supposed to wear it for the next few weeks. Marcus leans in, his mouth near my ear. "Are you joining me?" he murmurs, laughter in his voice. He nods at the shower.

I flash him a smile. "I'd love to, but I can't. My mom's waiting for me to go downstairs."

He flattens his lips together. "I'm not gonna be able to make love to you until we return to Chicago, am I?"

I press my lips to his cheek. "Don't worry. I'll think of something." And I will.

7

AMBER

When I was younger, and believed in Santa, I would wake up at four every Christmas morning. I would then sneak into Michael's room, and we would tiptoe downstairs to check out the presents Santa had left while we slept. I never had to wake my brother. He was always waiting for me.

Like the little girl I used to be, I wake to find my alarm clock glowing 4:00 a.m. While I'm no longer the girl with the brother eagerly waiting for her, I'm still the girl who sneaks downstairs to peek at her gifts.

And in this case, Marcus.

We haven't had a chance to be intimate since he arrived less than forty-eight hours ago, beyond small, chaste kisses or hugs. After almost losing him, I'm happy we can have even those. But they haven't been enough to stop my nightmares.

The only sound greeting me is the soft thud of my bare feet against carpeted steps, and the slight rustle of my pink satin robe. Underneath is one of my gifts to Marcus: a matching pink satin panties and bra.

The soles of my feet touch the cold tile floor and I pause. Once I'm positive Mom's super senses haven't kicked in, and she's realized what I'm up to, I tiptoe toward the guest room and inch the door open. The room is dark, other than the faint glow from the Christmas lights next door.

As my eyes adjust to the darkness, I spot Marcus sleeping. I stand in the doorway, wondering how I got so lucky. If I hadn't been failing my math class last term, I might never have given him a chance. A chance to prove he's more than the sexed-up guy everyone assumes he is. While I might not be thrilled that so many girls on campus are intimately familiar with his body, a warmth floods through me at the thought that he's *mine*.

"Are you planning to stand there staring at me," Marcus murmurs, "or did you have something else in mind?" His tone is teasing and edged with a desire to do things to my body. Things that will leave me beyond satisfied. My breath hitches and I struggle not to melt away.

He sits up and his bedding bunches around his hips, exposing his hard chest and abs. He clicks the bedside lamp on. A soft light snuggles him and leaves the guest room in shadows. The intimacy created sends a ripple of excitement through me.

The room hasn't changed much since Dad lived here. Unlike the rest of the house, which is modern in design, this room contains antiques. The bed, dresser and side table are made of dark maple and could be a hundred years old. At least. The armchair seems more modern, but not by much.

I step closer to the bed, shutting the door quietly behind me. "I thought I heard Santa," I whisper, then climb onto the queen-sized bed and crawl over to Marcus.

Still on my knees, I straighten and my robe slips open, revealing my bra and panties.

"Well, lucky for me he's already gone." Marcus slides the robe off my shoulder, his calloused fingers brushing my skin. I suck in a soft breath, too quiet to be heard.

He does the same to the other side, and the fabric cascades to the floor. His eyes never leave me as they consume every inch of my body. "Looks like he left me a present. I must have been a *very* good boy this year."

I roll my eyes. "You need to work on your pickup lines."

His finger traces the skin along the inside of my bra strap and continues its way under the satin fabric of my bra. Heat pools between my legs.

"No. I don't think I do," he says. "You're the only woman I want. The only woman I need. And right now, I need you more than you could ever imagine."

My gaze drops to his boxers and the unmistakable hardness. I laugh softly. "So I see."

Marcus grins. "That's not quite what I meant. I mean I want to hold you and kiss you." He plants a feathery kiss on my lips. "Though I'm not opposed to burrowing deep inside you." Another teasing kiss. "And making sure you're mine."

I climb onto his lap and straddle him. The molten heat between my legs brushes him and a throbbing ache pleads for me to relieve it. "I'm already yours and you're mine." I crash my lips into his and rock against him.

He moans into my mouth, the sound drowned out by my own moan and the headboard knocking the wall. I inwardly cringe, no longer rocking. God, I hope Mom's still asleep and didn't hear it.

Our tongues slide and stroke and reacquaint, while my fingers tangle in his silky hair. The faint smell that is all Marcus wraps around me, grounds me, makes me feel safe.

His mouth moves away from mine and his day-old facial growth scrapes along my jaw with his lips leading the way. His hands glide across my back to my bra. He unhooks it and tosses it on the floor.

His gaze sweeps over my body, his hazel eyes making me feel beautiful, strong, ready to face almost anything. "God, you're gorgeous."

I smile shyly. "You're not so bad yourself," I whisper and my fingers trace the ridges of his stomach. I rub the building throb between my legs along his hardness, careful not to cause the head-board to bang the wall again.

"You're killing me, Kitten," he groans, the sound only loud enough to be heard by me, and turns me so I'm lying on the bed. His mouth covers my nipple, and he alternates between sucking and teasing me with his tongue. My other nipple aches for his attention.

My entire body aches for his touch.

As if sensing what I need, he moves his mouth to cover the other nipple and thrills it like he did the first. I swallow a moan. Watching my reaction, he skims one hand down my stomach and along the waistband of my panties. His gaze never leaves mine.

His fingers inch between the fabric and my lower belly and keep going until they slide between the slick folds hidden beneath my underwear. They gently circle the throbbing mound and my body jerks, greedily wanting more. The movement, once again, sends the headboard banging into the wall.

We both frown at the offending wooden furniture. Marcus tosses the pillows onto the floor and creates an oversized nest with them and the duvet.

Not missing a beat, he makes himself comfortable on the floor. I join him, and he continues his exploration of my body, his finger easing inside me. I bite my lip to keep from making a sound louder than a soft whimper. Two can play at this.

I slip my hand into his boxers and wrap my palm around his shaft. He inhales sharply, and I smile as my lips find his. We deepen the kiss; then I pull away and gently push him back, my hand on his chest. His heart flutters rapidly beneath it, matching the pace of my own. I smile.

"Do you have condoms with you?" I ask.

"They're in my bag."

I fish through his bag on the floor next to us. Once I find a couple of foil packages, I remove my underwear and toss it on the floor next to my bra. With one hand, Marcus practically rips his boxers off and waits for me to straddle him.

The moment I do, one of his fingers is inside me again, tormenting me, pushing me to the edge. Another finger joins the first, and I can barely rip open the foil packet. I teeter there, ready to fall.

Not wanting to fall without him, I roll the condom onto his thick length. It's not the first time I've put a condom on him, but I feel clumsy doing it. I bite my lip as I focus my attention on the task. Marcus chuckles and his hand guides mine.

Without hesitation, I mount him. I think part of him prefers it this way, and it has nothing to do with his shoulder. He fears I'll get scared while we make love and flash back to last spring, and it will somehow drive me away. My being on top gives me a greater sense of control. Though I don't think it matters. As long as I focus on the amazing man making love to me, filling me with an immense amount of joy, I'll be okay.

I push us further to the edge. Sensing I'm about to come and scream out his name, he pulls my head down. His mouth is on mine seconds before my body clenches his length, seconds before I can make a sound beyond a muffled moan. He comes moments later, our lips still as one.

Even though I want to stay this way for a bit longer, as I regain my senses, I climb off him and collapse onto the bed. He gets up and tosses the condom into the garbage.

He returns and covers me with the duvet. He then relaxes under the covers with me curled around him. I make a mental note to remove the condom from the trash so no one else finds it. Especially Mom. I started the pill earlier this month, but I've got a few more weeks to go until we're safe. After that, I won't have to worry anymore about hiding the evidence.

"How's your shoulder?" I ask.

He tenderly kisses me. "I'm fine. At least I am now. Merry Christmas."

I kiss him back. "Merry Christmas."

We lie here for a few minutes, a tangle of limbs, both lost in each other, not wanting to move anytime soon. And we don't have to. Mom won't be up for another four hours. I just have to make sure I'm in my room before she wakes up.

"Tell me about your Christmases," Marcus says. "What were they like?"

I smile softly, caught up in the memories. "Wonderful. My brother and I would sneak down early and check out the presents Santa left us. Emma and Trent used to come over after lunch and we'd hang out. Then my grandparents would come over for dinner and Michael and I would stay up late." As hard as I try, I can't keep the sadness out of my voice. My grandfather died several years ago, so I'm used to his not being around for Christmas. It's Michael and Trent's absence that is new and fills me with an unwelcome heaviness. If Marcus weren't here, I have no idea how I would survive.

I snuggle closer to him and smile. Even though we were forced to be quieter than usual, the sex was amazingly hot. Hot enough to say what happened between us is now one of my favorite Christmas morning memories.

"Tell me about you and Ryan. What were your Christmases like?" I stroke the side of his face. This isn't just my first Christmas without Michael. It's Marcus's first Christmas without his brother. It's why I wanted him to be here with me during the holidays. No one should be alone today when they're filled with this much pain. And although Marcus pretends to be stoic when it comes to Ryan, I've noticed in the past week he, too, is experiencing the same heaviness.

He smiles, the emotion behind it filled with neither happiness nor sadness. It's more an act of comfort, for him, for me. What he has to tell me won't be something out of *It's a Wonderful Life*.

"Ryan and I were lucky, when I think about it," he says. "Mom and the step-jerk enjoyed getting drunk and hanging out at the local casino. We learned at a young age Santa doesn't exist. Or at least he doesn't exist for kids with parents like mine."

"That's horrible."

He shrugs. "It was hard, especially when Chase did believe in Santa. At first Ryan and I figured we had done something to make Santa mad at us. It hurt but we survived. Then we wised up and I realized Chase's parents were giving him and his sister the presents, not Santa. I used to lie to him about what Santa gave me so he wouldn't discover the truth."

A pain hammers my chest at his words, and I want to reach out and hug him. Not the man before me—the man who was broken as a child and used it to make him stronger. I want to hug the child he used to be. The one whose innocence was destroyed because he and Ryan got the crap end of the deal when it came to parents.

"Part of me looks forward to one day having kids, you know, so I can have the childhood experiences I missed out on." He kisses the end of my nose. "So I can hear them sneak down at four in the morning"—he brushes his lips against mine—"to see what Santa left them."

I laugh, the sound quiet so not to risk waking Mom. "The point of sneaking is so the parents don't know what you're up to." Until now, we've never discussed our futures. We've been living in the present, with me trying not to dwell too much on the upcoming trial. Hearing him say that he one day hopes to have children gives me a warm feeling. What his mother and stepfather did to him didn't completely break him. If anything, I can see him becoming a more loving father because of it. An overly protective and loving father.

"It doesn't matter. And as you can tell"—he pats my butt—"no one can sneak past me without me noticing."

I give him an impish grin. "I'll keep it in mind for next time."

"Hmm. I can hardly wait." He kisses me deeply, making me forget about everything else.

I OPEN MY EYES AND BLINK THE ROOM INTO FOCUS, MY MIND STILL fuzzy from the pleasant dream I woke up from.

A lazy smile stretches across my face as I snuggle into the warm body behind me. The rich aroma of coffee nudges its way into my awareness.

The smile vanishes and I sit up abruptly. What the hell was I thinking when I decided to stay in bed a little longer with Marcus, after we made love a second time?

I guess I was thinking I wouldn't fall asleep and wake up while Mom was in the kitchen making coffee.

Marcus stirs. "What's going on?" he asks.

"Shhh," I whisper. "My mom's up. She's in the kitchen."

"Shit!"

Shit is right. I scramble off the bed and search the floor for my clothes. Or more specifically, my underwear and satin robe. I can't even pretend I've been up for a bit and came to say "hi" to Marcus. And it's obvious we weren't chatting about math.

Marcus climbs off the bed and pulls on his boxers and jeans.

"I'll sneak upstairs and have a shower." I give him a quick kiss. "I'll see you in a few minutes."

I inch the door open, poke my head out to make sure the coast is clear, and scurry down the hallway to the kitchen.

I peek into the room. Mom's standing at the sink, filling a glass with water. In front of her, a large window overlooks the backyard, and in the dark it's a perfect mirror.

Since she's still staring at her glass, I make a break for it and run toward the staircase. Once I'm in the main foyer, my bare feet slap against the tiles. I don't stick around long enough to find out if Mom can hear them. I charge up the stairs, thankful for my extra-long legs.

I grab clean underwear and my black sweater dress and tights from my room, and head to the bathroom, desperate to hide from my mom. Humiliation twists in my gut at the possibility she spotted me making my not-so-heroic escape.

I turn on the shower and step into the tub. Hot water washes away evidence of my equally hot lovemaking session with Marcus. I stay under the spray, reminiscing about the steamiest parts of last night. I'm not even sure why I'm worried what Mom will think. I mean, I am eighteen now. Why wouldn't I be having sex with my boyfriend?

A voice in my head whispers, *Good luck with that argument.*

After taking longer in the shower than I need, I get changed, dry my hair, and put on makeup. Knowing I can't stall any longer, as I'll eventually have to face Mom, I drag myself downstairs.

Mom and Marcus are sitting at the kitchen table, drinking coffee, when I enter. "Morning." My tone is overly bright.

Marcus unfolds from his chair and kisses my cheek. "Did you leave me any hot water?" His back faces Mom, so she can't see the smirk on his face.

"Of course," I singsong; then I feel like a bigger idiot for sounding so phony.

"Good, but I still won't be long." He turns to my mom. "Thanks, Sarah, for the coffee."

"You're welcome."

Pretending not to watch his sexy butt as he leaves the room, I pour myself a mug and add a healthy helping of skim milk and sugar. Once I'm finished stirring it, taking longer than necessary, I join Mom at the table.

"Sleep well?" Mom asks, giving me a pointed look.

I smile, even though inside I'm shrinking from embarrassment. "Yes. I didn't have any nightmares." I sip my coffee, anything to avoid eye contact.

"I can imagine you didn't," she says, adding to the awkward moment. At least I don't have to worry about *the* talk. She's already had it with me. And so has Grandma. "I know you care about him—"

"I love him."

"You loved Trent, too."

I frown. "And that's a problem?" I hope she's not about to lecture me on soul mates and how we only get one real love. I thought she was more practical than that.

"You're young, Amber. You'll fall in love a few times before finding the right guy."

I put the mug down harder than planned. Hot liquid sloshes over the rim and burns my hand. I ignore the brief flash of pain. "What makes you so sure he's not the right guy?"

She opens her mouth, pauses, then says what's really on her mind. "He's got a criminal record."

"No, he doesn't. His stepfather's the one who shot him. Marcus was protecting someone." Alejandro. This isn't the first time I've explained it to her, minus the details she doesn't need to know.

"Amber, he's spent time in juvenile detention."

I stare at my coffee, unsure what I'm supposed to say. I had no idea. But the boy who spent time in juvie is not the man I'm in love with. That boy was abused and in pain. The man I'm in love with is smart and caring. He risked his life for Alejandro. He was willing to risk his life for me when I thought Paul was going to kill him for being my boyfriend.

"Whatever he did wrong in the past is no longer relevant," I say. "Or at least it isn't relevant to me."

"Maybe it should be."

8

MARCUS

"Amber, he's spent time in juvenile detention." My breath stalls in my chest, not daring to let them know I'm still here. I'd gone to my room to get a change of clothing and was walking past when I heard those dreaded words. I press my back into the hallway wall, away from where they can see me.

At first neither of them says anything; then Amber speaks, her voice soft and trusting. "Whatever he did wrong in the past is no longer relevant. Or at least it isn't relevant to me."

"Maybe it should be," her mom replies.

I've always thought Amber is too good for me, and deep down I know there's a good chance what we have between us won't last forever. When I mentioned this morning about having kids, I skipped the part about the only person I could see being the mother of my kids is Amber. There is no one else for me.

Never has been.

But as her mom pointed out, Amber has loved before. She's able to connect with people in a way I'm not. I'm waiting for the moment when she wakes up and realizes she can do better without me. She doesn't need me for her to feel alive.

The thought of that feels like someone's playing basketball with my heart and bouncing it into my ribs. Like the drills we used to do against the wall when practicing our passes. *Bang. Bang. Bang.*

Now that I know their opinions, I don't bother sticking around. I go upstairs and have a shower, in a bathroom that feels vastly empty, yet full of things that remind me of Amber, most notably the strawberry scent of her hair.

Knowing that she's waiting for me, knowing my past makes no difference to her, at least for now, and knowing that her mom doesn't trust me, I hurry to get ready. Every second I'm away from Amber is two seconds too long.

When I rejoin them, Amber's cooking what smells like eggs. I long to wrap my arms around her and press my body into hers, but considering her mother's at the table, drinking coffee, and considering their earlier conversation, I stroll over to Amber and lean against the kitchen counter instead.

"Do you like omelets?" she asks, peering up through her long dark lashes.

I've never tried them. Mom isn't one for cooking, and it's not the kind of food Ryan and I would have ever made. "I love them."

She smiles, making the lie worth it. I'd do anything to see that smile. With the fucked-up psychopath's trial rapidly approaching, Amber is smiling less than usual. Even with therapy, her nightmares are frequent. Her therapist told her it's not unexpected. It's going to take a while before things improve, especially given the stress of the trial.

I hope the therapist is right that it's just a matter of time.

Amber turns off the burner, and with a spatula, slides the omelet out of the frying pan. It falls apart midair and lands in a pile on the plate.

She grins at me as though she's made a prize-winning meal, looking neither surprised nor disappointed that the omelet didn't turn out perfect. A first for Amber. With everything she does, it's like she wants to be the best.

"Here you go." She hands me the plate.

"Thanks." Perfect or not, I don't care. I'm hungry either way.

We sit at the table, across from her mother. Even though it's Christmas and everyone is trying to be cheerful, sadness sits in the air like a dense fog. For all of us.

Amber's mom keeps shooting my chest sad glances, but her gaze never wanders to the empty chair next to her. *Shit*. Just my luck that I sat in Michael's seat.

Breakfast falls into a stilted silence. None of us seems too sure what to say. The small talk we started fades, and we focus on our food instead. I can't tell if the tension is because of Amber and her mother's earlier discussion, or if it's because Michael will never spend Christmas with them again.

Or both.

I'm relieved once we're finished and Amber and I have cleared the table. Like a little girl who's been waiting all night to open her presents, Amber grins and tugs me into the living room. The place is bigger than Chase's and my apartment. But unlike our apartment, nothing is secondhand. Even the expensive mismatched furniture somehow matches, as if it were designed that way.

Originally the plan was to celebrate Christmas at Amber's grandmother's house. Somewhere between now and the last time we were here, her mom decorated a tree. It's nothing like the scrawny trees Ryan and I used to get. Those resembled something Charlie Brown would have chopped down. This tree is straight from a Hallmark card, as are the decorations.

Amber slips her arms around my neck and kisses me. It's neither a quick kiss nor one filled with hunger and want. This kiss is slow and pure, the touch of a million unspoken promises.

Craving her body pressed against mine, I pull her to me. It's been a couple of hours since we last made love and I already miss every part of her, miss every erotic sound she makes.

A polite cough startles me from behind. Amber and I jerk apart.

I don't know about my expression, but if it's anything like Amber's, guilt's written all over it.

"Should we get started?" her mom asks, resigned, looking between us.

We both nod. I take hold of Amber's hand, and she leads me to the black leather couch. I sit at one end and sink into the under-stuffed cushion. Her mom drops onto the armchair across from me.

Amber searches under the tree and hands her mom and me each a gift. Mine is the size of a shoe box, but it's too light to be actual shoes. I point to the one I want her to open first. The one from me.

She joins me on the couch, close enough so our knees touch. That's as close as I dare go with her mom in the room. "You open yours first," I murmur in her ear. Her mom's too busy with her own present to pay attention to us. I drape my arm across the back of the couch. It barely touches Amber's shoulders. She snuggles closer. A sense of victory parades through me.

Her hair is pulled up in a messy ponytail, exposing the soft skin of her neck. The soft skin I love to nibble and tease. My cock twitches at the memory of doing exactly that a few hours ago.

I tear my gaze away from her neck and watch as Amber rips away the wrapping paper from her gift. She opens the box and a small gasp breaks free from between her pink-glossed lips.

"It's beautiful." She picks up the delicate silver bracelet with the two small charms: a lotus flower and a heart.

"I love how strong you are and how strong you make me," I say, voice low. Until Amber, I always thought I was strong. Strong enough to survive the crap Frank had put me through. But my idea of strong was screwing girls and keeping my walls up. As long as no one touched my heart, I was good. Until I met Amber, I didn't realize how wrong I was and what it meant to be strong.

Amber holds out her right wrist. "Can you do it up for me?"

With slightly shaky fingers, I fasten it. The bracelet is an odd contrast to the thick scars from when the sick psychopath handcuffed her to the basement wall. That's also why I bought it for her. Every time she wears it, I want her to think about me and not him. He's her past.

I'm her future.

She leans in and kisses my cheek. "I love it. Thanks." Her warm breath brushes my ear. "And I love you." Before I can say anything, she nudges the gift on my lap. "Okay, your turn." In a move I find adorable on her, she chews her lower lip.

I stare at my present for several long moments. It's like I've forgotten what I'm supposed to do with it.

Amber laughs softly. Shit, I could get lost listening to the sound of her laughter. "Tradition dictates you open it. The real gift is inside."

I tear off the paper and open the box. Inside is a bottle of edible body lotion—a gift I assume she didn't mean for her mom to see. I leave it in there. There's also a framed close-up photo of the two of us, locked in a private moment, about to kiss. From what I can tell based on the blurred background, we were outside at the time.

"Where did you get this?" I ask.

"A girl in my dorm is a photographer. She asked me if I wanted a copy. I also have one in my dorm room."

If Amber's past hadn't been filled with the horror of last spring, I would have made some wiseass comment about the girl stalking us. Instead, I say, "It's perfect." And it is. The picture shows the real us, with our walls down. The way we are when we're together.

Amber removes the picture. Underneath is a smaller box, similar to the one her bracelet came in. I lift it out and open it. Inside is a silver dog tag hanging from a narrow chain, with the words *Forever Yours* etched on one side.

"Turn it over." She chews on her lip again.

On the other side is an eagle.

"The eagle is a symbol of inner strength and healing," she explains.

"Healing?"

"You've been helping me heal, but I'm not the only one who has to. You do, too."

Somehow, I get the feeling she's not referring to my shoulder. "Thank you. I love it." And I do. She gets me. Other than Chase and Ryan, no one else has figured me out the way she has. While I once would have felt open and raw if someone else had made that observation, with Amber I feel safe. She's my safe.

Amber helps me put it on. With it against my chest, next to where my heart beats, it's as though part of her is now part of me. I kiss her temple. She smiles back, and once more I see the girl the psychopath almost destroyed. The girl Trent used to see all the time. The girl I hope to see more of once the trial is over, and she's finally released from her nightmare.

Amber shows her mom what I gave her and explains the meaning behind the lotus flower. How it symbolizes courage and awakening as the seed starts at the bottom of the murky pond and grows toward the light. By the time it hits the surface, it becomes the beautiful flower we see. Like the girl next to me—beautiful both inside and out.

Her mother smiles, and I can tell she sees her daughter the same way I do. After everything Amber went through with the psychopath, she was broken—and still is. But instead of sinking into the darkness like many people would, she held on to the light inside her. It's that light about her that I love. The light that saved me like it saved her.

I kiss her temple again to tell her that. Without her inner light, I'd be lost. I'd still be heading down the same self-destructive path I'd been living for as long as I can remember.

We continue opening the presents. Amber's mom gives me a blue dress shirt. I give her scented candles. Amber receives clothes and gift cards, none of which seem right for the girl I love, only her mom doesn't realize it.

After we're finished, Amber and I head to Emma's house. It's large like Amber's home, but there's an apartment above the garage, which is where we're meeting up with Emma, so she left it unlocked for us. Inside, the place is tidy and is more a bachelor pad than an apartment. The twin bed is pushed against one wall and is covered with pillows, like a couch. There's also a desk, TV, and posters of players from the Chicago Bulls. If the previous occupant hadn't had a girlfriend, posters of cheerleaders and models would no doubt also be plastered on the walls.

Amber's gaze wanders around the room. A mix of emotions twists on her face and her eyes gloss over. A jealousy I have no right feeling pinches inside me....I shove it aside.

She sniffs and walks to the desk. I remain by the door, unsure what I should do. Do I let her have a few moments alone, to once again grieve for her dead boyfriend? Or do I hold her and let her cry on my shoulder?

The need to comfort her overrules all other thoughts. I gather her in my arms. She's holding a picture of her, Emma, and Trent, all smiling at the camera. It's the same photo I saw in Emma's dorm room last term, when I almost hooked up with her at a party. Back before I started to tutor Amber in math.

"I'm sorry," she whispers, her voice filled with tears. "This is the first time I've been in his room since he died."

"It's okay. You loved him. His death won't change that."

"But it's not fair to you."

I hold her a little tighter. "It doesn't matter. I know how you feel about me." And hopefully one day my love for her will help heal the hole in her heart.

I can't even be pissed at her boyfriend for hurting her, as much as I want to. It wasn't his fault. And if he were alive, she'd be in his arms, and I would be the one never knowing what it felt like to be understood, to be loved.

She twists in my arms to face me and gives me a weak smile. "Thank you for being here for me."

I run the pad of my thumb across her cheek, wiping away the tears. "Anytime." I lean down to kiss the remaining damp streaks.

My lips don't have a chance to make contact; the apartment door clicks open.

We turn around, Amber still in my arms. Releasing her, I step away, suddenly feeling awkward holding her while in her old boyfriend's room, even though it shouldn't bother me. I didn't know him.

"Guess I should have knocked first," Emma says, seeming much smaller than normal, which is hard to believe given she's just shy of six feet.

Amber hugs her best friend. Emma holds on to her tightly, as if that's the only thing keeping her together.

They separate and Emma's gaze roams the room. "My parents refuse to come in here." She continues glancing around. "After he died, I used to curl up on his bed whenever I couldn't sleep. My parents never knew. They still don't." She shrugs, looking back at us. "That sounds kinda crazy, huh?"

"No crazier than me sleeping with Michael and Trent's old T-shirts," Amber says. "Or wearing Trent's hoodie all the time because I couldn't cope without part of him always being with me."

The last part is a kick in the stomach until Amber reaches out and squeezes my hand. I remember that hoodie. She used to wear it pretty much all the time when we first started hanging out. Now she only occasionally wears it.

"I brought something with me." Emma pulls out a bottle of rum and a two-liter bottle of Coke from her messenger bag. "I thought we could do a toast or something to our brothers."

Before she said it, I hadn't realized how much the three of us have in common. We all lost our brothers this year. And all three guys were murdered. I wish it was a bond we didn't share, but I've long since learned wishes don't come true—except maybe in fairy tales.

Amber finds glasses in a kitchen cupboard. Emma pours the rum and Coke into them, going a little heavy with the rum. Normally Amber and I don't drink alcohol. The asshat my mom married is an alcoholic. Amber's mom is a recovering alcoholic. We know how destructive the stuff can be, especially when you're using it to dull the pain. But once in a while, it's hard to refuse the one thing that can help the day go by a little bit easier.

Emma has us sit on Trent's bed, with Amber sandwiched between us. A wall of solidarity on either side of her, for what she's about to face next month.

"I thought we could each share a memory about our brothers," Emma says.

Amber and I both agree to that and let her go first. Emma's obviously given it some thought.

"I remember Trent coming to our basketball games and cheering louder than anyone. Then after each game, he would recount all our highlights."

Amber laughs. "He was like a proud parent, only ten times more so."

Amber goes next and takes a moment to think about what she wants to say. "Michael used to sneak me into the house when I lost track of time with you and Trent. He knew I'd get in trouble with Mom because I kept missing curfew. So he'd help me sneak in through his bedroom window." I suspect it was more Trent that she lost track of time with.

Now it's my turn. I want to mention how Ryan suffered the brunt of Frank's abuse to keep me safe, but that's not a happy memory. This needs to be a happy one. "Ryan was a huge fan of *Harry Potter*. He used to read them to me at night when I was a kid. I think he secretly hoped Hagrid would one day show up and whisk us to Hogwarts." I used to secretly hope that, too.

Amber places her hand on my thigh and gives it a little squeeze. She knows how much my brother means to me. How I tutored her in math last term so I could raise enough money to buy my brother a gravestone. Something I never managed to do in the end. Amber has offered to give me the money, but I refuse to accept it. It doesn't feel right now that she's my girlfriend. Besides, it was Brittany who helped Amber get an A in math in the end, not me.

We raise our glasses. "To Trent, Michael, and Ryan."

We finish our drinks and Emma pours us another round. There's still rum in our glasses, but a little less than before. Or maybe it seems that way after Emma was a little heavy-handed the first time.

Amber leans her head on my shoulder and for the moment, everything feels so right.

9

MARCUS

Two weeks after Amber and I return home from spending Christmas with her family, she and Jordan come over to watch a movie. Jordan flops next to Amber on the worn navy couch and blows out a huff of air. Her springy black curls brush Amber's arm. Lucky hair.

I hand the two girls their Diet Cokes and sit next to Amber.

"I can't believe we start classes tomorrow already," Jordan says.

In the beat-up recliner next to us, Chase points to her with his beer bottle. "I hear ya. How 'bout we consider the first week an extended vacation? Then we don't have to go back till next week."

Both Jordan and Amber stare at him as if he suggested we spend an enjoyable evening at home, snapping heads off live chickens.

Laughing, I drape my arm around Amber's shoulders and pull her close. "He's kidding. Chase was the king of perfect attendance in high school. I wouldn't be half surprised if he still has his old crown."

Chase smirks. "You're just jealous."

I snort. "You're right. I am. You know damn well that crown should have been mine."

Chase cracks up, and I chuckle. Having perfect attendance in school had never been a burning ambition of mine. It's a miracle my old math teacher managed to convince me to show up and study, period. Missing school and getting laid were two of my greatest achievements—until I pulled my act together.

I grab a handful of microwave popcorn from the oversized bowl on Amber's leg. Smoky is resting against the other one, between Amber and Jordan. Not the most exciting way to spend our last night of freedom before we start back at school, but I don't care what we do, as long as I'm with Amber.

Still laughing, Chase turns the TV on and selects *Superman*. We've been watching it for forty-five minutes when Amber's phone vibrates on the scratched, fake-wood coffee table. She picks it up and checks the display.

"It's Emma." She hands me the popcorn bowl and walks toward my bedroom. Smoky gives a disgruntled meow at being disturbed and jumps off the couch.

"Hey, what's up?" Pause. "Why?" She listens for a moment. "Okay, okay." She returns to the couch and removes the phone from her ear. "Chase, change the channel to fifty-nine." The twenty-four-hour news channel.

"What's going on?" Jordan asks.

Amber shrugs. "I have no idea. She said to watch the news."

Chase flips channels.

"...For those who aren't familiar with the news story, Amber Scott was the seventeen-year-old who was allegedly kidnapped by Paul Carlson and held captive for eighteen days during the spring. According to Mr. Carlson's sister, Rosemary Carlson, Amber was never kidnapped. Rosemary reported that she has handed over love letters to the police that were written by Amber to the accused. Miss Carlson claims the teen seduced her emotionally unstable brother and convinced him to stop using his meds. The letters imply that the teen was into brutal sex, including beatings and manacles, and outlined in graphic detail what she

wanted him to do to her. The police have confirmed that they have received them…"

What the fuck! The reporter continues talking, but I'm no longer listening.

Amber's face is stripped of color and she stares openmouthed at the TV. At some point during the report, she dropped the phone. Emma's higher-than-normal voice shrills from it. "Amber? Are you there?"

Amber doesn't make a move for it. I can't tell if she's having a flashback or is in shock. Or maybe even both.

I grab the phone from the floor. "Emma, she'll call you back."

"Why would they say something like that?" Emma whispers, though I can't tell if the words are for me or for herself.

I don't have time to deal with Emma, so I hang up. I have to figure out what the hell is going on. That's more important than anything else.

I glance between Jordan and Chase. Both are looking at Amber, waiting for her to say something. Anything. Amber and Jordan have been friends for only four months, and most of that time Jordan didn't know the truth about Amber. I know Amber better than any of them. None of what the reporter said is true. The woman doesn't know Amber. If she did, she wouldn't be reporting these lies. There's no doubt Amber's been violated. The scars, the nightmares, and every time we make love, there are the little things, which she probably doesn't realize she does, that tell me she's been abused. If the reporter knew Amber like I do, there would be no question that the psychopath's sister is lying. They wouldn't be reporting this crap on the news.

"You believe her." Amber's voice is empty. Destroyed.

Frowning, I whip around to face her. *What the fuck?* How can she believe that? She knows how much I get her and get what she's been through.

She shifts away from me, the emptiness mirrored on her face. Her body shakes violently, like it did when we were at the youth center last semester and she had a flashback during a thunder-storm. She's not even paying attention to Chase or Jordan. Her pain is directed at me.

"That's not true," I say.

Her phone vibrates in my hand. Thinking it's Emma, I'm about to return it to the table when I spot the name. *Shit.* I hand Amber the phone. "It's your mom."

She takes the phone from me, her hand trembling, then answers it. She stands and walks to my room. The door closes softly behind her. Her muffled voice reaches our ears, but I can't make out what she's saying.

I turn back to Chase and Jordan. "It's a lie. There's no way she's capable of any of that."

They both nod, looking as hollow as I feel.

Jordan buries her face in her hands. "I can't believe I just sat here and didn't say anything." She directs her gaze at me. "I bet she thinks Chase and I don't believe her either. Which is crazy. Of course we know none of what they're saying about her is true." The words steamroll out of her, unwilling to wait for her to take a breath.

"It's me she's angry at, Jordan. Not you." And I have no idea how to fix this. I'm not good at this relationship stuff. Amber made it easier, but that was when she wasn't pissed at me.

I stand. "I'll talk to her."

Jordan nudges Chase's arm and unfolds her long body from the couch. "Chase and I are going to leave you guys for a while, okay?"

Chase flashes me a look that says it all: *Good luck. You'll need it.*

I'll need a helluva lot more than luck to make things right, especially since I have no idea what I did to fuck things up. I nod and watch them leave. Even after the apartment door clicks shut, I stay rooted on the spot, unable to move, listening to the silence coming from my room.

Unsure what to say, other than I love her and know she's not capable of what the woman claimed she did, I will my body to move and enter my room.

Amber's lying on the bed, arms wrapped around her knees. Her eyes are closed, face damp. My heart squeezes into a tight ball until I can barely breathe.

I kneel on the floor and brush her hair out of her face. "The cops will prove those letters are fake. They'll prove she's lying."

I expect Amber to yell at me, tell me I'm a shithead, and dump my sorry ass because she thinks I didn't believe her when we first heard the report. Like Trent hadn't believed her at first when she started receiving letters from the psychopath and he thought she was cheating on him.

But she doesn't do any of those things. She opens her eyes, and my heart squeezes even tighter at the pain still in them. "I didn't know he had a sister. He never talked about his family."

"Maybe she isn't his sister. Maybe she's someone looking for her fifteen minutes of fame. What did your mom say?"

Amber pushes herself up and sits on the edge of my bed. "She told me not to say anything to the media or to anyone else, and she'll get back to me once she finds out what's going on....Can I ask you something?"

"Of course you can."

"Why were you in juvie?"

I flinch, even though I knew this question would eventually surface. "My mom and Frank never left me and Ryan any money for food, and they rarely bothered buying groceries for us. I was fifteen and an idiot and tried shoplifting DVDs to sell to kids at school. I got caught and the judge decided I needed to be taught a lesson even though I had no previous record.

"I was in juvie for a month. It was the best damn vacation I've ever had. I got fed three meals a day, and the beatings I got there were nothing compared to what I was used to with Frank. And at least after that, my mom made sure we always had money for food.

They didn't want to risk social services breathing down their necks."

Amber's gaze drops to her lap. "My mom told me you spent time in juvie, but she didn't know why." Her voice is quiet, filled with shame.

"I know."

Her head snaps up, eyes wide.

"I overhead you two talking." I kiss her temple. "I also heard you tell her that whatever I did wrong was in the past. It wasn't relevant to us."

"I meant it. You had a rough childhood. No one should have to endure what you did, Marcus. Who you were back then isn't the man you've become." She reaches up and kisses me, her lips a soft caress. "What are Jordan and Chase doing?"

"They left so we can talk."

She kisses me again. "Maybe we should make the most of it while they're gone." Her fingers inch their way under my T-shirt and spread across my abs. My muscles contract and relax at her touch.

I study her, trying to gauge her emotions, trying to read her thoughts. She's using sex as a distraction. But what I don't know is, if I'll be a dickhead if I have sex with her when she's so broken, or if this is the best way to comfort her.

"I'm all for that," I murmur, hoping I'm not about to make a huge mistake. This feels like a test, and I'm not sure how to pass.

THE WARM, SOFT BODY UNDER MY ARM JERKS, JOLTING ME AWAKE. I open my eyes to find my room is still dark, and Amber's whimpering and moving restlessly on the bed.

I run my hand along her bare arm. "Amber, you're having a nightmare."

She mumbles something and her knee lashes out. She makes a

direct hit. Against. My. Fucking. Package. A white light blinds me and I squeeze my eyes shut. Groaning, I fold in two at the same moment Amber starts screaming. *Shit.*

Somehow, despite the mind-numbing pain, I manage to pry my eyes open. I need to calm her down before she wakes up the whole goddamn building with her screams.

"Kitten, it's okay. It's just a nightmare."

She continues tossing and turning in her sleep. I can't believe she hasn't woken herself up with the noise she's making.

Pushing past the pain, I scoot closer to her and touch her arm again. She sits up abruptly, still screaming, arms flailing. The sheet drops away, revealing her breasts. For once, my cock isn't interested.

I sit up, and while risking all kinds of injuries, gather her in my arms. Unlike a moment ago, she relaxes at my touch and her screams fade away, to be replaced by gentle sobbing.

Amber rests her head on my shoulder as Chase bursts into the room. At the sight of a half-naked Amber, he twists away, mumbling, "Sorry."

I pull the sheet up to cover her breasts. "You can turn around. She's covered."

Chase turns back to us, face redder than I've ever seen. He doesn't embarrass easily, and it's not like he's never seen a naked woman. Pride rushes through me at his reaction. He knows Amber's mine. He respects both that and her.

"You guys okay?" he asks. "I heard you groaning and her screaming, and neither of you sounded like you were having a good time."

"She had a nightmare," I tell him. Chase knows she suffers from them. She's woken up before, screaming, but never this bad. At least not while she's been with me.

Amber lifts her head from my shoulder. "I'm sorry I woke you," she whispers, voice hoarse.

Chase steps up to the bed and smiles. "Scooch over," he tells her. She does and he sits next to her. "You gonna be all right?" He's not just referring to what happened. He's referring to the fake love letters and everything else she's dealing with, no thanks to the psychopath.

It's something we're all wondering. Me. Her mom and grandmother. Emma. Jordan. None of us want to see her destroyed because of what the sick fuck did to her. She's so strong, but even steel has its limits.

She nods. "I think so."

Chase glances at me. I give a small nod. I have to be okay, for Amber.

"I want you to know, Jordan and I didn't doubt for a second that you've been set up. We should have said something sooner, but we were in shock." He looks at me. "We all were."

"I know," Amber whispers.

Satisfied we're okay, at least for now, Chase leaves and shuts the door.

"That's not true what you told him." My words are quiet, not because I want to avoid Chase hearing me. I'm afraid what I'm about to say is true. "You doubted me. I thought you understood me, understood me better than anyone. But when it came down to it, you didn't have enough faith in me to accept that I would know the difference between the truth and the lie."

She covers my hand with hers. The warmth of her skin eases its way in, like it always does whenever she touches me. And the warmth melts away some of the fear that leaked in since the news report. Her hand then moves to my face. I lean into her palm, absorbing more of her warmth, her love.

"I'm sorry, Marcus. I was scared. I shouldn't have lashed out at you. You're right. I understand you...like you understand me. You've seen the scars. You know the truth. I never doubted that."

I kiss the palm of her hand and we lie back down, her head on my chest.

I blanket her in my arms and stroke her shoulder. "Do you want to talk about the news report?"

"Not really."

"You sure? You might feel better."

"I'm sure. Talking isn't going to fix this. Only the cops can do that." But the way she says it makes me wonder if she trusts that they will—or if she's already given up hope.

10

AMBER

Jordan and I hurry to our first class, taking care not to slip on the icy sidewalks. The freezing wind nips my cheeks and nose and burrows through my jeans.

"When did you get back to the dorm last night?" I ask.

"'Round eleven."

My eyebrows shoot up my forehead. Mom called me around eight thirty. Jordan and Chase left the apartment around then and hadn't returned. Or at least they hadn't returned while I was awake. "Where did you guys go?"

"The pub near their place."

I flash Jordan a teasing smile. "And what did you guys talk about?"

She rolls her eyes. "It's nothing like that. We're just friends."

"You sure about that? You've been spending a lot of time with him."

Her grin widens. "Okay, close friends. And you're doing that thing again."

"What thing?" I say even though I know what she's talking about. Because she's about to do the same. She does it every time I bring up her and Chase's friendship.

"Redirecting."

I laugh. Jordan has that effect on people. "You're definitely going to be a psychologist." I loop my arm with hers as I scan the area, keeping an eye open for anything suspicious. The side effect of being a victim of stalking.

A gust of wind sends our hair flying forward and into our faces. My straight dark-blond hair and her black textured curls. I brush a strand behind my ear in time to see a guy from my math class last term watching me from the intersecting paths ahead of us. He's with a group of guys and elbows one of them in the ribs. Once he has his friend's attention, he nods toward me as he says something. Like a single unit, the entire group turns and their gazes run appreciatively over my body. I might be wearing a winter coat, but it feels as though they can see past my layers, stripping me naked.

"So things are okay with you and Marcus?" Jordan asks. She either doesn't notice the guys or can't be bothered to give them a second thought.

"He knows I didn't write the letters." And in a few hours, everyone else will know.

"But are things okay between you two?" Her expression turns serious. And like with those guys we passed, it's as if she can see through my layers. But unlike with those jerks, she's delving deeper, to the most vulnerable part.

"Seriously, we're fine." All I have to do is survive the trial and everything will be okay.

Jordan goes off to her class and I enter the room for Community Psychology. Emma's already here, seated in the third row. I tried calling her this morning but ended up with her voice mail. I sit next to her. Emma doesn't look at me, her attention focused on the empty page in front of her.

"Hey," I say. She startles. "Is something wrong?"

She turns, her expression a mix of emotions, none I can get a firm grasp on beyond exhaustion. Her normally bright blue eyes are dull above dark half circles. "Why are the reporters accusing you of writing those letters?" she asks quietly.

"I didn't write them. I loved Trent. You know that." I fight to keep my voice low and even, none too thrilled at the prospect of providing a free source of entertainment for everyone in the room.

If I thought Emma looked startled before, that's nothing compared to now. She opens her mouth to say something.

"Okay, class," a tall woman says, wearing black pants and a cream-colored sweater. "Let's get started. I'm handing out the class outline." She passes a stack of papers to the person at the end of our row and moves to the row behind us. The girl takes a handout and gives the pile to the guy next to her. "As you'll see, there will be two midterms, a term paper, and an oral presentation..."

She continues talking, but I don't hear what she's saying. All I hear in my head over and over and over again are the words *oral presentation*. I remove a handout and pass the rest to the person next to me. We spend the remainder of the class listening to the professor talk about her expectations and what the course will cover. Once it's over, we pack up to leave.

Emma hasn't rushed off, and even though I'm meeting up with Marcus to study in the library, I hold back to talk to her.

"I swear, Emma, those letters are fake. You have to know how much I loved Trent." At the thought of losing my best friend over this lie, my insides begin to crumple. I sniff. "I need you," I whisper.

Lines pucker between her eyebrows. "Am I missing something? Why would I think you wrote them?"

My head droops forward. God, I'm such an idiot. My friends believe in me, but I couldn't get past my fear of losing them. So instead, I assumed they thought I was capable of doing what I've been accused of.

I gave Paul power over me once. And due to my own stupidity, I almost gave it to his sister, too.

"When you went missing," Emma says as we leave the class-room, "your story was constantly on the news. At one point they announced you had been found. I'd lost Trent but you were still alive. I cried so hard because I was happy. But the report was wrong. The cops didn't have a clue where you were. You can't believe everything you hear on the news. They screw things up like everyone else."

A couple of students pass us, laughing at a private joke. It's easy to laugh when your private life isn't splashed on television and newspapers. How the hell do celebrities survive all the gossip that hits the tabloids? I couldn't do it.

"I'm hoping that's the last of it. The reporter wasn't even supposed to mention my name, because I was a minor when it happened and because I was raped." I practically whisper the last part.

"So why did she?"

I shrug. "Maybe she figured it didn't count since the letters were supposed to be love letters. According to Paul's sister, I wasn't kidnapped. I was there with Paul willingly." I cringe at the disgust on Emma's face each time I mention Paul's name.

"Maybe," she says, slowly sounding out the word.

We hug, and I head to the library. Marcus isn't at a table in the library when I arrive. I continue to the rear of the room. That way I won't be noticeable. That way I can hide and make sure no one pays more attention to me than they should.

A few people look my way as I pass, but no hint of recognition crosses their faces.

I'm safe.

I STRIDE THROUGH THE CROWDED FOOD COURT, DODGING PAST TABLES as I search for my friends.

A hand grabs my arm from behind me. "Hey, babe, what's the rush?"

My body stiffens at his touch. I turn to find a tall, bulky guy I don't recognize leering at me. His hair is buzz-cut short and he has a large star tattoo on the side of his neck. I might not recognize him, but I do recognize the guy from this morning at the table next to us watching the exchange. Like this morning, he's checking me over.

I jerk my arm away and keep walking.

The guy snatches my arm back. "Hey, I wanna talk to you. I hear you're into the heavy stuff."

Frowning, I try to wrench my arm free. "What are you talking about?"

His fingers curl into my arm to the point of causing me pain. I gasp, too stunned by his actions to do anything else.

He lowers his voice to a seductive purr. "You know, as in sex. Whips. Bondage. The good stuff." My stomach crashes to my feet and my body starts shaking. I want to run, but my fight-or-flight reaction has bailed on me.

"Get your hand off her." Marcus's tone is as sharp as the blade of an ax. He rests his hand on the curve of my spine, his message unmistakable.

To anyone but this guy.

Buzz Cut scowls. "What's your problem?"

Everyone at the surrounding tables watches us with growing interest. The food-court noise is nothing compared to the silence emanating from near us.

"My *problem* is you're touching my girlfriend."

Buzz Cut's hand drops away from my arm. "Well, then, you're a lucky guy." He winks at me and joins his friends.

With his hand still protectively on my back, Marcus guides me over to Jordan and Chase.

"You're shaking," he says as we take our seats across from them. "What did he say to you?" Unlike everyone else in the general area, Jordan and Chase are both deep in conversation, oblivious to what happened.

"He knows."

"Knows what?"

"He knows about the news report. He thinks I get off..." I shudder, the cruelty of the words choking me. "That I get off on being beaten during sex."

Marcus turns around in his seat and throws Buzz Cut a dark look. Not that the guy sees it. He and his friends are preoccupied with their current topic of interest—which hopefully doesn't involve me.

"What's going on?" Chase asks.

"People saw the news report last night about the letters to Paul," I say.

"Has anyone else said anything to you about it?" Marcus inquires.

"No. He's the only one. But his friend, who was in my math class last term, was pointing me out to some other guys this morning."

"Give it a day or two and everyone will move on." Chase's tone is optimistic, but the emotion in his eyes is far from it. He believes that like he believes in the Easter bunny.

"It's a good thing we're starting our self-defense class tonight." Jordan's serious expression transforms into a grin. "Then you can kick the butt of the next guy who harasses you."

"Unless if he's like that loser." I jerk my head toward Buzz Cut. "That might turn him on."

Marcus glares at the guy again. "In that case, I'm staying with you twenty-four-seven. Until the news gets their ass together and releases the truth about the letters. I'm not risking another shithead thinking he has the right to touch you."

I place my hand on his forearm. His muscles are bunched up tight. I gently rub them, trying to ease the tension out of him. "You can't miss your classes, Marcus. They're too important. Paul's already screwed up enough people's lives. I'm not letting him screw up yours, too."

Marcus opens his mouth to say something as a redhead in painted-on jeans places her hand on his shoulder. Her equally skinny friend with straight black hair hungrily eyes him. An expression mirrored by the redhead.

He turns to them. "Yes?"

"We've missed you, Marcus." Redhead's voice drips like molasses off a spoon.

Jordan rolls her eyes, and I press my lips together to keep from laughing. At Jordan. Not at the two girls. Though from the way they're paying attention to Marcus and not us, I doubt they would have even noticed if I did laugh.

I unwrap the egg sandwich Marcus made me this morning, willing the girls to go away.

"There's a party this weekend and we're hoping you'll come." Redhead leans over, her hand high on his thigh, her cleavage inches from his face. "Maybe we could have some more two-on-one action." She moves her hand higher, her little finger getting way too intimate with my boyfriend.

My appetite vanishes and I dump my sandwich onto the plastic wrap. Marcus has been involved with more girls than I care to think about, but it doesn't mean I want to know all the details about their pasts. Especially details like this.

Unable to bear seeing the sympathy in Jordan's and Chase's eyes, I pick apart my sandwich and pretend I'm anywhere but here.

"I have a girlfriend."

"Who doesn't like to share," I say without glancing up. The heated words fall from my mouth before I even realize they were there.

Jordan coughs to hide her laugh. Chase and Marcus are watching me with amusement twitching at their lips. Only the two girls don't find my comment funny. They check me over, clearly deciding I don't meet their level of blatant sex appeal. And it's true. I don't.

Marcus wraps his arm around my waist and smiles at them.

The black-haired girl pouts. "Well, if you change your mind, you know our number."

"That's what they think," he mutters as they walk away. He turns to me, beaming as if he's proud of something. "I've only kept your number, Kitten."

"You mean you don't have a little black book?" Jordan asks, seemingly shocked at what she assumed would be a given.

He shakes his head. "Never needed one. I rarely had sex with the same girl twice." Other than with Tammara. Until she wanted their friends-with-benefits arrangement to become something more.

"So why did you ask for their phone numbers if you weren't gonna keep them?" Jordan's tone isn't filled with disgust, just curiosity. Like she's planning to write a how-to book on dating and this is research.

"I didn't. Girls just give 'em to me." He flashes me a smile. "Except for Amber. It took me a while to convince her to give me her number." And the only reason I did was because he was tutoring me in math. We needed to be able to contact each other if there was a change of plans.

As I watch the girls sashay away, I wonder how sex has become, to everyone else, the thing that defines me and Marcus—even if everyone is wrong about what they perceive to be the truth, that I'm into violent sex and Marcus is a man-whore. Though the bigger question is: How can we change it if no one wants to believe us?

11

AMBER

The next evening I stuff my psych book and change of clothes into my knapsack. "If anyone's looking for me, I've gone to Marcus's to study."

Brittany, my roommate, smirks. "Study? Is that what you're calling it?" Her gaze drops to my bag. "Do you usually bring a change of clothing when you study?"

"Sure, don't you?" I ask with feigned innocence.

She flicks an eraser at me. It bounces off my shoulder. I flinch, even though it didn't hit hard, and let it fall to the floor.

On the desk are her latest manga drawings she's currently working on. She's pre-med majoring in criminology, but whenever she's procrastinating or is pissed at something, she sketches.

This picture is darker than her usual ones. A fierce dragon rears above a young woman, ready to tear her to pieces. The girl's long brown hair flows around her shoulders. She's wearing a black dress and thigh-high boots. The same dress and boots I've seen on Brittany.

"Has Jake tried contacting you again?" Her boyfriend who raped her last semester. Well, now ex-boyfriend. The last time she drew a picture of this dragon, he'd called her to tell her he was sorry and wanted to get back together with her.

"I hung up on him like last time."

"Good. But you should tell the cops that he's harassing you."

Brittany picks up the eraser from the floor. "What good would that do?"

"They could tell you how to get a restraining order so he leaves you alone." And hopefully he's not one of those guys who ignores it. I decide not to share that part with Brittany. But at least then the DA can hit him with more charges, beyond rape and battery.

She continues working on her picture.

"Promise me you'll tell the cops."

She sighs, eyes locked on the drawing. "Okay, I promise." I can't tell if what she is saying is the truth or not, but I decide to let it go. For now.

I grab my knapsack and laptop and leave the room.

Glancing around every few seconds, I slip down the hallway, hoping I can escape the building before anyone interrogates me about the allegations that I enjoy being beaten during sex. I can't believe how everyone is reacting to the erroneous story. I was kidnapped and tortured by a guy who was stalking me, but no one cares about that. They're more interested in the lies. Not once since the news broke, and people realized I am *the* Amber Scott, has anyone asked me how I'm doing. It's like the truth isn't sensational enough to bother with, at least not compared to the sex scandal.

I'm about to head downstairs when a cop steps out of the RA's room, followed by Becca the RA.

"Amber," she says. "Officer O'Neil is here to talk to you."

Ignoring her, I ask him, "About what?"

"This is something we need to discuss at the station."

"Why? Am I in trouble?"

His expression isn't very reassuring. "I have questions for you regarding some letters we've received."

"I'm allowed one phone call, right?" I squeak even though there's no reason for me to be nervous.

"You're not being arrested," is his nonanswer.

He escorts me to his cruiser and opens the rear door for me. The few people milling about watch with interest. I slide onto the back seat and with shaky hands, I phone Mom. She tells me not to worry. She'll contact someone and they'll meet me at the station.

Then I call Marcus and update him on what's happening.

"I'm on my way," he says. Despite everything going on, a comforting warmth spreads through me. Hanging out at a police station can't be up there on his list of favorite places, not with his past experiences, yet he plans to go there. For me.

As the cruiser pulls up to the station, a crowd surges forward. Reporters, I'm guessing, from the camera and video gear some are sporting.

"What's going on?" I ask, checking to see if I spot any familiar faces. I haven't heard of any more mall shootings, and don't they usually hang around the mall when that happens?

"They found out we need to question you." He flashes me a sympathetic look in the rearview mirror. The first one he's given me since showing up at the dorm.

But instead of making me less jittery, it exacerbates the panic flooding me, to the point where I'm drowning. I pull my knees to my chest and make myself smaller.

The cop parks the cruiser and escorts me to the building. Several other cops help with crowd control.

But it's not enough to prevent a reporter from slipping past. He sticks a microphone in my face. "Amber, can you tell us why you wrote those letters to Mr. Carlson?"

Don't speak to reporters, Amber, Mom's voice says in my head. *Don't give them the opportunity to twist your words.*

I remain silent and focus on the sidewalk, trying to block out their voices.

"Do you love Paul Carlson?" someone yells.

I know you love me, Amber. Paul's voice replaces Mom's. I cringe at the memory of it and at the memory of him stroking my hair, like my mom used to do when I was scared of storms. *You might not be ready to say the words yet, but you will. And then we'll be together forever and ever.*

My body trembles as his words wrap around me. I pull away from myself to keep from being yanked into a flashback. I'm here but I'm not. Numb, but not numb enough.

The cop directs me inside the brick building to a small room with a mirror on one wall, and a table with three chairs. All the walls match with their dingy white color, but the other three are empty, without as much as a window to make the place less claustrophobic.

A small female cop joins us, dressed in a navy pants suit. She might look tiny, but I don't doubt she could kick some major ass if need be. She smiles at me. It's not enough to drive away the fear. "I'm Detective Hale. Would you like something to drink?"

"No, thanks." My voice is as shaky as my body. I take a deep breath while trying not to be obvious about it. *I've done nothing wrong. There's nothing to be nervous about.* It doesn't matter how many times I tell myself this, I can't convince my body and brain that it's true.

To distract myself, I play with the lotus charm Marcus gave me. Strong. I can be that. Right?

The door opens and a woman my mom's age, wearing slim-fitting jeans and a flowery blouse, enters the small room.

"Hi, Amber." She holds out her hand for me to shake. "I'm Sheryl Kenyon. Your mom and I are old law school friends. She asked me to be here with you since she couldn't."

"I don't get what I've done wrong."

"You haven't done anything wrong, Amber. Despite what Mr. Carlson's lawyer is claiming, you're still very much the victim. But we need to prove it in light of the recent evidence."

"You mean the letters? I didn't write them. I swear I didn't."

Sheryl takes the seat beside mine. Detective Hale sits across from us and places a thick file on the table.

She opens it and removes a piece of paper, which she slides across the table to me. "Does this look familiar?"

I read it and frown. "It looks like my writing, but I never wrote this." The letter is embarrassingly sappy and it sounds like I was horny for Paul when I supposedly wrote it. It's not something I would have written, even for Trent. "Don't you have someone who can analyze handwriting? They'll tell you it's a fake."

"Someone did analyze it with a writing sample your mother gave us. It was a match."

Part of me wants to curl into a tight ball and pretend none of this is happening. It's not the part that says, loudly, "But that's impossible. I. Didn't. Write. It."

Sheryl puts her hand on mine. It's not to comfort me. It's to shut me up. "Handwriting analysis isn't a perfect science. Handwriting can be faked by someone who knows what he's doing." She isn't telling me this. I'm just in the room as far as she's concerned. This conversation is directed at the detective. "It's my understanding that the letters claim Amber is involved in masochism. But there is no proof that she is. The letters prove nothing. And even if she were involved in it, it does not entitle anyone, including Mr. Carlson, to rape her."

Detective Hale removes a photo from the file and slides it across the table to us. In it, I'm standing at the counter in the adult store with Emma, and the salesclerk is showing me the whip. The picture resembles one from a store security camera.

My eyes widen, and I stare at the photo. I'm nothing more than a puppet whose strings are being moved at someone's whim. "It's not what it looks like. Emma and I were searching for gag gifts for our boyfriends. All I bought was body lotion."

"Why is he showing you the whip?" the detective asks.

"I don't know. I saw them and he mistakenly thought I was interested. He showed me one and I zoned out."

"Zoned out?"

"Yes. I was there and I wasn't. Paul whipped me once because I wouldn't talk to him and because I wouldn't eat." I subconsciously move my hand to my shoulder. Below it is the worst of my scars. "But I'm sure you already know that." My gaze falls to the file.

"Amber was severely injured by Mr. Carlson's actions," Sheryl points out. "The wounds were allowed to fester and were what one would hardly call the result of consensual sexual activity. If she hadn't been found when she was, she would have died from them."

I close my eyes, attempting to block the memory of lying on my side, afraid to move due to the pain. When the firefighter found me in the burning building, I was burning up as much on the inside as I was on the outside.

"You have to believe me." The words trip over themselves, my voice growing rough with tears. "I was never interested in Paul that way. He was my friend at the animal shelter. That's all. I loved my boyfriend, Trent. Paul knew that. It's why he killed him."

"If you didn't write them, who did?"

"How would I know? This is the first time I've seen them."

Detective Hale removes a small stack of pink paper from the folder and pushes them toward me. I start reading the letters, and with each word my stomach churns more and more, until I'm positive I'm going to hurl. The first letters are nothing compared to the later ones, which describe in gruesome detail what I want him to do to me.

My stomach reacts as though I'm on a roller coaster, and I'm hurtling down a massive drop, sending the contents rushing in the opposite direction. "I'm gonna be sick," I say weakly.

The detective jumps up and retrieves the trash can seconds before both women see what I had for lunch.

12

———

MARCUS

I push the shopping cart down the vegetable aisle, scanning the possibilities.

"What about cooked baby carrots?" Chase asks. "Who doesn't love those?"

"I guess so." Amber's never said she doesn't like them, so they should be a safe enough choice. I think.

Chase tosses the small package into the cart. "Does she like Indian food? 'Cause my mom started buying kits for making butter chicken. It's really good. Plus it's easy to make."

Easy to make? I can deal with that. "We haven't discussed foods she likes, other than she loves pizza and chicken noodle soup and chocolate ice cream." I shrug, feeling a little lame at not knowing these things about the girl I love.

The look he throws me confirms he's thinking the same. "Butter chicken it is. Frozen pizza isn't very romantic, and the deli pizza here sucks." He grabs the shopping cart and leads me to the Asian food aisle. Several minutes later, I have a box of butter chicken mix and a small bag of basmati rice; then he drags me to the meat section to find chicken breasts. Next, we pick up candles... at Chase's insistence.

I laugh. "Dude, you need a girlfriend."

Before he can argue or agree or whatever he'd planned to do, a tall brunette, who would leave most men panting at the sight of her, steps up to my cart and smiles at me. Her bright-green eyes glow with an edge of seduction.

Relief that Amber isn't here rushes through me. I don't recognize this woman, but that doesn't mean anything. I've slept with so many girls in the past, their faces are all a blur. Though I doubt I'd forget this one.

"Marcus Reid."

"Yes," I say even though it was a statement, not a question.

"I'm Angelina Mathews from Channel Four News."

Chase glances over my shoulder and groans. I don't have to look to know why. She's not here alone. She's got her cameraman with her.

"Whatever you want, I'm not interested." Whatever it is can't be good.

"I want to talk to you about your girlfriend."

"No comment," I snap.

"Is it true the two of you participate in more violent forms of sexual activity?"

"What kind of fuckin' question is that?"

A mother pushing a cart down the aisle with her two young kids glares at me as she hurries past.

Chase steps in between the reporter and me. "Unless you want us to file a complaint against you for sexual harassment, I suggest you leave. C'mon," he says to me under his breath, "let's get out of here." He nudges me forward and pushes the cart toward the self-serve checkout.

"Can we really file a sexual harassment complaint?" I ask, intrigued at the idea but at the same time suspecting he was bullshitting.

"Who the hell knows? I just had to get you outta there before you did something both you and Amber will regret."

I turn on the TV. The spicy scent of butter chicken fills the small apartment as the chicken, rice, and carrots cook on the stove. Smoky jumps onto the couch, then flops against my thigh. I scratch him under the chin. He misses Amber as much as I do.

I'm about to flip channels when the anchorman says, *"The story surrounding Amber Scott and her alleged kidnapping earlier last year has taken a new turn. In light of the love letters she wrote to Paul Carlson that have recently surfaced, the Chicago Police have been interviewing anyone who can provide additional leads."*

The news cuts to the outside of my apartment building, to the eighty-year-old woman from next door. Chase sits on the beat-up recliner and we exchange confused looks.

She tells the reporter about hearing Amber screaming on more than a few occasions. *"I've been close to calling the cops several times, because the young lady has been quite disruptive with that good-for-nothing boyfriend of hers who the police frequently visit."*

"You bitch," I hurl at the TV. "She screams because of the fuckin' nightmares that fuckin' asshole caused." I'm ready to storm down the hallway and repeat it to her face, but Chase's don't-even-think-about-it expression glues me to the couch.

My cell phone rings from my bedroom. Still cursing the stupid bitch, I retrieve it and check who's calling. Amber?

"Hey, Kitten. You're still coming over, right?"

"I can't. A cop is taking me in for questioning." Her voice is so small, scared, my heart breaks just hearing it.

"Why? You haven't done anything wrong." I don't give her a chance to respond. "I'm on my way."

Hanging up, I stalk into the living room and grab my keys from the kitchen table. "The cops are dragging Amber in for questioning." Smoky meows at her name.

"Is she okay?" Chase asks.

"I don't know."

I arrive at the station to find it swarming with media. *What the fuck?*

After parking my car, I push through the crowd. Thank God the reporter from earlier isn't part of this lot. That's the last thing either Amber or I need. As it is, I don't know how the woman even found out that Amber's my girlfriend. While we haven't been hiding the truth, we also haven't painted it on a billboard.

I enter the building. Not a single reporter harasses me. Most seem bored, talking to other reporters or texting.

I tell the cop behind the counter that I'm here for Amber, and I'm directed to the plastic chairs along one wall. I don't bother sitting. I pace back and forth, restless, as though I'm the one locked behind bars. This isn't the place I was dragged to when I was arrested for shoplifting, but it might as well be. Everything about it, including the stench of desperation and power is in this place.

I've been pacing for at least an hour when Amber emerges, pale and more broken than I've seen in a while. I silently curse everyone responsible for that look and gather her in my arms. Her usual strawberry smell, with a touch of mint this time, engulfs me, along with the urge to hold on to her tighter.

"Are you Marcus Reid?" The woman's gaze moves to Amber and I see the concern in it.

"Yes." I keep holding on to Amber, afraid if I let go for even a moment, she'll disappear.

The woman smiles softly, but it's not enough to erase the concern. "Take her home and take care of her. She's been through a lot."

"Is this about the fake letters the psychopath is claiming she wrote?"

The smile fades away. "I'm afraid so."

"But you know they're fakes, right?"

She nods. "I believe Amber when she says they are."

Amber pulls away, and I reluctantly let her go. "But what about the cops?" Her voice is heavy, as though she's carrying the weight of several buses on her shoulders. "They don't believe me, do they? I mean, with the evidence they've got against me, I'm not sure I'd believe me either."

"Amber, they're doing their job," the woman says. "They believe you. It might not seem like it, but they do believe you. They know you're the victim. But they have to gather all the evidence so the DA can prove without a doubt that Mr. Carlson is guilty of everything he's been accused of. If they don't, it could put the trial in jeopardy. We just have to hope they turn up something soon to prove the letters are fake."

The woman hands me her business card and we leave the building, my arm around Amber's waist. The two cops with us do their best in keeping the media from getting too close. You'd think Amber was a rock star and they were the paparazzi the way they're acting.

Whenever one of them asks a question, Amber's lawyer tells them no comment. Amber doesn't look at them. She focuses on the ground, her face even more pale and wary than when she first stepped out of the interrogation room.

I drive Amber back to the apartment. While she describes what happened during her interrogation and about the evidence against her, my hands tighten on the steering wheel, coming close to snapping it in two. I avoid mentioning the reporter at the grocery store and my neighbor's need to destroy me, to destroy us.

And all I want to do is hit something.

13

AMBER

I wake up in Marcus's bed, his arm keeping me close. This is the only time I feel truly safe, even though it's when I'm at my most exposed. I snuggle closer to him, absorbing his safety and warmth. No one has ever made me feel this way, not even Trent. I loved Trent, but what I feel for Marcus goes beyond that. I might have had doubts about him after I misinterpreted his reaction to the news report, but he came through for me by coming to the police station, the last place he wanted to be.

Eventually I wiggle out of bed, needing to go to the bathroom. Marcus doesn't stir, and he looks more at peace than he has for a while. He won't admit it, but he suffers from nightmares, too. Nightmares based on the horrors he went through as a kid.

I silently slip out of the room. Smoky meows from his treehouse scratching post, jumps down, then rubs against my leg.

"You hungry?" I scoop him up in my arms and smile as he butts his head under my chin. He used to do it a lot, along with kneading my arm, during the time when Paul held me captive and tortured Smoky to force me to cooperate. It was Smoky's way of keeping me alive. It was like he knew that once I allowed myself to slip into unconsciousness, we were both dead. I was the one thing saving him from an early grave, and he was the one thing saving me from mine.

Once he's fed, I check my phone. Mom called and wants me to phone her right back. She phoned over two hours ago. She must be frantic by now. I'm sure she's already spoken to Sheryl, her lawyer friend, and I'm not ready yet to discuss what happened with anyone. Not even Mom.

Emma also left a message.

> Emma: I saw the news. Are you okay? I can't
> believe that old witch said those things
> about you.

What old witch?

Curiosity and fear pulse painfully through my veins, and I reluctantly turn on the TV. I flip through the channels until I find the local news. A minute or two later, I discover what Emma was talking about.

Once again, in the eyes of the media, the evidence makes it appear as if I get off on violent sex and I seduced an emotionally unstable man. But even if it were true, what about Michael and Trent? Even if Paul is found innocent of his crimes against me, there's no way he can talk his way out of what happened to my brother and boyfriend. He can't pin their deaths on fake love letters.

Unless there's something in them you don't know about, a voice in my head taunts. I didn't read all the letters. The ones I skimmed were bad enough.

I stare at the television, vaguely aware it's on. All I can think about are my options. The media is painting me as someone I'm not, and Marcus's neighbor hasn't helped. Maybe I should talk to them. Tell them my side of the story. Maybe even explain the screams she heard are due to my nightmares.

But would they buy it? What does more for their ratings: me screaming because of nightmares, or me screaming because

Marcus and I are VIP members of an S&M fan club?

The footage of Marcus leading me from the police station flashes on the screen. I look like hell. Worse than hell. But what do I expect after puking? At least the media didn't get footage of that... or maybe it would help me if they had.

I pick up the remote and mute the volume, then call Mom.

"Sheryl told me what happened yesterday," she says. "Are you all right?" It's clear from her tone that she knows I'm not. There's no point in lying.

I skip the answer and bulldoze forward. "The media is telling nothing but lies about me. Isn't there something we can do to stop them?"

Mom sighs heavily. "I wish there were, but they aren't exactly lying. They're reporting the evidence as they see it. Whether you wrote those letters or not, Amber, it doesn't matter. They do exist, and Rosemary Carlson sent copies of the earlier ones to the media. Right now our concern is proving they're fakes."

"But if we can't prove they're fakes, he can at least be charged for statutory rape, right?"

Mom doesn't answer right away, and dread fills me with each millisecond of silence. Her voice is weary when she finally responds. "The age of consent in Illinois is seventeen." Which means they can't charge him for statutory rape. I was seventeen when I had sex with him.

"Shouldn't I at least issue a statement?" I whisper.

"The DA's office will do that. Amber, I can't stress enough how important it is that you don't talk to the media."

"But doesn't that make me look guilty?"

"What will make you look guilty is when they reveal things taken out of context. Anyway, the media isn't the court of law. And you're not going on trial. Paul Carlson is."

It only feels like I'm being tried by my peers. It's my reputation that's being destroyed. I'm the one who has to put up with guys thinking they have the right to sexually harass me, all because Paul's sister is doing whatever she can to save her brother.

I flop back on the couch. A large part of me is relieved I don't have to talk to reporters, even though I want to clear my name as soon as possible. Speaking in front of a class is bad enough. I shudder at the thought of doing so in front of the camera and in front of everyone at Paul's trial. One I can avoid. The other I can't.

There's one other reason why I need to avoid reporters. "You used to say the media drove Dad away. Is that true?"

The line is silent, and for a moment I wonder if Mom's hung up. "Yes," she eventually says. "It was too much for him. He couldn't handle the attention from having a wife who was a high-profile defense lawyer. I think it scared him, too."

"That's what I thought." I'm no longer talking about my father. How long will it take before Marcus has had enough and also walks out of my life?

14

MARCUS

I check through Alejandro's math equation and grin. A smattering of college students are sitting in the food court and joking with their friends now that classes are done for the day. "Looks good. I think you'll get another A on your next quiz."

Alejandro fist-pumps the air. "Now there's no way coach is kickin' me off the team."

"As long as you don't mess up your other classes."

"Not a problem. I'm good in those." He packs away his books so we can head to the gym to play ball. I desperately need to blow off steam after the last few days, and this was my way of bribing Alejandro into talking to me.

The redhead from lunch the other day approaches, wearing tight jeans and an equally tight T-shirt. "Hi, Marcus." Her eyes flick to Alejandro. "Is this your brother?"

The only things Alejandro and I have in common is we're both tall and have black hair. Smiling at her, he rattles off something in Spanish. I might not understand everything he says, but I know enough to realize his comments would get most guys slapped.

My insides freeze as I remember how Frank touching me led to

100

my man-whore reputation. I was searching for a way to deal with the numbness and for a way to prove I wasn't like him. Having sex with any girl eager to spread her legs seemed the perfect solution.

Shit, I hope Alejandro isn't headed down my old self-destructive path. It won't drive away the pain. It will make things worse.

The girl smiles at him as if he's an adorable puppy.

"Is there something you need?" I glance around, making sure Amber isn't nearby. She's supposed to be with Emma, Brittany, and Jordan in their self-defense class, but I don't want to risk her leaving early and seeing me with this girl. I don't need any more of my sexual past returning and hurting her.

"I saw the news the other day about your girlfriend. You know, that blond you were with." Her gaze drops to my lap. I scoot forward so the table covers her view. She licks her lips. "I know she doesn't share"—she leans down. Her breath brushes my ear—"but I can do things that'll make you both feel good. Make you both come screaming. I'm especially talented with whips." I don't doubt it.

I push her away. Alejandro's eyes are about to pop across the Marketplace. "Not interested," I say firmly.

She laughs. "From what I've heard, you're more than interested. Both of you."

Alejandro's mouth flops open.

"One, don't believe the lies you hear on TV," I tell her. "Two, neither my girlfriend nor I are interested, so quit harassing me. Apparently you and I had sex once. It's a mistake I won't be repeating." I might as well have slapped her. And judging from her wide eyes, my words stung as if I had.

She walks off in a huff.

Alejandro doesn't watch her leave. He's watching me, the shocked expression still on his face. "You don't even remember having sex with her? How can you not remember? I mean, did you *see* her?"

"Look, I thought by having sex with girls—a lot of girls—it

would erase what Frank did to me. That it would erase the pain. And maybe it did for a while. But that was all a lie. I didn't realize it till I started dating Amber." I lock eyes with his. "Don't make the same mistakes I did, Alejandro. Don't let Frank win."

Alejandro glares at me. "I'm not telling anyone what happened, so don't even go there."

I open my mouth to say something but slam it shut as a man approaches our table. The smell of garlic lingers on him.

"Marcus Reid?"

"Cop or reporter?" I grunt.

Alejandro's gaze jumps from me to the man, a million questions written all over his face.

"I'm a reporter with the *Chicago Post*. I want to ask you about—"

"I don't give a damn what you want. What *I* want is for you and the rest of your idiotic friends to leave me and Amber alone." I stand and grab my books, hinting to Alejandro to do the same.

"It will—"

The look I give him causes him to step back. "Do I need to report you to security?"

"No." He says something else, but Alejandro and I are walking away. Now more than ever, I need to play ball.

"What was that all about?" Alejandro asks.

"It's nothing," I grumble.

He stops abruptly, his eyes dull with fear. "It wasn't nothing. Did he want to talk to you about Frank?"

I glance around, checking no one's within earshot. Fortunately my threat about security was enough to keep the reporter from following us. He's skulking in the opposite direction. "No. It's about Amber."

"What about her?" The fear turns to concern and protective-ness, and my heart swells that he feels that way, even if he doesn't know her very well.

"She was kidnapped last year by a stalker and badly hurt. Now his sister claims Amber wrote love letters to him, and everything he did to her Amber wanted. The media's been twisting things."

"That was Amber? ¡*Meirda!* I heard my parents talking about it. They said her name should never have been mentioned. Now everyone knows she was raped."

I cringe at his unspoken thoughts. "The reporters haven't mentioned anything about her being raped. And just because Amber's name was leaked it doesn't mean yours will be."

He narrows his eyes. "How can you be sure?"

"Amber's name was released when she went missing. The media stopped using it once she was found, 'cause she was a minor, but her name was already public record. Your name won't be."

"But if I tell the cops what happened to me, people might figure out what he did to me."

"They're not going to figure it out."

"How can you be so sure?" His voice is loud enough to gain us a few curious glances.

I want to give him the answers he's looking for, but I can't. I can't be sure the media isn't going to be sniffing around, searching for their next story.

Alejandro walks toward the exit, his next words soft, spoken more for his benefit than mine. "That's what I thought."

15

AMBER

Marcus checks his phone, his body pressed against mine on the narrow dorm bed. I already miss his warm lips on my neck, and I almost groan my complaint. But he's been waiting for a text from Tammara for several days.

"Tammara finally responded. She's back in town." He replies to her. Thirty seconds later, she responds. "We're on. She'll meet me at my apartment in half an hour." He pushes himself off me and the bed and holds his hand out to me. "Let's go."

"Are you sure? I don't think she's going to be too thrilled to see me." Especially once she learns that we know she was the one who sent me the fake letters from Paul last semester. Especially once she finds out they aren't the only fake letters we want to know about.

"I don't care if she's thrilled or not." Marcus's mouth spreads into my favorite sexy, one-sided smile. "You're there to protect me from her."

"Smoky will protect you." I lean in and briefly kiss Marcus. "He likes you." Which is saying a lot. Smoky doesn't like too many people. Not after Paul abused him to keep me in line.

We leave my room and I turn to lock the door.

"Amber Scott?" a powerful male voice rumbles behind me.

I swivel to find two cops approaching with Becca, the RA. My body tenses and I look wildly between her and Marcus. They don't know what's going on any more than I do, but I need the confirmation that everything will be all right.

Except they can't do that. It'd be a lie. I can tell from the way the two cops regard me that once again I'm the criminal, not the victim.

"Yes?" The word comes out as a squeaked whisper.

"We have a search warrant for your room and backpack."

"What for?"

The bulky cop doesn't answer. He hands me a folded piece of paper. I open it and read. According to it, they're looking for any items that are sexual in nature linking me to the letters I supposedly wrote to Paul. They're also looking for letters written to Paul from me, or letters he may have written to me. The latter I gave the cops when he was stalking me, but Paul never signed them.

"You're wasting your time." I hand the paper to Marcus. "I don't have any of those things. And I have a roommate. You can't search through her stuff too." I know nothing about search warrants, but doesn't Brittany have rights? She's done nothing wrong.

Like I've done nothing wrong but they're treating me as if I have.

"The warrant is only for your personal possessions," the smaller, bald-headed cop explains. "The places we can search are outlined in the warrant."

"But shouldn't she be here at least?

"It's not mandatory."

I open the door and stand to the side with Marcus.

"Which is your side of the room?" Bald Cop asks. I point to it.

"It's gonna be okay, Amber," Marcus says. "You've done nothing wrong. But you should call your lawyer and your mom."

I nod and pull out my phone. I call Mom first, since she'll know what to do. Like Marcus, she tells me everything will be all right. I've done nothing wrong. It's police procedure. I have a feeling she's not telling me everything, but I have to trust her. She knows more about this stuff than I do.

"Should I call Sheryl and tell her?" I ask.

"She already knows."

Huh? "How can she already know?"

"The police are here, too, and at Grandma's. They're searching for more evidence to connect you to the letters."

"But there is nothing to connect me to them. I didn't write them." Panic writhes in my voice and my stomach is a pit full of unsettled snakes. I can't believe this is happening.

"Which means you have nothing to worry about, Amber. They have to do their job, or else it puts the court case at risk if procedures aren't followed to the letter. They don't want to give the defense any opportunities to win the case. You have to trust the police to do their job. They want Paul Carlson locked away as much as you do." So, pretty much what Sheryl told me. "There's something else I should tell you. The pipes froze in the courthouse. Which means the trial has been delayed."

"Delayed?" I'm not sure if I should be relieved or upset. Or both. "Till when?"

"They pushed it back to March thirteenth." So instead of the nightmare being over in two to three weeks, I have to put up with it for another six or more weeks. I'm not sure if I can.

Sensing what I need, Marcus caresses my hand with his thumb, grounding me before the numbness can creep in. He raises his eyebrow in question. Once I'm off the phone, I fill him in as Bald Cop searches under my bed with a flashlight.

He reaches under and pulls out several magazines, a DVD, and a small whip. The writhing panic grips my stomach hard.

"I don't enjoy doing this, Amber. But it's for your own good." A sharp slap snaps through the air and an equally sharp pain slices my upper back. I scream.

"Screaming will only make things worse."

"Kitten, you're safe," Marcus's voice breaks through the distant sounds of the whip tearing my body apart.

I blink the world into focus and find myself on the floor, tears spilling down my face. Marcus is crouched beside me, brushing my cheeks dry.

The cops are watching me with a mix of concern and confusion and curiosity on their faces.

"I had a flashback," I tell them through a Sahara-dry mouth. I didn't have one in the adult store. Why now?

Marcus helps me to my feet. I lean into him, needing him more than ever. He's always reminding me how strong I am. And I am to have survived what Paul put me through. But there are times I don't feel so strong.

"I have no idea where it came from." The words rush from my mouth.

Bald Cop holds up the magazines with half-naked women on the cover dressed in leather and holding what I'm guessing to be sex toys. "And what about these?"

Shaking my head, I step away. "They're not mine."

"Are you saying they belong to your roommate?" Bulky Cop asks.

"I don't know who they belong to. I just know they're not mine."

Becca shoos away two juniors who live next to Jordan's room. They ask her what's going on. I don't hear her reply. But it doesn't matter what she says. Everyone knows who I am. They've heard about the letters and the lies about my sexual preferences. The cops searching my room will only fuel the rampant rumors.

Bald Cop searches through the magazines and pulls out pink paper similar to the ones I saw at the police station when I was questioned. "What about this?" He holds it for me to see.

It's my writing, like with the other letters, but I never wrote it. "It's not mine."

He bags the evidence. I can't even lie to myself and pretend it all belongs to Brittany, because why would she have that letter in the magazine? She's an artist. She's not a forger.

Once they're finished searching the room and my backpack, they leave. All they found are the magazines, DVD, the letter, and the whip. But that's more than enough to damage my story in the court's eyes.

"I don't get how those things got in my room." I flop onto my bed, grab my pillow, and hug it to me. Marcus sits next to me. "I seriously don't believe they're Brittany's."

He fires off a text to Tammara, telling her he'll be late. "Which means someone else entered your room and planted them. Did you leave your door unlocked?"

"No. Brittany and I always lock it. We're both kinda paranoid that way."

"Even when you're going to the bathroom?"

I want to say yes, but there have been times lately where I've been less strict about it. When I first moved in, I automatically locked the door even when I was in my room. "But who would plant the stuff in my room? It's not like anyone can simply walk into the building. You have to get past security."

"Unless you live here."

"Which means it has to be a joke. No one has a reason to hurt me." Except that doesn't explain the letter. Even if it was a joke, how would the person have forged it? It can't be that easy to do, otherwise anyone could do it. "But the only person trying to discredit me is Paul's sister." A thought smothers me, and my mouth drops open. "Paul never mentioned a sister. Maybe she's a student here. She could be living in this building."

Marcus tucks a strand of hair behind my ear. The tenderness of the moment helps settle my stomach, a little. "That's what we need to figure out."

We head to Becca's room and knock on her door. She opens it and blushes at seeing me.

"Those weren't my things the cops found," I hastily explain.

"Someone hid them in my room and I'm trying to figure out who."

She nods, the movement barely there. I can't tell if she believes me. "That's why it's important to keep your door locked when you're not in your room. I hounded people all last term to remember that."

"Is there a Rosemary Carlson living in the building?"

"I can't give out that information. It's confidential."

"How so?" Marcus asks. "It's not like everyone keeps their name a secret."

I tilt my head to the side and give the most pleading look I can muster. "Please. All we're asking for is a yes or no. That's all."

Becca thinks about it for an excruciating moment, then nods. "All right. Give me a few minutes." She retreats into her room and shuts the door. After what feels like an hour, she re-emerges. "There's no one here either with Rosemary as a first name or Carlson as the last name."

The air rushes from my lungs as if someone heavy sat on them. "Thanks," I manage to say. It would have been easier to prove Paul's sister is framing me if she lived in my building.

Marcus and I hurry to his car. On the way to his apartment, I call Mom and tell her what happened.

"I'll talk to the DA and Sheryl. They'll at least check into the possibility of a link between Rosemary and the university, but I wouldn't get your hopes up. All I know is that she's a waitress in Chicago."

"Where?"

"I don't know, and you can't go searching for her either, Amber. Nor can Marcus. If you do, you could make things worse than they already are. You have to trust the police and the DA."

I groan. The police don't have a great track record of protecting me as far as I'm concerned. Otherwise, they would have discovered Paul was the one stalking me a year ago and would have put an end to it before Trent and Michael were murdered.

But that was the Crossfields police. Hopefully the Chicago

police do a much better job.

I glance at Marcus. If the Crossfields police had a great track record of protecting me, Trent would be alive and Marcus and I wouldn't be together. But would things be any different between Trent and me to what they were a year ago, when he planned on us having a future together—and I lived one day at a time? Unable to fully commit because my father walked out on his family. Unable to fully commit for fear of history repeating itself. Things aren't much different between Marcus and me, except he hasn't talked about us being forever. Not like Trent had.

Chase isn't at the apartment when we arrive. Just as well, since he and Tammara don't see eye to eye. Never have, from what Marcus told me.

I wrap my arms around Marcus's neck. "So, what do you want to do now?" I ask, desperately needing a distraction from what happened at the dorm. We have a few minutes until Tammara is due to show up.

The building buzzer screeches through the apartment, and disappointment floods me. She's early.

"Someone's eager to see you," I say. "I'm guessing she has no idea I'm here."

Marcus presses the button to unlock the main entrance. "I didn't say you *weren't* going to be here."

I roll my eyes. "The woman's been after you for months now. You seriously can't believe she's stopped wanting you."

He shrugs. Apparently he does.

I swear Tammara sprinted up the stairs, because a minute later there's a knock at the door. Curious if my theory's right, and to prove to Marcus he's the kind of guy girls have trouble letting go, I hide in the bathroom. He flashes me a panicked look as I close the door, chuckling.

The apartment door clicks open and I lean my ear against the bathroom door.

"I'm glad you called," Tammara purrs, and I roll my eyes again.

"We need to talk," Marcus replies somewhat stiffly.

"There's nothing to talk about."

A soft thump near the door, like someone bumped into the wall, leaves me frowning as all kinds of unwanted images pop to mind.

"Tammara, you have things wrong." Panic and desperation strangle his tone.

Deciding that I've proved my point long enough, I open the door. Marcus's back is pressed into the wall, his hands on her shoulder like he's going to push her away. Only a few inches separate their bodies. Her head jerks toward me and deep lines form across her forehead.

"Hi." I say it cheerfully even though the desire to yank her off him by the hair courses through me.

"Hi," she responds, tone flat, and steps away from Marcus.

"We might as well sit for this." I point to the living area.

Tammara looks at Marcus. He nods in response, his eyes locked on hers. I walk around them and take my usual spot on the couch, legs curled to the side. Marcus joins me, forcing Tammara to sit on the recliner. She's wearing black pants, which will be covered in gray fur once she stands. It's Smoky's favorite seat.

Marcus threads his fingers with mine. "We know what you did, Tammara."

She huffs, her eyebrows pinched together. "You had me drive all this way to tell me something I already know. In case you've forgotten, we've already had this conversation." When Marcus told her he knew that she had drugged him so she could take photos of her kissing him and send them to me. She thought I would dump him, and then she would become his girlfriend.

"That's not what I'm talking about."

"Then can you be more specific?" If Tammara were a poker player, she'd have no trouble winning every hand. Her expressions are perfectly tooled to hide what she's thinking. Something she learned from her politician father.

"I'm talking about the fake letters you sent to Amber before Christmas that you pretended were from the psychopath who kidnapped her. The letters that threatened my life and then Amber's."

"I have no idea what you're talking about."

If Emma hadn't filled me in on the conversation she'd had with Tammara, when she told Tammara about Paul and what he'd done to Trent and Michael, I would believe Tammara. She's that good.

"So you'd have no problem if Emma tells the cops what she knows about them?" Marcus asks.

Tammara shifts in her seat. "What do you want from me?"

"We want you to promise that you'll leave us alone. If you can't do that, we will report everything we know to the cops. I'm not saying they won't figure it out on their own. They've been investigating where the messages came from. But leave us alone and we won't tell them anything. Can you live with that?"

She nods, eyes averted.

"Also, we want to know about Rosemary Carlson," I add.

"Who?" There's no surprise in her voice, only confusion.

"Fake love letters mysteriously appeared, supposedly from Amber to the psychopath," Marcus says. "And since you're the queen of fake letters…"

Her eyes widen. "I had nothing to do with those. I swear." The panic in her voice seems genuine, leaving me unsure what to believe.

"Look"—he scowls at her—"if you're not telling us the truth and the cops discover you were responsible for *all* the letters, you could be facing serious time." We don't know if it's true, but we're betting she doesn't either.

Tammara pales, her skin a stark contrast to her bright-auburn hair. "I'm telling the truth. All I wanted was to scare Amber away so you'd come back to me. I'd never do anything that would cause the killer to be set free."

At least we agree on something.

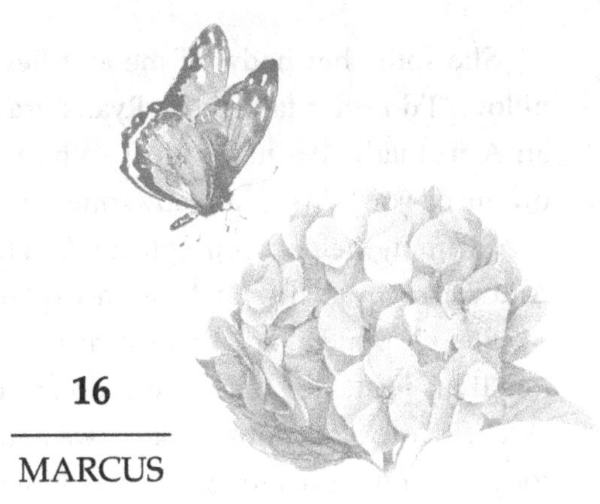

16

MARCUS

"How're you doing?" I stroke my fingertips along Amber's spine. She shivers at my touch, and I smile at how she responds to even my smallest gestures. I have almost as much power over her as she does over me. Almost.

Her eyelids drift shut and a small smile curves on her lips. "Mmm." Her head is on my naked chest—one of my favorite places for it—and her gentle hum vibrates through my heart.

I laugh at her telling nonanswer. She opens her eyes and traces her fingers down each rib and along my stomach muscles.

Reluctantly, I capture her hand. "I know what you're doing, Kitten, and it's not gonna work."

"I don't know what you're talking about," she says, looking away.

Except she does. She was hoping to distract me so we wouldn't have to talk about what happened earlier in her dorm and how the fucking trial date has been delayed. Her plan worked. She distracted me. Just not for as long as she would have liked.

I let out a heavy breath. "I'm worried about you. You're supposed to be getting better, but with everything going on, things are getting worse. Your nightmares are getting worse."

She shifts her body off me and lies on her side, elbow on her pillow. "I'd rather talk about Ryan's gravestone. You helped me get an A in math. We had a deal. Why won't you take the money I promised you?" We've already gone through this. I didn't earn it.

"Brittany helped you get the A. That wasn't part of the deal. And you're my girlfriend. I can't accept money from you."

She gives me a look that warns me what she thinks of my opinion. If my pride had nuts, I don't doubt that she would knee it there. "Well, if you're not gonna take it, we need to figure out another way for you to raise the money, especially since you haven't been able to work."

Frank fucked up my job at Chase's old man's garage. Until my shoulder is fully healed, Tony doesn't want to take a chance that I could make the injury worse.

"You could tutor again." She leans over and teases my lips for a heartbeat, then pulls away a fraction of an inch. "But you better not fall in love with your student this time."

I grin. "You don't have to worry about that. I've had my quota. You're the only girl for me."

"Glad to hear it." She smiles at me in the way that makes me both weak and horny.

I roll over and skim my fingers along the curve of her breast. She sucks in a sharp breath. God, can I ever get enough of this woman?

I close my mouth over her nipple and circle it with my tongue. As much as I want to honor my brother for his sacrifices, and the sacrifice that cost him his life, I'd rather spend the day making love to Amber. Making love to her and distracting her from her fears and currently messed up life.

"Marcus," she moans and my cock is hard and ready for action once more.

"Hmm?" I hum against her nipple.

"We could do a fundraiser." She struggles to get the last word out as I play and suck my way to complete distraction. "Jordan and her parents do...they donate...the proceeds to a charity that...that helps kids deal with domestic abuse."

I vaguely hear her last words as my lips find hers, and my fingers find another of her body parts to keep me entertained—and render her unable to talk.

17

AMBER

The bitter wind blows through my winter coat and I shudder. The only thing that will warm me is seeing my friends and Marcus. Coffee wouldn't hurt either.

I rush to the Student Services Building and buy a large coffee with extra milk and sugar. As I spot Jordan at our usual table, a weird feeling that I'm being watched creeps through me. I swivel. Unlike outside, where people were more interested in escaping the cold, the Marketplace is filled with curious onlookers, their eyes focused on me.

Even though I have a thick coat on, I wrap my arms around myself, preventing them from seeing the real me instead of the image the media has inadvertently painted in their heads. The real me is more likely to break.

I sit across from Jordan and force a grin on my lips. "Hey."

She gives me a weak smile in return. "I heard about what happened yesterday in your room. Brittany freaked when Becca told her."

"About which part? That the cops searched our room or about what they found?"

"Probably a little of both."

I close my eyes for a moment. "She hates me, doesn't she?" We didn't have a loving relationship when we first became roommates. That was my fault. Well, more like my nightmares' fault. Things improved when I helped Brittany after she was raped by her now ex-boyfriend, but there's only so much she can handle before she changes her mind about our friendship. I'm just relieved the cops didn't find anything she didn't want them to see.

"She doesn't hate you. She's worried about you. We all are."

"Not everyone is." My gaze jerks to a nearby table where guys keep checking me out, their perverted thoughts written on their grinning faces. "Anyway, I'm fine."

She looks at them for a brief moment, then powers on. "Is that what you're saying or what your therapist says?"

Therapy is supposed to make a difference, but even my therapist admitted I'll experience delays in my recovery due to everything going on. The goal is to keep things from getting too deep.

I sip my coffee and welcome the heat, which is ready to scorch away the chill growing inside me. "She said I'm fine. Anyway, Brittany might not hate me now, but I'll have to spend more time in our room and less at Marcus's. Did you hear what his neighbor said about me on the news?"

"Everyone did, but what does that have to do with anything?"

"Now everyone thinks Marcus is into violent sex and he isn't."

"Marcus is a big boy. He's not going to care about that. He wants to be with *you*. And he already had quite the reputation before you guys started dating. What's one more thing to add to it, even if it isn't true?"

"What's this about my reputation?" Marcus asks, sliding onto the chair next to me—minus his sling. Chase joins Jordan and hands her a hot chocolate.

Marcus scowls at the table of guys next to us, who've been eyeing me up the entire time. They turn away from us, laughing.

I ignore them and touch his injured arm. "You don't have to

wear your sling anymore?" I say, hoping to distract him from getting into a fight.

"Nope. Got the all-clear to stop using it, but I'm supposed to go to physio for a few weeks." He screws up his nose and places his palm on the curve of my spine. Heat radiates through my body and jolts back memories from last night. In his bed. "So, what's that about my reputation?" he prompts.

I open my mouth to respond, but a newspaper is slammed down hard on the table, narrowly missing my coffee. I startle and my words still in my throat.

"Have you read this yet?" Emma snaps, glaring at the newspaper. Scared to find out what she's talking about, I can only shake my head.

"According to this"—she stabs the newspaper with her finger—"Melissa told the reporter that she witnessed you and the murderer making out a few weeks before you went missing."

I open and close my mouth, unable to make a sound. My friends stare at me, waiting for me to say something. Anything.

"She told the reporter she never mentioned anything to Trent because she didn't want to hurt him. And she said she was even more shocked after Trent's death, when she saw you again getting all cozy with the murderer."

The guys at the next table over whisper to each other while watching us. I don't have to turn to know they aren't the only ones being entertained.

I want to say something, but I can't. Numbness fills me as I stare at the paper. I'm that girl from last spring. The girl who'd had her whole life ahead of her. The girl who would have one day played college basketball. The girl who dreamed of becoming a vet. The girl who spent two weeks, five days, and eight hours either handcuffed to a wall or curled up on a bed with a kitten who was her sole source of comfort.

The girl who wondered each day if she would live to see the end of it, and who almost didn't when the man who professed his love set his house on fire. *"Don't worry, Amber. You and I were meant to be together. Forever and ever."* The words ring like funeral bells in my brain. He had it planned all along. My murder. His suicide.

Amber.

If only he had doused the house with a flammable liquid, he would have been nailed for arson and attempted murder. Instead, he made a romantic candle-lit dinner for me, and "accidentally" set the house on fire.

Amber. I blink, then realize the voice isn't a memory in my head. The numbness slowly recedes until it's a shadow lingering at the edge, waiting for another chance to push me under.

"Amber." Marcus touches my face. "What happened?"

I lean into his hand, grounding myself once again, like I did when the cops searched my room yesterday. But I can't rely on him. I need to learn to ground myself on my own. Eventually he'll grow tired of the craziness that's my life and walk away.

He'd be insane not to.

"What happened?" Marcus repeats.

"I'm not sure." I smile, but judging from the frown on his face, he doesn't buy it. "I'm okay now." I glance at Emma, ready to explain that it's all a lie. I never kissed Paul. At least not until my life depended on it.

The anger on her face from earlier is gone. "I know Melissa hates you," she says, her voice soft against the murmurs around us. "I can't believe the bitch would do this."

"Why does she hate you?" Jordan asks.

"She had a thing for my brother," Emma explains. "It wasn't mutual, and she blamed Amber for that."

Everyone stares at me, waiting for me to elaborate. "Trent and I were best friends for years before we started dating. I knew she was crushing on him, but then who wasn't? He was cute and sweet and funny."

Marcus stiffens, and I kick myself. While he tries to act like it doesn't bother him that Trent is part of my heart—and always will be—I can tell it upsets him whenever I say anything nice about my old boyfriend. I can see it in his eyes. He feels like he'll never be able to compete with Trent even though Trent's never coming back.

I reach for his hand and thread my fingers with his, telling him that I love him. Trent will never have my whole heart. Only Marcus has a chance for that.

"Anyway, I began developing feelings for Trent, beyond us being best friends. I should have told Melissa, since we were friends at the time and she'd been asking me to set her up with him. But I didn't. And then out of the blue he kissed me, and everything between us changed. To say Melissa was mad would be an understatement."

Emma makes a face that tells me I'm right, and pulls up a chair from a table behind me as I study the newspaper.

"What the hell am I going to do?" What I want to do is scream. "I'm not sure how much more I can take of this. It's like everywhere I go, people are watching me and judging me. And I keep getting this weird feeling someone's stalking me. Am I always going to feel this way? Will I ever feel normal again?"

"It'll get better, Amber," Jordan says. "You have to believe that."

"I don't know if I can anymore. If I'm the victim, why is everyone treating me like I'm the fucking criminal?"

They all look at me, eyes wide. If I weren't so upset at everything, I'd laugh at their reaction to my swearing.

Marcus recovers first and lightly squeezes my hand. "Because Paul's sister is determined to make you into the criminal so her brother goes free."

Emma turns white, and I silently curse him. "Emma, it's gonna be okay. Paul won't come after you."

"How can you be so sure? He killed my brother."

"He killed Trent because Trent loved me and stood in the way of Paul's delusions. So unless you plan to make out with me in front of him, I think you're pretty safe."

Chase snort-laughs.

Jordan shoves his arm. "God, you are such a guy."

"Glad you've noticed," he says, tone oddly serious. His expression then switches to a goofy grin.

While Marcus and Jordan give Chase a hard time, a weird feeling that someone is watching sets me on edge. I glance over my shoulder. No one is looking in my direction, but I still can't seem to shake my old paranoia.

18

MARCUS

I enter the Student Services Building, the freezing air still clinging to me. I survey the open area and spot Amber. I'm about to call her name, to stop her before she disappears into the Counseling Center for her weekly appointment with her therapist, when I spot a guy checking her out from several yards away. He pretends to read a brochure he picked up someplace, but his spy skills need a lot more work.

Something about *this* guy unnerves me.

Amber strides down the hallway, oblivious to him. The guy places the brochure on a table and walks after her.

And I follow him.

He stops when she gets close to her therapist's office, and he whips out a small camera. *What the fuck?* I grab hold of his arm, preventing him from taking a photo.

Amber pulls the Counseling Center door open and steps inside, not once turning around.

"What the fuck do you think you're doing?" I ask, glaring at him. He's a good several inches shorter than me and his muscles have never been introduced to weights.

"It's none of your business." He yanks his arm from my hand.

"Well, since that's my girlfriend you were planning to take a photo of without her consent, I'm making it my business."

"I wasn't gonna take a picture of her. I-I was going to take a picture of the Counseling Center."

"Bullshit. I saw you back there." I point in the direction we came from. "I saw you check her out and I saw you stalk her. Now tell me the truth, or she'll be filing for a restraining order. And that's gonna make your life real tough if you really are a student here." I'm bluffing. I have no idea if Amber can get a restraining order unless she can prove this isn't a one-time event. But since she complained the other day that she felt as though someone was stalking her, I suspect this isn't the first time he's followed her.

The guy holds his hands up. "Okay. Okay. I'll tell you. I'm a journalism major. She's a hot topic right now, and I figured a different angle on the story would be great for my portfolio. It's not like I'm hurting her."

"She's a person, not a hot topic," I growl, my face inches from his. I can smell the fear seeping from him. "And you don't have the right to harass her."

"You're wrong. I have the First Amendment backing me."

"The First Amendment doesn't give you the right to harass her, asshole."

"I'm not harassing her. The public has the right to know if an innocent man is being convicted for a crime he never committed."

Something inside me detonates in a series of explosions and I shove the jerk into the wall. "The psychopath is not an innocent man. He killed two people and nearly killed her."

"Some people don't believe that. They believe your girlfriend is guilty, not Paul Carlson."

I slam him into the wall again. "You don't even know what the fuck you're saying." I'm ready to keep smashing him against the wall until he finally realizes Amber's the victim.

"Let him go, son," a man says behind me.

Still holding on to the asshat, I glance over my shoulder and groan. My hands drop away from the guy and I turn to face campus security.

"He assaulted me for no reason," Asshat whines.

"He's stalking my girlfriend," I counter. "And taking photos of her."

The man looks from me to Asshat. "I don't have time for this. If you're serious about the stalking, you can file a report with campus police."

Asshat blanches and I weigh my choices. I file the report, and he can counter with charges of assault. "I'll need his name for the report."

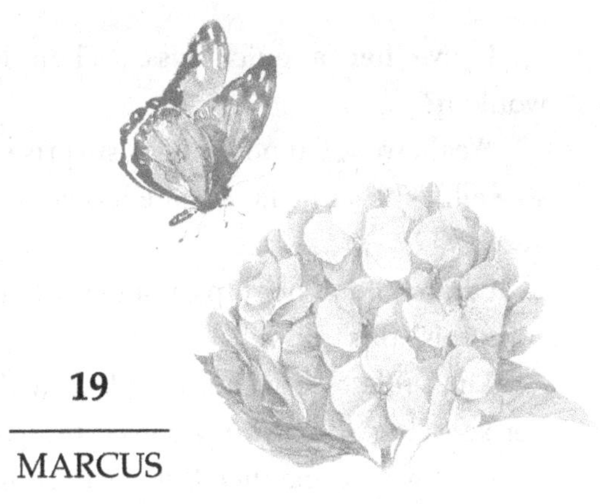

19

———

MARCUS

Amber removes an envelope from her mailbox. "So, are you gonna tell me where we're going tonight?"

"It's a surprise."

She pouts, though it's not very convincing with the way the corners of her mouth try to curl up. "How am I supposed to figure out what to wear if you won't tell me where we're going?"

"You can wear whatever you want." *Because you won't be in it for long. Chase's sister is bound to have another outfit in mind.*

"Okay."

We go upstairs to her room. Brittany isn't here. Normally I'd make the most of it, but we have plans. Plans I don't want to delay much longer.

Amber opens the envelope and removes a letter. She reads it, then frowns.

"Something wrong?"

She refolds it and shoves it and the envelope into her desk drawer. "It's nothing. It's from someone I once knew, but it's no big deal." Smiling, she wraps her arms around my neck. "Are you positive you can't tell me where we're going?"

I give her a quick kiss. "Then it wouldn't be a surprise, would it?"

"Yeah, well, I'm not one for surprises. They don't always end up so well." The smile fades. She lets go of my neck and begins to pull away.

I grab hold of her hips, not ready to lose the contact between us. "I promise this one will."

The smile returns but it's edged with uncertainty. I want to kiss her senseless so she forgets everything. Everything except for how amazing we are together. But we don't have time.

Amber surveys her closet.

"You can wear what you have on now if you want."

She glances at her jeans and light-pink long-sleeved T-shirt. She's not trying to look sexy, but there's something about the way her clothes skim her body that makes my cock twitch.

She shrugs. "If you say so."

The drive through Chicago's wintery streets to Shannon's apartment stretches to forty-five minutes. I can tell Amber's itching to ask for the fifth time where we're going, but she knows I won't tell her.

I park in an empty visitor's spot and lead Amber to the building.

"Are we going to a party?" she asks.

"Nope."

"Are we having our fortunes told?" She smiles in a way that tells me she's trying to amuse me now. Then her expression turns wistful. She doesn't believe in that stuff, but some idea of what we're both facing when it comes to the men who tried to destroy us would be great.

"Nope," I say.

"Am I getting warmer?"

I grab her hand. "I don't know about that, but if you want to get warmer, I can take you back to the car and see if we can steam up the windows."

She laughs. "Sounds good to me."

We haven't had too many chances to make love since she started staying in her dorm again. Even though she gave me a lame-ass reason, it has more to do with the old bitch who insinuated Amber and I get off on pain than because Amber finds it easier to study in her room.

I open the main doors and let her in, then buzz Shannon's apartment.

"Hello?" a female voice crackles through the intercom a minute later.

"It's Marcus."

The door buzzes and I pull it open. The elevator is empty when we enter. We don't have much time since Shannon's apartment is on the fifth floor.

My mouth is on Amber's as soon as the doors close, my fingers in her silky golden hair. She parts her lips, ever eager for me to explore her with my tongue. I try to maintain some level of control, but it's next to impossible. I'm starving from being unable to touch her like I've wanted to in the last few days.

All too soon the doors open. I reach for Amber's hand and lead her to apartment 510. I open the door and we step inside. Shannon wheels down the short hallway, grinning.

"So this is Amber," Chase's sister says, checking her over.

I lean in and hug her. "Don't get any ideas," I whisper in her ear.

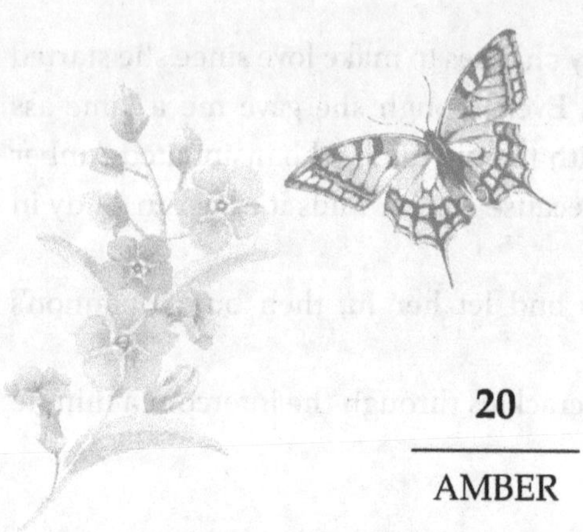

20

AMBER

I knew Chase's sister had been paralyzed in an accident when she was twelve years old, but I had no idea what to expect. The girl is nothing like her older brother, who is tall and blond. She's delicate in size, yet there's a subtle fierceness about her. I can't pinpoint what it is exactly, beyond the ripped muscles in her arms and shoulders revealed by her tank top.

Marcus whispers in her ear and she giggles. "Don't worry. As cute as she is, she's not my type." She winks at me and puts me instantly at ease, like Chase has a habit of doing. "Is he always this overbearingly projective of you?"

I laugh. "Always. He forgets I can take care of myself."

"I know you can take care of yourself, Amber. You've already proved that. But where's the fun if I can't chase off the competition? In case you've forgotten, you once hired me to do exactly that."

Shannon's eyes light up. "Oh, I can't wait to hear about this." Looking at Marcus, she points toward a brown couch in the tidy but sparsely furnished living room. On one wall is a collection of framed black-and-white photos of historic buildings. "Go watch a game or something while I work my magic."

"Magic?" I ask, glancing between them.

"You haven't told her?"

"I thought I'd surprise her," Marcus explains, his eyes lighting up the same way Shannon's did. "Where's Debbie?"

"She's on shift at the hospital." To me she says, "My girlfriend's a nurse."

She ushers me into a bedroom and points at a stool by the bed, which is covered in an array of clothes. "Marcus wants me to alter your appearance so you guys can go out without being harassed."

"Alter?"

"I'm going to be a theater major next year. Mostly behind-the-scenes stuff, like makeup and costumes."

"You're not gonna give me a moustache, are you?"

She laughs. "No. Marcus would kill me if I did that." She studies me for a minute, her gaze sweeping over me. "You really have him wrapped around your finger."

"What do you mean?"

"First"—she holds up a finger—"he's never introduced me to any of the girls in his past, and it has nothing to do with me being a lesbian. Those girls didn't matter."

Her words don't come as a surprise. This is something Marcus has already told me, when he said I was the only girl who's ever made him feel alive—even before we made love the first time. "What's the second?"

"Second, I don't think he's ever gotten jealous when a guy pays attention to a girl he's with. He'd more than likely pass her on with his compliments. But I bet he'd kill to keep guys from getting within ten feet of you. Never thought I'd see this day." Her mouth moves into a wide grin; then her smile fades away. "Just promise me you won't hurt him, okay?"

"I won't." I smile softly, touched by how much she cares about Marcus.

The grin returns to her face. "Okay, let's get started on mission Outsmart the Media." She riffles through the clothes on the bed. "Marcus said you have scars on your body you're self-conscious about. I borrowed some stuff that I think will be perfect."

She pulls out a black dress. It's short and sleeveless, but the back is high enough to keep my scars hidden.

She passes me the dress and a thick pair of purple tights. "I've got thigh-high boots that will cause guys to come in their pants at the sight of you."

My face heats a hundred degrees as I pretend to study the outfit.

She laughs and maneuvers her wheelchair to face away from me. "Tell me when you're ready, and I'll do your hair and makeup."

I quickly change and check the dress in the full-length mirror on the closet door. It's shorter than any dress or skirt I've ever worn, but the tights cover the patchwork of skin grafts on my leg. The neckline is scooped and skims below my collarbone.

"Okay," I say. "You can turn around."

Shannon does and nods her approval. "Sit, and I'll start on your makeup. Even Marcus will barely recognize you once I'm finished." She brushes my hair into a ponytail. Next, she works on my makeup. Even without seeing what she's doing, I can tell she's applying more than I normally wear in an entire week.

"Do you know where Marcus is taking me?"

A secretive spark gleams in her eyes. "I do, but I'm not telling you. What I will tell you is that you're going to look perfect for where you're going. You'll blend in with the crowd." She attaches long, thick eyelashes and a layer of muted red lipstick. *God, I'm going to resemble a prostitute.*

She wheels over to the bed and opens a wooden box. From it, she removes a Styrofoam head covered in a black chin-length wig with bangs and purple streaks that match my purple tights.

Now no one will recognize me. Tonight I get to be someone who isn't Amber Scott. Tonight, I get to be the wild girl I've always dreamed of being, the one inside me who was strong enough to survive Paul's torture and abuse.

Shannon helps me put the wig on and I check my reflection. My mouth drops open at the sight of me staring back. Or rather, the girl who looks nothing like the real me. I don't even have to wear sunglasses to hide my true identity.

The final touch is two wide metal bands that hide the scars on my wrists. My forget-me-not tattoo, with Michael's and Trent's names, is visible on my forearm. But since the media has never mentioned it and only a few people have seen it, no one will associate the tattoo with me.

Smiling, I run my finger over the names and the flowers, thrilled that for once I can show them off. Thrilled that for once I can show how much I loved two of the most important males in my life.

Shannon studies me and nods. "Marcus won't want to keep his hands off you for fear of someone swooping in."

"I don't think he has to worry about that. I'm not going anywhere."

"I'm glad to hear it, and so will my brother. He's never been a fan of Marcus's past relationships. Not that you can call most of them relationships." Her eyes widen. "Oh, God. That sounds terrible. I'm sorry."

"Don't worry about it. I know he was a man-whore before he met me. His past flings aren't exactly subtle about it."

She sighs. "I can't imagine they would be. Okay, show time." She gestures to the bedroom door.

Marcus is busy watching a basketball game on TV when I enter the living room.

"Nikki's ready," Shannon says behind me.

He turns and drops the remote as his intense hazel gaze trails up my body. When most guys do that, I feel dirty. When Marcus does it, I feel stronger, more desirable.

It takes a moment for Shannon's words to sneak their way into my brain. "Nikki?"

"You can't go around using your real name," she explains. "The less connection you have to who you really are, the less likely anyone will add two and two together."

"She's right." Marcus strides toward us, his eyes never leaving me.

"How come you don't have a disguise?" I run my finger across his day-old growth, and a thrill trembles down my spine. My lips beg to trace along his jaw as I breathe in his subtle spicy scent. The scent that's one hundred percent Marcus.

"My picture hasn't been on the news," he says. "And anyone who knows me and sees me with you will think I've gone back to my old habits."

I give him a questioning look. "You mean being a cheating man-whore?"

"I never cheated on those girls. Not even Tammara. She knew where things stood, like the rest of them. Only fucked-up guys would cheat on their girlfriends and wives." Like his stepfather. He might not have been cheating on his wife in the typical sense of the word. But he still cheated on her every time he touched a boy.

I take Marcus's clenched hands and caress them with my thumbs. "I know you wouldn't cheat."

His hands relax and thread with mine. His gaze drops to my mouth and the tip of his tongue runs along his parted lips. Just when I think he's going to kiss me, he says, breathing slightly fast, "You ready to go? Jordan and Chase are meeting us there."

A momentary sense of power courses through me at the way I affect him. The same way he affects me. "Are they wearing disguises?"

"No. Only you needed one. Anyway, the last thing Chase needs is for his sister to make Jordan sexier."

"Chase has a girlfriend? How come I'm the last to know?" Shannon fakes a pout.

"They aren't dating. Jordan has a boyfriend at the University of Texas. She and Chase are just friends."

"Oh, that's too bad. It's about time he gets a girlfriend. Dad will be happy. Right now he's worried that both his kids are gay. One he can handle, but not both of us."

After we thank Shannon for her help, Marcus drives us to a bar where a live rock band is playing. There's a line, but Marcus knows the bouncer and we get in without waiting. With his hands on my hips, he weaves me through the crowd to a corner table where Chase and Jordan are sitting, chatting.

"Hey, guys," Marcus says. Chase glances at us and grins. Jordan starts to look up. The smile wipes off her face when she sees me and it turns into an uncharacteristic frown.

And then she glares at Marcus, ignoring me. "Hi."

Chase whispers in her ear, and her expression shifts through several different emotions. It settles on grinning.

"Hi, I'm Nikki," I tell her as if meeting them for the first time. I make a move to sit next to Jordan, but before I can claim the seat, Marcus sits on it.

"Wow, you look amazing." Jordan's gaze shifts to Chase. "Your sister did this?"

He nods.

Marcus pulls me onto his lap and settles his hand on my upper thigh. The heat of it burns through my skirt and tights. "I want everyone to know you're mine," he murmurs in my ear.

My cheek hovers next to his. "Good. 'Cause I want everyone to know I'm *yours*." Especially if members of the I've-had-wild-sex-with-Marcus-and-want-an-encore club are here. Though I'm sure it won't stop some of them from attempting to stake their claim.

The waitress shows up and we order drinks. Shannon's right. With my disguise, I fit in perfectly. Even the old me never dressed like this. I feel sexier than I ever have. I wiggle my butt in Marcus's lap. He groans. I laugh and kiss him.

What starts off as the brushing of lips quickly becomes more heated. Our tongues glide and stroke to the music; our breaths grow rapid. Marcus moans into my mouth and the sensation vibrates through my body.

By the time we reluctantly pull apart, Jordan and Chase have joined the crowded dance floor. I want to dance, but I don't want to risk the wig coming off. And the thought of getting sweaty in the wig doesn't sound too appealing. Instead, I let the music flow through me. I've never felt freer than I do now.

Marcus tenderly kisses my bare arm. His touch sends a wave of heat rushing between my legs. As if sensing the effect this has on me, he slides his fingers along the inside of my thigh and beyond the hem of my dress. Normally I'd be uncomfortable with such blatant PDA. But I'm not Amber for this one night, and Nikki is definitely not complaining. Besides, with the table providing cover no one can see what he's doing.

Marcus's mouth claims mine, while his fingers continue stroking my thigh. They might not be touching the throbbing ache, but they're coming pretty damn close. I whimper against his lips.

His finger moves slightly and brushes me. I groan, "Oh, God," my mouth still on his. My body jerks, and I'm not the only one affected. The thickening length in his jeans presses into my hip. I smile, wishing we were at his place, but at the same time enjoying the game going on between us. Maybe there's something to be said for pretending to be someone else...even for a short time.

"So, is it Amber or Nikki who turns you on the most?" I murmur in his ear.

His hand moves away from my thigh, and his fingers trace their way up my stomach until his palm is over my heart. It pounds against my ribs, eager to show him what he does to me.

"This is what turns me on the most." His hazel eyes burn into mine. "It's what's inside you that makes me feel like I've never felt before. That's what turns me on." A mischievous one-sided grin slides into place. "Though you in this outfit is hot. You're more confident than normal, and that's ultra sexy."

The way he's consuming me with his eyes, I expect him to kiss me hard, like he'll die of hunger if he doesn't.

That's what I expect. Instead, he tenderly brushes my bottom lip with his thumb, lowers his mouth to mine, and gently kisses me. There's more heat and desire in the kiss than if he had ravished me.

We settle back and watch the show. Marcus keeps his hands on me the entire time, either of them resting on me or stroking my arm. The only time he isn't touching me is when I go to the bathroom with Jordan, and even then he escorts me.

Marcus blames himself for what happened to Ryan, the abuse and his brother's death. I suspect it's why he's overly protective of me. I wish he would realize that he hasn't failed me like he sometimes thinks he has.

I survived hell, and I did it on my own.

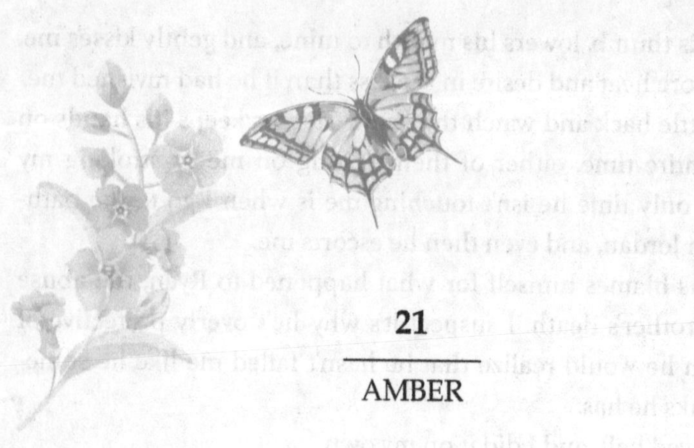

21

AMBER

At the soft knock on the bedroom door, I open my eyes. The low angle of the sunlight catches on the dust motes drifting in the air, creating a magical mood.

I stir, shifting my body against Marcus. A voice in my head tells me to get my butt out of bed. I have to work on my psychology presentation.

I hit the voice's imaginary snooze button.

"Mornin'," Marcus murmurs, his breath brushing my ear.

The soft knock comes again. "You guys awake in there?" Jordan asks.

"We are now," Marcus grumbles, then presses his lips to my lotus tattoo, like he does every morning and whenever I wake up from a nightmare.

"Chase and I are going to The Coffee Shack," she says. "You want anything?"

"Yeah, maybe three more hours of sleep." Marcus pushes himself up and checks the alarm clock on the tower of books by his bed. "Make that four hours." He drops back down and covers his face with his arm.

Chase laughs, the closed door muffling the sound. "The last I saw, dude, neither of those was on the menu."

Without getting out of bed, we tell them our order.

Marcus yawns. "I can't believe those two are already up."

"That's because they didn't have to deal with nightmares last night." I rest my head on his chest and listen to the steady beat of his heart. My favorite sound in the entire world. It means he's alive.

He holds me closer. I can't tell if that's to soothe me after the nightmare I had last night, or to remind himself that he's okay after his. While I didn't wake up screaming this time, Marcus did have to nudge me awake. I was tossing around and muttering in my sleep. And then once we finally fell asleep again, Marcus had a bad dream and jerked me awake. A bad dream he refused to tell me about.

I stroke his jaw. "Maybe you should see someone at the Counseling Center."

He shakes his head. "I'm fine."

I scoot away. "No, you're not. There's no way you can be fine after what you've gone through. If you had been fine, you wouldn't have slept with all those girls and blocked most of it out."

"Yeah, but I'm only sleeping with *you* now." He smirks, thinking he's won the argument.

"And now you're having nightmares." And the last I heard, nightmares aren't contagious. He didn't catch them from me. "What would it hurt to talk to someone?"

"You're still having nightmares and flashbacks. Not exactly a glowing recommendation for therapy." His tone is stiff, his wall returning, preparing to shut me out.

In the past I might have let it go. But I can't. Not this time. "Therapy isn't a quick fix." I wish it were. I'd be cured by now.

"I'm fine, Amber," he snaps and glares at me. "I'm not you."

I frown. "What's that supposed to mean?"

"You were tortured and raped."

"And your stepfather abused you and sexually assaulted you and raped your brother. I don't see what the difference is."

"I'm coping better than you are."

I sit up, holding the sheet against my otherwise naked chest. "Just because I have flashbacks and you don't doesn't mean you're coping better. It means you're coping differently."

Marcus scrambles out of bed and snatches his clothes off the floor. "Forget it. I told the cops what Frank did, and look how well that went. I'm not telling any more strangers the truth. There's no point. And I'm definitely not seeing a therapist. You're still messed up over what happened to you. I'm not." He storms out, slamming the door behind him. Less than a minute later, the pipes squeak to life and water showers the bathtub.

Sighing, I climb out of bed and head for the bathroom, not bothering with my clothes. He's right; I am damaged. I'm never going to be the girl I was before Paul violated me. He made sure of that. But once this ordeal is over, I'll keep getting better, keep getting stronger. Why can't Marcus admit he needs help, too?

I should be pissed at him. I should say screw it and walk away. But I can't. He's been hurt and betrayed so many times, he doesn't know who or how to trust anymore. I'm not going to be yet another person to turn my back on him.

I open the bathroom and enter the tiny steam-filled room. I can barely make out Marcus's naked body through the fogged-up glass door. I slide the door open and step into the tub. Marcus doesn't turn. He's standing in the stream of water, head drooped forward, his hands pressed against the wall.

Hesitantly, I place my hand on his ribs and curl my fingers around them. I don't say anything. I wait until he's ready to talk or kick me out. Or a combination of the two.

He slowly turns, and his tortured eyes meet mine. He places his hands on the wall on either side of my face, leans in, and kisses me. Unlike the tender kisses last night during the show, these kisses are filled with heat, passion, anger, pain. Everything we're both feeling...and maybe something more.

The kisses swell with hunger and need. A need to release everything boiling within us before it consumes us, before it's too late.

I hug the base of his fully aroused length with my hand. Marcus moans. He reverses me into the wall and his hands slide down my body to the backs of my legs. In an easy move, he lifts me up and my legs automatically wrap around his hips. He shifts so his tip is at my entrance, and in a swift move he's inside me, my spine against the wall.

What comes next isn't about making love. It's about the release that comes when emotions don't have a safe place to go. When they become too big, too overwhelming no matter what you do.

We pour everything inside of us and beyond into the moment, focused on feeling good, so damn good, and nothing else. I don't regret the usual tenderness isn't there. This is about power and control and forgetting ourselves.

It's about letting go.

I scream out as the softest part of me clenches Marcus hard and my body shatters into a million pieces. The sound is partly drowned out by the rush of water hitting the tub. Marcus comes seconds later.

We stay this way for several long moments, me locked around him, his cock buried deep, as we fight to regain our breath, our senses.

Eventually I slide from his body and stand in the stream of hot water. Why can't he see that he's as broken as I am? Just like in the past, he used sex as a way to deal with his emotions, his pain. Except this time, we both did. We're both guilty.

I rest my head on his shoulder. His arms engulf me and hold me tight. I could remain like this forever, pretending we're standing under a waterfall on a tropical island with no other worries. But reality has a way of pushing its way in when it's not wanted, and reminding us that what we want is usually not what we can have.

"I have to go. I've got to work on my presentation." I'd ask him if he's okay, but he won't tell me the truth. He and Ryan kept the truth hidden for so long, he's become skilled at the art of lying to himself and others.

I climb out of the shower and wrap a towel around me as Marcus turns off the water. I open the door and walk into Chase.

"Um, hi?" I manage to say, face heating up twenty degrees hotter than the shower water.

An amused smile slips onto Chase's face. "Have a good shower?"

Oh, God. He heard. My entire body temperature shoots up, and I'm surprised the drops of water clinging to my skin and hair don't vaporize into steam.

"Hi," Jordan says with the usual grin on her face. It then slips away. "We have a problem."

You mean other than me standing mortified in the hallway wearing nothing more than a small towel? "What kind of problem?"

"The media's outside swarming the building."

"What for?" Marcus asks behind me. He rests his hand on my shoulder; his thumb caresses my lotus tattoo.

Chase shrugs. "No idea. It might have nothing to do with you, Amber. For all we know, the police found a stash of drugs in someone's apartment and the news caught wind of it."

"Were there any cop cars?"

Jordan and Chase shake their heads.

"Then it's not drugs," Marcus points out. "Something else is going on." No one voices it, but it's not hard to figure out it has something to do with me—or Marcus. That's the only reason the media has been sniffing around here lately.

Marcus and I quickly dress, neither mentioning what happened earlier. There's no point. He's already made his opinion clear. The question is, how long will he put up with me if he thinks I'm so broken? He's got enough problems as it is without mine weighing him down, without mine weighing us both down.

With my coffee and muffin in hand, I follow Marcus and Chase downstairs. Jordan walks with me, shooting me curious glances. "Are you okay?" she asks as we arrive at the main floor.

"I have my presentation in two weeks and I'm getting nervous."

It's not a complete lie. Emma, I'm not. She's great at presentations.

"Really? But you used to play basketball. Are you telling me no one ever came to your games?"

"That's different. I was playing, not talking to the crowd."

"So, pretend you're playing basketball."

I give her a funny look, then remember Jordan doesn't play sports. She doesn't understand how different the two are.

The guys push the main door open and step into the cold January air. Six or so individuals are milling about. If it weren't for the cameras and oversized camcorders, I'd think they were hanging out for a smoke.

Like cats waiting for an unsuspecting mouse to scurry past, their heads perk up and they pounce. Except they're throwing out questions at the same time and it's giving me a headache. I drop my head forward, hiding the fear in my eyes—or whatever else they might interpret it to be and mention it in the newspaper or on the news.

Marcus takes my hand. Chase walks in front of us, Jordan beside me. If it weren't for the annoying reporters, I'd laugh. My friends resemble secret service agents, minus the black suits and sunglasses.

A reporter's voice breaks through the buzz of unintelligible questions. "Amber, what do you think of the DA's move to reduce the charges against Paul Carlson?"

My head snaps up, but before I can say anything, Marcus replies, "No comment," and gives me a warning look. Until I've confirmed things with my mom, there's no point reacting to the question. It's probably a lie anyway. If the DA had reduced the charges, Mom would have called me as soon as she found out.

Muffled music from my cell phone plays in my purse. Still walking, I fish the phone out and glance at the screen. *Mom.* The weight on my shoulders just got heavier. What are the chances the call and the question are a coincidence?

Still shooting questions at me, the reporters follow us to Chase's car. Marcus opens the rear door and climbs in after me. Jordan joins Chase up front. Unlike in the movies, the reporters don't converge like a pack of zombies. They move back as Chase reverses the car, and watch us drive away.

With my heart racing us to the dorm, I check Mom's message. She tells me to phone her ASAP. I call her, silently praying she phoned to tell me I'd forgotten something in my old room and she found it the other day. That would be better than the alternative.

Mom answers the phone. "Amber." She sounds breathless.

"Is it true?" I somehow manage to squeeze out the words. "The charges against Paul have been reduced?"

"He's got a new defense lawyer. Some hotshot who's pushing for a motion to drop the charges of rape. He claims the evidence states otherwise. He's been leaking this to the press. He's also pleading not guilty to the two charges of murder, since he believes there's not enough evidence to prove this."

"But that's not true," I say through the building tears. "Paul confessed to me that he killed Trent, and I saw him shoot Michael."

Silence draws out long and impatient as I wait for Mom to respond. She sighs, the defeat deafening, and I almost pull the phone away from my ear, too afraid to listen to what she has to say next.

"Paul claims you shot Michael as part of an elaborate scheme to be with him. And that Trent's accident was just that, and had nothing to do with Paul."

I stare out the window, barely taking in the world moving past in a striped blur. I can feel Marcus and Jordan watching me, and I let my head fall against the back of the seat. All I want to do is disappear and pretend none of this is happening. That my worst nightmare isn't about to become real.

"Does that mean the DA doesn't believe me anymore? Are they going to send me to jail and let him go free?" Though from what I've learned about stalkers, jail might be the safest place for me. Then there's no way he can come after me. If he's given a short sentence, he will come after me. He will kill me. That's what stalkers do. They never let go of the object of their obsession until it's destroyed.

"You're not going to jail," Mom says. "The DA does believe you, but she's worried the jurors won't. The evidence stacking up lately doesn't look good, or it's weak at best. But the DA also filed for charges of forced confinement, aggravated kidnapping, arson, and attempted murder." Her voice lacks the conviction I'm used to hearing when she was a defense lawyer and was confident she'd win a case.

"But...?"

She doesn't say anything for almost a full minute, then sighs. "The evidence that Paul Carlson was responsible for the arson is flimsy, especially since it was started by candles placed too close to the curtains. Defense is going along with the idea it was an unfortunate accident."

My stomach tightens. "So what does this mean?"

"It means the only thing the DA has the strongest case on is forced confinement and physical assault. But that doesn't mean she's not pushing for all of the charges." The lack of confidence in her voice is staggering.

"How long would he get for those two things?"

"A minimum of six years for kidnapping with no chance of parole. But the judge could also sentence him for up to thirty years."

Six years. Six years and he'll be free to stalk me again if his obsession for me hasn't died.

"What about if he was found guilty of everything?"

"It's hard to predict what the judge will decide, but there's a good chance Paul would never be released." Which means he'll never be able to hurt me or anyone else I love. I wouldn't have to keep checking over my shoulder, wondering if he's stalking me again once he was released.

We talk for a little longer, though I suspect that's Mom's attempt to distract me. It's not working. Marcus watches me, waits for me to end the call. He covers my free hand with his. I disconnect and stare out the window, not seeing anything beyond the blur of houses and dead-looking trees.

He squeezes my hand. "What's going on?"

Without making eye contact, I tell him what my mom said. Tension streams from him with each word, to the point I'm positive I'll suffocate.

"How can anyone think he's innocent?" Jordan asks.

"I'm not sure if anyone does. But it's not his lawyer's job to protect me from his client. He's paid to ensure that Paul is either found not guilty or serves the minimum amount of time possible."

"But that's not right."

"I know, but there's not much I can do about it. The damage has already been done to my reputation." Both in the courtroom and with the scumbags who think I'm some sort of sexual plaything for their entertainment. Fortunately, they haven't acted on that belief yet, beyond the guy who grabbed me in the food court and the inappropriate comments some guys think I deserve because of what they've heard on the news—and because of the twisted rumors.

"Your mom said the psychopath has a new defense?" Marcus asks.

I nod. "He now has some hotshot lawyer."

"So Paul has a lot of money?"

I think for a moment. "We never talked about money, but I didn't get the idea that he had much."

"You mentioned that the house burned down."

"He set it on fire because he planned to kill me in a murder-suicide. The place was engulfed in flames when the firefighter found me. I have no idea how much of it survived. I didn't want to know." I only know that the fire destroyed most of the evidence.

"He could have gotten insurance money and used it to pay for the lawyer," Chase suggests.

"It wasn't his building, so that's a no."

Chase pulls into the parking lot near the dorm and easily finds a spot since it's Sunday. Marcus wants to make sure the reporters haven't scouted out my dorm like they did his building, so he and Chase walk with Jordan and me.

I chuckle. "What, no bodyguard formation this time?" As soon as the words come out I realize I'm doomed. There are as many reporters at the main entrance of my building as there were at the guys' apartment.

"This is unbelievable." Grooves form between Chase's eyebrows. "They're like piranhas to fresh meat."

Except the piranhas aren't watching us approach. They're circling another piece of meat and looking enthralled by whatever Brittany is telling them.

"Two freshmen have mentioned they've heard Amber screaming at night. Are you denying this?" a male reporter asks.

"Amber has nightmares. If you went through what she did with that psychopath, you'd have nightmares, too. And those two freshmen are skanks. Maybe you should be more interested in their sexual escapades than Amber's." She says it so matter-of-factly, it catches me off guard. She doesn't even have a scowl on her face, which is not like Brittany when she's pissed at someone.

"What about the evidence the police recently seized from her room?" The cops never reported specifically what was found, but someone leaked to the media that the cops searched my room and found items of interest to the investigation.

"We live in a building where people come and go all the time. Anyone could have planted the evidence. If you're determined to do it, it wouldn't be too hard to find a way. Maybe you should ask why the cops aren't doing a better job protecting Amber from someone who is clearly trying to hurt her."

Why can't I be strong enough and stand up for my rights like Brittany? Hell, I can't even stand up in front of a classroom and do a presentation without feeling like I'm going to puke.

A reporter turns her head and spots me. Her body shifts around and she lurches toward me. "Amber, how do you feel about the charges against Paul Carlson being reduced?"

"Shit," Chase mutters under his breath.

"No comment." My voice cracks. I'm the girl trapped in the concrete room all over again, barely surviving. Except this time instead of a defenseless kitten keeping me from dying inside, the man I love threads his fingers with mine and pulls me past the reporters, many who are shivering in their coats. Several of them look as thrilled to be here as I am to see them.

Once we're in the building, we go upstairs while Brittany fills us in on what happened this morning. Some people who live in the residence demanded that the reporters leave me alone. Some have been enjoying their fifteen seconds of fame, at my expense.

By the time Marcus and I head to the library, the reporters have disbanded. I'm not a celebrity who is hounded for the elusive million-dollar photo, and for that I'm extremely grateful. They get stalked by crazies, too, and I don't mean the paparazzi. But how many celebrities are blamed for their overeager fans' obsessions? How many of them are treated like they're the criminals?

And how many times does one of them—or someone they love —wind up dead because the fan felt justified in his actions?

I shudder, and it has nothing to do with the freezing temperature. That's what it comes down to. Paul felt justified to stalk, torture, and kill me. His sister feels justified to protect him by doing whatever she can to destroy the case. And in the end, with everything that's happening, including our argument this morning, Marcus might feel justified to walk out of my life.

At the library, I sit at an empty computer. Marcus takes up residence at the one next to me. I have to locate books for my report, but there's one thing I must do first. I pull from my bag the letter my father sent me last week—the only letter I've ever received from him since he abandoned us—and type *Lily Cummings, Chicago*.

22

AMBER

"**A**m-ber. You and I were meant to be. Forever and ever. When will you realize your boyfriend didn't love you? Not the way I do. You and he were never meant to be."

With what little will I have left, I lift my head and peer through slitted eyes. I'm alone and in the same concrete room I've been in for the past three, four, or maybe five days. Next to me is a plate of lasagna. One of my favorite foods when I was a kid. Paul knows this. He knows everything about me. Because I told him when I thought we were friends.

"No," I whisper, "Trent loved me. He wanted to marry me one day." I have no idea who I'm saying it to. No one is here with me. I'm not even sure where Paul's voice is coming from. Maybe it's just in my head.

"If that were true, why did he leave you? That doesn't sound like true love to me."

"He didn't leave me," I scream through a raw throat. "He was in an accident."

Laughter thunders through the enclosed space. "It was no accident, Amber. It was fate."

"There's no such thing as fate."

"Are you so sure? It was fate that we met. It was fate that your boyfriend's brakes failed. It was fate that I found you stranded alone with

147

a flat tire. And soon fate will have it that we will be one, like husband and wife."

I shudder at the implication behind the last part and get lost in the part about Trent. The police hadn't released that information about the accident. How did Paul know?

"What did you do to him?" I sob. "What the hell did you do to my boyfriend?"

The room turns into the same one I've seen many times in my night-mares. The room of mirrors. And like all the other times, the mirrors shatter for no reason and shards of glass slice through my skin. But the pain they cause is nothing compared to the pain of knowing the truth.

"I had to kill him, Am-ber. For you. His death is my gift to you."

And like I do every time I have this dream, and like I did in reality when Paul told me what he had done...I scream.

"Amber," Emma says from a distance. Someone shakes me. "Amber."

"Things are getting worse." Brittany's voice also sounds distant as my nightmare fades away.

I slowly open my eyes and the room comes into focus. Pushing myself up, I shake away the sleep slogging around in my brain, and glance at my alarm clock. 3:15 p.m. I've been asleep for maybe thirty or forty minutes. That explains why I feel like a zombie who's been partying hard for several days. "I wasn't screaming again, was I?"

Brittany shakes her head. "No. You were restless and muttering in your sleep."

I don't want to know what I said, so I don't ask. I remember what I was dreaming about, and I don't want to mention it in front of Emma. Or anyone, for that matter.

Emma studies my face, a frown on hers. I scoot my legs off the bed and she sits next to me. "You look like you haven't slept in months." Feels like it, too.

"Maybe I could get an oversized teddy bear." For the days I sleep in my dorm room. Which is sad when I think about it. I should be stronger. I shouldn't need Marcus or a teddy bear to help me sleep through the night.

Brittany grunts. "I prefer the idea of sneaking Marcus into our room. I can't study with a glassy-eyed, giant stuffed toy staring at me."

A small smiles flits at the corners of my mouth. I can't imagine Brittany being disturbed by a stuffed animal. She tends to scare people away. Or at least the people she doesn't give a chance to get to know her—which is most people.

"Not much longer and the trial will be over," Emma says. "You know what you need?"

"Caffeine. And lots of it."

"Yeah, that's one possibility. But I've got another one." She scrambles off the bed.

No, I'm pretty sure caffeine is the *only* possibility.

Emma riffles through my drawers. I'm tempted to collapse on my bed and go back to sleep...at least until the bad dreams hit again.

"Here, put these on." She tosses me the gym clothes I wore when I played basketball with Marcus at the youth center. Before winter hit Chicago.

I catch them and eye the pile in my hands, half expecting them to bite me. I don't even wear them when I work out, since I'd rather keep the scars and tattoos hidden.

"Trust me, you'll feel better," Emma says.

"What are we gonna do?"

"It's open gym time. We're going to play ball. And you're not going to say no, because you know I'm right. You need this."

Brittany snorts. "The girl can barely stand and you expect her to play basketball? Wow, you really are blond, aren't you?"

Emma glares at Brittany. "I know what I'm talking about. I know her better than you do." She turns to me. "And we can get coffee on the way if you want."

I do want. Maybe the sugar and caffeine will give me an energy boost.

Once I would have been self-conscious about stripping with Emma and Brittany in the same room as me, but both have seen my scars. I change into my clothes and pull my yoga pants over my shorts, then grab my coat.

"Have fun." Brittany fuels her words with a heavy dose of sarcasm. "And be sure to let me know when you want me to sneak Marcus in."

Emma and I push through the bitter wind clawing at our faces as we make our way to the sports center. It's enough to wake up any warm-blooded creature, even one who is past due on her sleep.

We decide not to bother with coffee. Now that the idea we're going to play basketball has chased away the fog in my brain, I can't get to the gym fast enough. I pick up my pace as the building comes into view through the blowing snow.

A game's already going on when we hit the court. All guys. None are from the men's team, but they sure can play.

Emma and I head over to them. Once they stop long enough to catch their breath, Emma's in there, asking if we can join them.

They give us the once-over, their gazes lingering on my scarred wrists and leg. Instead of looking disgusted, which is the reaction I usually expect, they nod and let us play. One of them recognizes Emma from the women's team.

"Shit, you're good," Troy, one of my teammates, says after I nail another lay-up. We high-five. These guys are even better than the teens Emma and I played with prior to Christmas.

"You're not so bad yourself. How come you're not on the men's team?" They all could be. I wipe the sweat from my forehead with the back of my hand.

He reaches for his water bottle near the sideline, where the rest of the guys' stuff is piled. "I used to be. We all were." He gestures to the guys, all taking a quick time-out. "But I'm in grad school now and no longer eligible to play. Nor do I have the time. Same deal with everyone here. What's your excuse?"

"My excuse?"

He lifts an eyebrow. "You're not on the women's team, even though you obviously should be. So what's your excuse?"

"That's what I'm wondering, too," a tall woman, with the same golden-brown coloring as Jordan and wearing a tracksuit, says as she approaches. Coach Willmott. As in, the coach for the women's basketball team. "I haven't seen you play before, so I know you aren't playing for another collegiate team. So what's your excuse?"

Emma breaks away from the guys on her team and joins us. "Hey, Coach."

The woman grins at Emma. "I take it you couldn't wait until practice to play?"

"Something like that. Amber"—Emma points to me—"desperately needed to play. And you know how sacrificing I can be."

I laugh. "You wanted this as much as I did."

Coach Willmott doesn't seem too surprised to hear this. "You still haven't explained why you aren't playing collegiate ball."

"I was recovering from burns on my leg"—*among other things*—"and missed out on my senior year. No games. No chance of being scouted."

"That's too bad. Well, if you're interested in trying out for the team next year, I'd be happy to put you through the paces and see what you can do."

"Th-thanks! I would love that." I do my best not to shriek my response.

"Don't worry, Coach," Emma says. "I'll work her ass off to get her ready."

Coach chuckles. "I bet you will, Emma." She nods at the guys playing ball. "I'll let you two get back to your game, but Emma, try not to wear yourself out before practice in twenty minutes. Deal?"

"Deal."

Coach Willmott strolls off, and my best friend hugs me. "Oh my

God, I can't believe our dream might come true after all." Trent, Emma, and I had planned to play for the University of Chicago. It had been our dream since we were kids. But our dream was destroyed last year, and instead of going there, Emma and I applied to the University of Illinois at Chicago. While this might not be UChicago, being able to play for a collegiate team would put me a step closer to being what I was last year, prior to Paul stepping into my life.

Emma and I hug again, not caring that we're both sweaty.

"Unless you're planning to make that a group hug, and I'm game for it if you are," a guy from Emma's team calls out, "would you two ladies get your asses over here? We need you."

Laughing, we jog over to join them, and the game resumes.

It's almost time for Emma to leave when Troy says, "Do you know there's a guy over there"—he nods at something over my shoulder—"who's been videotaping you for the past ten minutes?"

I whirl around. A balding man in his midforties is holding a video camera. The woman with him has long dark hair and seems familiar.

"How can you be sure he's not videotaping everyone?" I ask.

"Because every time I look over at him, the lens is pointed at you."

Before we can dwell on it more, the woman hustles over to us. "Hi. Amber Scott, right? I'm a sports reporter and I'd like to do a story on you."

"Why? I'm not on any team."

Emma and the guys join me. Like Troy, they're standing with their arms crossed in a stance that signals "Keep your distance."

A warmth spreads through me. Not the same warmth that consumes me when I'm with Marcus and he's kissing me. This warmth comes from knowing people, strangers, care enough to want to protect me from all potential threats.

"Since when were you a sports reporter?" one of my teammates asks. "I thought you did general news stories. I'm a huge fan of yours." His face is red, but I can't tell if it's from a hard game of basketball or because he admitted to being a fan.

"You're right. But I thought I could pitch the story to the sports team."

Something seems off. She wasn't anywhere near us while I was talking to the coach. She has no idea I've been offered a chance to try out.

"No comment." I turn away.

"So you have nothing to say about the sex video that was leaked showing your boyfriend? A video that shows he's into S-and-M."

I can only stare at her. My mouth opens and closes in an attempt to formulate a reply, but there are no words that can convey what I'm thinking and the panic seeping in.

She says something else before Troy and another guy escort her away, but whatever it was is lost on me as I stand frozen, my body growing numb.

This is the evidence that could destroy me.

23

MARCUS

"**T**rue or false?" I ask Alejandro as I line up the pool stick with the white ball. "During the nineteen-ninety to ninety-one season, the Chicago Bulls won sixty-five games." I tap the ball with the stick. It rolls toward the red-striped ball but only nicks it. Alejandro and Matt laugh while Juan releases a stream of Spanish curses.

"False," Alejandro says, still laughing at the same time Juan mutters, "You suck," and then another stream of words slips out that I'm probably glad I don't understand.

"They won sixty-*one* games," Alejandro continues, ignoring his friend's rant. Of the three of us, he's the only one who understands what Juan is saying.

Outside, the wind howls against the cracked window, reminding us that even though it's basketball season, it's too fucking cold to play it unless you have access to indoor basketball courts. And in my old neighborhood, that's as likely to exist as Santa in a Speedo.

"Hey," I say to Juan, "some of us were too busy studying in high school to have time to master the game of pool." That's complete

154

crap. I've always sucked at the game, even after Ryan tried to teach it to me. He was the pool champion. But that didn't bother me. I was the pool stud. Girls didn't care how good I was at the game. It was how I handled my own stick that counted, but I'm hardly explaining that to the guys.

Matt surveys the balls, walking around and checking the best possible angle to shoot from. He's nothing like his two friends. Whereas Alejandro and Juan are loud, athletic, and always ribbing each other, Matt is quiet, and sports isn't his thing.

With the exception of pool.

Matt hits the cue ball and it slams into the red one. The red ball steamrolls into a pocket. Juan groans again, but this time keeps the cursing to himself.

My cell phone rings from my jeans pocket. I pull it out and check who's calling. Amber.

"Hey, Kitten, what's up?" I haven't seen her in the last two days, and my entire body aches to be with her.

Amber doesn't say anything. The only sound is her jagged breathing. Panic hammers in my chest at all the possible reasons for this. "Amber? What's going on?"

She lets out a long slow breath. "Have you...have you ever participated in any sex videos?"

I want to lie but there's no point. She knows or she wouldn't be asking. "Yes. Last year," I say, walking away from the guys. I have a feeling this is a conversation I don't want them to hear. "But it's not something I'm into normally. Ryan had just died. I was drunk and thought at the time that it was a great idea. Why? What happened?"

"I'm going to text you a link to a video. You need to see it."

At the pain in her voice, I scrub my hand over my face. I've never seen the video. I just know it exists. I also know the girl I did it with hadn't planned for it to go public. At least that's what she told me. I guess I should have known better, but in all honesty, I had forgotten about it until Amber mentioned it.

"Give me a second. I'm at the youth center. Let me ask Dave if I can check it out on his computer. I'll call you right back."

"Okay."

Dave's office door is closed but I knock anyway. Part of me hopes he'll say no and that's the end of it until I get home. But the other part wonders why Amber's upset. It happened well before I met her. She's got to know that.

"Come in." The former marine sounds distracted.

I open the door and enter. Dave's attention is focused on the computer screen. A jumble of documents is spread across his desk. "What can I do you for?" he asks, not glancing up.

"Can I check something on your computer? Amber wants me to look at something on the Internet."

"Sure, knock yourself out. I could use a break." He stands and lets me take his chair, but it's obvious he's not going anywhere. I don't blame him. It's *his* computer after all.

I stare at the screen, summoning all my strength. Having Amber and Dave watch me screw a girl doesn't exactly make it to the highlight of my day.

"You want a coffee or something?" Dave asks after a few seconds.

I nod, and once he leaves the room, enter the URL. The page opens to a still shot that is definitely me, wearing only jeans. The video isn't new but the download is. It went live five hours ago. I click on Play.

The picture isn't the best quality, due to the poor lighting, but it's clear enough to see what's going on. The girl comes onto the screen and runs her fingers down my chest. Although that night is a vague memory, I do remember a few vivid details about her that cause a shudder to race through me. While I have no complaints when sex gets a little rough, her preferences went way beyond that. I was drunk, but I wasn't that drunk. I told her I wasn't interested and she had been fine with it.

Dave enters the office as the video progresses from me kissing the girl to me tearing her clothes off and her doing the same to me. Neither of us appears concerned at our nakedness. Whereas Amber's still shy with my seeing her naked and vulnerable, there's nothing vulnerable about the woman in the video. Her confidence, even in her drunken state, is obvious.

"Oh, my," Dave says, which would have been funny if it weren't for what is happening on the video. My eyes widen as the girl bends over the bed, leaving her ass in the air, and I whip her exposed backside. I didn't do that. I'm positive. That's just not me.

But according to the blurry picture of a guy who could be me, that's exactly what I did.

I bury my face in my hands. The girl's moans of ecstasy reach inside my chest and clench my heart hard, killing all hopes of a future with Amber.

A clicking sound comes from the computer mouse and the moaning ends. I glance up to find the video has been closed. But even though I no longer have to look at it, no longer have to see what I did that night, the image is burned in my brain.

"I don't know what to say, but my guess is you weren't expecting any of that." Dave pulls up a chair and sits. "You want to talk about it?"

Shame at what I did screams at me, and I bury my face once again in my hands. I can't bear to glimpse the disapproving expression that is no doubt on Dave's face. It's too much to take in as part of my already screwed-up life.

"I vaguely remember the girl and I vaguely remember us making the video. I was drunk at the time and stupid. But I swear I don't remember whipping her." *And God knows what else happened after that.*

"When did you make the video? Do you remember?"

"Last summer." I remove my hands from my face and stare at the wallpaper of a dramatic lightning storm on the computer screen. "After Ryan died, I was upset and reckless and got drunk. I met her in a bar and went to her apartment. I don't get why I don't remember doing that stuff. It's not my scene. You'd think I'd remember doing that, wouldn't you?"

"What else do you remember about that night?"

I shrug. "Not too much. It's not like she was the first girl I'd had sex with. As far as I remember, sex with her wasn't any different from any other girl I've been with. Certainly nothing like in the video."

"Has Amber seen it?"

I let my head hang, elbows on knees, and nod. "She called me and told me to watch it." My heart clenches even tighter at what she had to watch, at what this could mean to Paul's trial. Except none of it is real. Not the whipping at least.

"I don't know what happened, but I swear it wasn't me doing that stuff." I peer back at the computer screen. "I need to watch it. I need to know what I supposedly did after that." *Even if I can't bear to watch it.*

Dave pats my leg and stands. "Call me if you need anything."

"Thanks." I reach for the mouse and reload the website as he leaves. I close my eyes. The door clicks shut and I sit unmoving, waiting for the courage to hit Play.

The video is forty minutes. Forty minutes of me doing things to the girl that I've never done and would never do. I can be adventurous under the covers like any other male, and there are tons of positions Amber and I haven't tried yet that I have with other girls. But I would never hurt a girl just to get off. Even if she was willing.

The guy does look a lot like me, but the more I watch, the more I'm positive it's not a repeat of last November with Tammara, when she slipped me a roofie and I didn't remember her taking photos of her kissing me. This guy isn't drunk. He's not stumbling around like I would be for me not to remember any of this.

The girl's either been videotaping herself having sex with plenty of guys, including one who resembles me when the picture is blurry. Or she hired someone who looks similar to me and staged this video. The setting is the same, or at least the furniture is the same. She took the two footages and spliced them together to make one convincing video.

Now I have to convince Amber of this—as well as the DA.

24

MARCUS

I return to my apartment two hours later. I haven't talked to Amber since she called me about the video. I drove to the lake, to where Ryan and I used to escape when we needed a break from life and the hell known as Frank. It was too cold to sit on the beach, so I stayed in my car, staring at nothing, wondering what to do about this new piece of evidence that could be used against Amber. Struggling to remember the girl's name, and anything else that could help the cops.

After I sat for over an hour, freezing because I was low on gas and didn't want to keep the engine running, I drove to the police station and explained everything. I'm not sure they believed me. I got the sense they thought I was just trying to save ass with my girlfriend.

But it's not my ass I'm trying to save. It's Amber I'm worried about. The media will eat up this new piece of information. I've given them the best news story so far. I've given the defense a reason to celebrate. I don't know much about the law, but I do know all the jury has to do is find the psychopath not guilty on all the charges, or find him guilty but sentence him to only a few years in jail—and then he'll be free to stalk her again. He'll be free to stalk and kill me, if he so chooses, like he killed Trent. And if there's the slightest risk of that happening, I know Amber. She'll disappear from my life to protect me. She did exactly that when she thought the letters Tammara sent her were from the psychopath, and the threats to kill me were real. Except this time she will disappear so the psychopath can't find her. This time she'll disappear so I won't be able to find her. Ever.

I park my car. Chase isn't home yet. I haven't told him about the video, but as soon as Amber tells Jordan, my best friend will find out what happened. He'll know how I screwed up big-time, like he's always suspected would happen one day.

Each step toward the building feels like the world is shaking under my feet, eager to knock me down and keep me there. I need a beer. I need several beers, but that won't solve fuck all. Being numb won't solve fuck all. If I knew someone from the computer science department, I'd ask them to analyze the video. At least then I'd know something is being done about it. But who am I kidding? Amber's mom won't ignore it. She'll be on top of it to prove it's not authentic as soon as she learns I'm not the only guy in the video. I need to call Amber and tell her the truth about that night, or at least the truth as best as I remember it.

Shit, Amber's barely holding on as it is, and now my past is coming back to destroy her. The video is one more reminder of how she deserves someone better than me.

I enter the building, and the shaking under my feet becomes a full-out earthquake, easily measuring seven on the Richter scale. Amber's mom is standing in the lobby, and based on her scowl, she doesn't have good news. She's dressed in a business suit under her designer winter coat. Slung over one shoulder is a briefcase-style leather bag. Her chin-length blond hair is slightly damp from the falling snow.

"I need to talk to you." Her tone is as warm as a winter blizzard.

The coldness of her words reaches inside me and turns my blood to ice. Inwardly, I shudder. "If it's about the video, it's not what it looks like. I've already told the cops that."

"I would rather not discuss this here." She nods at the locked entrance door, indicating she would prefer to discuss it in private. I'd prefer that, too.

We ride the elevator to my floor in silence. I can't be bothered with small talk, and she's not in the mood for it, either. The tension is so heavy, I'm surprised we haven't surpassed the elevator's weight restriction and crashed into the basement.

After what feels like several hours, the door opens, and I lead Amber's mom to my apartment. Her disgust coats me like mud when she sees where I live. Chase and I aren't slobs, but our place is a far cry from what she's used to. Our furniture is worn, scratched, and mismatched.

Smoky glances up from his carpeted tree, meows, and goes back to sleep. His tree is the nicest piece of furniture that we own, which is sad when you think about it. Until now, I didn't care. What we had was functional, even if not always comfortable. But for Amber's mom, this is a reminder of where I came from, how I was brought up in the projects, and how she wishes I would crawl back there and leave her daughter alone.

I don't invite her to sit. I suspect she wouldn't want to even if I offered.

"I want to you stay away from my daughter, Marcus."

"The video is a fake." My tone lacks all hint of life, my insides slowly fracturing at what she's suggesting. "Parts of it are me, but the S-and-M parts aren't. I told the cops what happened. They're checking into it."

"That might be so, but the damage has already been done. The fact that you even made the video suggests your obvious lack of judgment. A lack of judgment that I cannot risk, will not risk, destroying Amber. She's already been through enough. She doesn't need you adding to her stress, too."

"But I love Amber." I struggle to keep my tone calm, to keep it from revealing what this conversation is doing to me. Though she is partly right. It was due to faulty judgment on my part. I shouldn't have agreed to the video for any reason, and if I could take it all back, I would. "I'd never do anything to hurt her. I would do anything for her. But you have to realize I never intended for the video to be released. My brother had just been murdered and I was angry and upset. I got drunk and made a mistake."

She flinches at the part about my brother being murdered, but the movement is small, barely noticeable. "Your reasons for making the video are not relevant. You did, and now it's hurting Amber." What she doesn't say, but we both know is true, is the video is hurting Amber beyond the court case. She was forced to witness me having sex with another woman, even if the video was made before I met Amber. She knew about my past man-whore reputation, but watching me in action is probably a million times worse, especially since most of it was a lie and she doesn't even know it.

"I have connections at the university," Amber's mom says. "Connections who won't be happy at what your video could mean to the school's reputation. For you, this could mean termination of your scholarship."

If she were a vampire, she couldn't have drained blood from my body as fast as she did with those simple words. I remain silent. There's no point saying anything; she hasn't finished with where she's going with this.

She unzips her bag and removes some papers. "If you continue to see Amber, I will ensure that you are removed from the school. But if you cease your relationship with my daughter, I'll smooth things over with the school, and your scholarship will remain intact. Do I make myself clear?"

Perfectly. I'm being forced to choose between the girl I love and the promise I made my brother. The promise I made to pursue a future he was deprived of due to our circumstances. He gave up everything when he moved away from home, taking me with him to keep me safe. But how can I give up Amber? She means everything to me, too. She's my reason for living, my reason to keep fighting against what Frank did to me.

25

AMBER

I walk through the Marketplace, coffee in hand, toward our usual table for lunch. Jordan is sitting there alone, reading a textbook. Chase usually sits with us, but he and Marcus have a project they need to work on. At least that's what Jordan told me. I haven't heard from Marcus since I called him about the video two days ago. He hasn't responded to my messages or texts, and I have no idea why. I even told him in one message that I don't blame him for what happened. He was upset by his brother's death—I get that. What I don't get is how the guy who is tender with me in bed could be so different from the one on the video. That guy is nothing like the Marcus I know and love. And Marcus has never given me any hints he's into that stuff—just the opposite. Which is why I wish he would talk to me and tell me what's going on. I wish anyone would tell me what's going on.

Someone grabs my arm. Buzz Cut. The asshole who grabbed my arm a few weeks ago, when the media first mentioned the phony letters to Paul. He smiles at me, but there's nothing friendly about the gesture. In his other hand is a local newspaper. I can't read the entire heading, his thumb is covering it, but I can see enough to know the article is talking about me, the video, and Paul.

I snatch my arm away from his hand and scan the area. People are watching us with the same level of interest that's been directed at me ever since the first news story broke about the letters to Paul. No one seems interested in helping me. Why put an end to the free lunchtime entertainment if you don't have to?

Buzz Cut steps closer, leaving mere inches between our bodies. Instinctively I move back. "Rumor has it you and your boyfriend broke up," he says. "I take it he wasn't man enough for you. Only a certain type of man can handle a woman like you." Before I can move away, he runs his fingers down my arm. "Only I can handle a woman like you." His words are slow, no doubt intended to sound seductive. He misses the mark by several light-years.

I remove the plastic lid from my coffee. "Handle this." I hurl the hot contents at his hoodie-clad body.

Laughter thunders around us, matching the sound of my pulse pounding in my ears.

Buzz Cut's face reddens and he pulls the soaking fabric from his body. "What the hell did you do that for, fuckin' bitch?"

"Thought you liked it rough," I spit at him, and instantly regret it. The last thing I need to do is encourage his misguided beliefs.

I don't give him a chance to say anything else; I storm past him. He doesn't come after me, and I don't check to see if he's where I left him. The laughter dies away, and a murmur of excitement fills the food court as I sit across from Jordan at our table.

Jordan closes her book. "Are you all right? You look like you've seen a ghost."

I shake my head, but I'm not sure if it's due to me not being all right or because I haven't seen a ghost. "Apparently there's a rumor circulating that Marcus and I broke up." I try to swallow back the growing ache in my chest, but it leaks into my words. Is that why he hasn't called or texted? He finally decided he'd had enough of me.

Bit by bit, my wall returns as my insides shrivel at what this means. Marcus must have started "dating" again, and that's how Buzz Cut knew.

Her eyebrows pinch together. "What do you mean?"

"Marcus hasn't called me since he told me about the video. And now guys believe I get off on being tortured during sex, because the cops haven't issued a statement saying the letters are forged"—*which they haven't been able to prove*—"and because Marcus's sex video went viral. This morning Brittany found a letter shoved under our door. It was a very graphic drawing of what a guy wants to do to me." I close my eyes at the memory, but the pornographic image is embedded in my brain.

I shudder and reopen my eyes. "I don't even know who sent it."

"Did you tell Becca?"

I nod. Fortunately the RA hadn't left for her class yet. And it wasn't the first letter I've given her since Marcus's video went viral. Plus, I told her about some of the sexual comments and innuendos the guys on our floor have been saying to me. At her encouragement, I filed formal complaints for each letter and comment.

I'm hoping it does more than when Marcus filed a complaint against the man he caught photographing me in the Student Services Building. There wasn't enough evidence to prove he was stalking me and for things to go further than that.

"She didn't know who it was either," I tell her, "but she's going to talk to the appropriate individuals so further action can be taken." Beyond her having words with some of the offenders.

I tell Jordan what happened with Buzz Cut.

She pinches her lips together, and I wish more than anything I had kept quiet about what happened. Right now, I need her to be the Jordan who's always grinning. "So what are you going to do? Keep coming here for lunch and let those assholes harass you?"

I raise an eyebrow at her swearing, something I've never heard her do before. "Until it all blows over, I'm going to hang out in the library where no one can bother me."

"You mean hide out."

I shrug. With everything going on, it's not like I've been hungry. Now I don't have to pretend that I am.

Jordan sighs and toys with the bread on her sandwich while I play with the heart and lotus charms on the bracelet Marcus gave me for Christmas. A reminder of him I'm not sure I'm ready to give up yet.

"I wish more reporters were like Oprah," Jordan says.

"What do you mean?"

"She did things to help her ratings. There's no doubt about that. But she did things on her show that would make a positive difference. She cared about her ratings, but she also cared about people. She gave people a voice to be heard. Really heard."

And I bet Oprah doesn't get nervous talking in front of a million viewers. I bet if she faced in court a guy who had brutalized her, she wouldn't fall apart. She'd be strong.

She'd be the person I want to be. Need to be. I'm just not sure if I can.

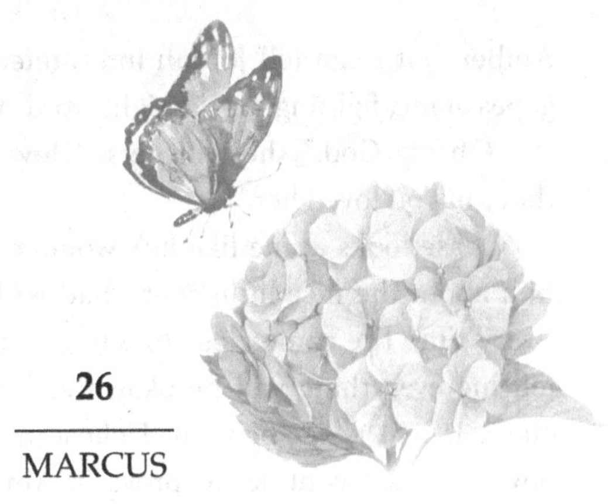

26

MARCUS

I step out of the elevator with Chase right behind me. Jordan is standing across from us, scanning the main floor of the engineering building.

Figuring she's here to see my best friend, I turn to Chase. "I'll see you later." I'm about to walk away when he grabs my shoulder.

"She's here to see you."

There's only one reason Jordan would want to talk to me. Amber. I stride over to her, not caring if I'm bulldozing into anyone. "Is she okay?"

"Are the rumors true? You broke up with Amber?" Her voice holds a note of anger I didn't think would be possible with Jordan. She's one of the most optimistic people I know.

I can't even answer the question. Technically, I haven't broken up with Amber. I can't bring myself to say the words to her. Instead, I'm the asshole who's not saying anything at all. I've read her texts and listened to her messages over and over and over again. Each time I do, I feel like I did every time Frank hit me, every time I feared I could be the one he raped next. Helpless.

I might not say the words to confirm that I've broken up with

Amber, but I can tell Jordan interpreted my silence correctly. She gapes at me, fighting for the right words to respond with.

"Oh my God," she whispers. "How can you do that to her? I thought you loved her."

Chase looks at me like he's wondering the same. I haven't told him about the nice little chat I had with Amber's mom last week. Every time I've come close to telling him, so he can lie to me and tell me everything will be okay, the words remain wedged in my chest. It will never be okay. I chose my education over Amber. I have a signed contract to prove it. Amber's mom came prepared and didn't give me the chance to dwell on it. It was sign the contract or she would've contacted the university and destroyed my future. But without Amber in my life, my future is destroyed either way. All I can hope for is that one day she'll meet a guy as great as Trent, a guy she deserves.

Jordan lifts her hand, and her palm strikes my face. I swear everyone in the hallway heard. They watch us with growing interest. Jordan is oblivious to this as she glares at me. Chase glances back and forth between us, unsure if he should defend me or support the girl he's falling for.

"You selfish jerk." Tears fill Jordan's voice. "Ever since your video showed up on the Internet, guys have been harassing her. And now that you're no longer a threat, because of the rumors you dumped her, it's been open season on Amber."

Fuck. As if she didn't have enough to worry about with the trial. "Who?" I snap, and ball my hand into a fist, suspecting I know who one of the assholes is.

Chase puts his hand on my shoulder. "Dude, don't shoot the messenger. Jordan and Amber don't know who the guys are."

I glare at him. "What do you mean they don't know?"

Jordan answers. "One of them is the guy you almost got into a fight with in the food court. He grabbed her yesterday at lunch."

"Has anyone else touched her?"

"No, but guys have been sending her drawings and letters that are pretty explicit. She's filed complaints with the university and police, but until they can discover who's sending them, there's nothing anyone can do about it."

I drag my fingers through my hair. When did things get so fucked up?

BY THE TIME I RETURN TO MY APARTMENT BUILDING SEVERAL HOURS later, after driving aimlessly, Chase's car is parked in his usual spot. I left the engineering building after my run-in with Jordan, and since then, I've been trying to figure out what to do about Amber's situation. As long as I'm not around to protect her, she'll be at risk. Her mom never thought of that when she planned to eradicate me from her daughter's life.

Feeling like I haven't slept in a thousand years, I plod to the building. I have a test this week I need to study for, but I don't have the energy right now. Soon Amber's mom won't have to worry about my attending the same university as Amber. The way I'm going, I'll flunk out on my own. In my head I hear Frank laughing, telling me I'm just a worthless piece of shit.

I enter the apartment. Chase is sitting on the couch, TV off, a beer in his hand. He's slouched forward with his elbows on his knees, staring at a pile of papers on the table in front of him.

"What's going on?" I ask.

He glances up, face pale. "What the hell is this, Marcus?" He lifts the top piece of paper.

I shrug. "Looks like paper to me. Why?"

"It's a contract. A fucking contract you signed." He slams it on the table. "Why the hell did you sign away your rights to see the girl you supposedly love?"

Compounded with everything else, his anger and staggering disbelief at what I did goes beyond what I can handle. I slump against the wall, my legs barely keeping me up. Chase is used to my crazy shit, but clearly he never expected me to pull a stunt like this.

"Why were you in my room?" I mentally kick myself for leaving the contract on my desk.

"My calculator batteries died. I figured you'd be okay with it if I borrowed your calculator for my math assignment." He's not the slightest bit remorseful for entering my room without permission, even though we respect each other's privacy. That's why I hadn't been worried about leaving the contract out. Reading it again and again and again has been my punishment for walking away from Amber.

"Why the hell did you sign it?"

"I didn't have a choice. If I didn't, I would have lost my scholarship. And then I would have lost Amber for sure." I would've had nothing to offer her.

"Shit," is all Chase has to say.

"It's killing me. I can't even explain it to her, because if I do, I lose everything." Her mother covered all her bases to keep me away from Amber.

"Shit. What are you going to do about it?"

I flop onto the couch next to him and press my elbows into my thighs, my face into my hands. "The hell if I know."

I somehow manage to hold back the bitter laugh boiling inside me. Ryan sacrificed himself so I could have a future. And now I'm sacrificing myself—my happiness and my dreams—for Amber's future.

And like with my brother, I won't be around to see her live it.

Her mom made sure of that.

27

AMBER

I nhale. *Exhale.* I walk across campus, my mind a jumble of emotions. The side effect of watching an all-night *Friends* marathon after I woke up from a nightmare, combined with a *grande* dose of nervousness.

Not a good way to start a presentation.

I sit in my usual seat near the back of the classroom and wait for Emma. People keep peeking over their shoulders at me. They know my presentation is today.

My palms grow clammier. I tighten my grip on my phone. It's been two weeks since Marcus's video surfaced and since the last time he called me. Jordan talked to Chase about it, and he couldn't tell her anything. I'm not sure if that's a "couldn't" or "wouldn't." But despite the silent treatment, I keep checking my phone in case Marcus finally decides to contact me. In case he has a good reason for not telling me that we're through.

Ahead of me, several students are bent over a newspaper and frequently glance over their shoulders at me. It's got to be the latest news about Paul and the trial. And the petition someone started, claiming that I should be the one on trial and not Paul. It's already garnered several thousand signatures, thanks to Marcus's video.

The regular news has at least decided to ignore it, but that hasn't stopped the local tabloid from running the trash. It hasn't stopped people from believing a petition is enough to change the justice system.

Emma slides onto her seat and throws me a look that says she's sorry for being late.

"How are you holding up?" she asks.

"I'll be glad when it's over."

Emma laughs. "I don't get how you can play basketball in front of a huge crowd and not be even the slightest bit nervous. But do a class presentation and you're ready to hurl."

"That's different. I don't pay attention to everyone watching and cheering. I only notice the ball and my teammates. Everything else doesn't exist."

Emma nods. It's the same for her. The difference between us, though, is her confidence goes beyond the court. Mine stops at the out-of-bound lines.

"Okay, class," Professor Hale says. "We have a number of presentations to do, so let's get started."

The presentations begin, but since I'm last, I get to sit, bouncing my fingers on my thigh, wishing time would either speed up so that I'm finished sooner or screech to a halt so I don't have to go up there yet. For the next forty minutes, it's all I can think about.

"Amber Scott, you're next."

I take a deep breath. *I can do this.*

"Good luck," Emma whispers.

I've never been jealous of anything about my best friend. She's gorgeous, an amazing player, smart, popular. But as I walk down the steps to the front with everyone watching me, knowing I'm *her* —the girl the media loves talking about—I'm jealous at Emma's ability to not let things like this bother her. If our places were reversed, she would own the audience and make the most of her situation.

My legs feel like I'm skating across a frozen lake. At any moment the ice could crack and I'll disappear into the deadly waters. They're shaky, uncertain, wondering if it's better to turn and run and hope for the best—or to keep going and take a chance that everything will be all right.

I'm not eager to start new rumors, like I'm pregnant with Marcus's child and had to run to the bathroom to puke—especially since puking is a real possibility right now—I stand my ground and take my place behind the lectern.

A few individuals lean toward the person next to them and say something. Their friend either giggles or whispers in reply. I swallow, trying to ease the sudden dryness in my mouth, and shuffle my index cards.

Emma smiles and nods for me to begin. While everyone else wants to believe the lies, Emma's here for me. Even when her brother died because of me. Even when I turned my back on her due to the overwhelming guilt. Even when I caused her and her family insurmountable pain, Emma has been there for me, except when I wouldn't let her.

Relieved no one can see my fingers tap-tap-tap behind the lectern, I take in another slow breath. "We, as members of our community, have an obligation to protect children and their fundamental rights. But often children are the forgotten members of society because they aren't vocal. They're expected to trust adults, but often it is the very individuals they are supposed to trust who let them down the most."

I pause and gauge the audience's reaction. They weren't expecting me to talk about the role of advocacy in children's rights. I can see it on their faces.

I continue my presentation, and with each word I gain a little more strength. It's no longer Emma I see in the back row. It's a younger Marcus and Ryan, as well as Alejandro, who watch me, silently cheering me on. My heart beats fast. If it had wings, it would soar around the room. I'm lighter and freer than I have felt in a while.

The words slip out easily. A little too easily. And I have to focus hard on not sounding like an out-of-control train. I want to make sure that even on some deep unconscious level, everyone is thinking about the most vulnerable part of society, the part with the least voice.

I conclude with why community psychology is important for children's rights. Everyone's attention is solely on me. They're not thinking about Rosemary's allegations that I seduced her brother, or the allegations that I'm into violent sex. They're thinking about the forgotten kids like Marcus, Ryan, and Alejandro.

I smile as everyone applauds. The relief of being finished surges through me and chases away the last of the adrenaline overload, which has plagued me since the beginning of class.

I scan the audience, one last time. A girl near the back row bends down.

And that's when I see him.

28

———

AMBER

I blink at the sight of Marcus. He's not really here. He's a delusion brought on by my lack of sleep. My body aches at the sight of him. If this is how it responds to my delusion, how would it respond to the real deal?

I keep staring at him, afraid if I blink again, my delusion will vanish. If I can't have the real Marcus, the delusion will have to do.

"Amber," Professor Hale says, intruding on my runaway thoughts. "Amber," she repeats. "Are you all right?"

Groaning inwardly at how stupid I must look, I tear my gaze away from Marcus and turn to her. "Sorry." I gather my index cards from the lectern.

"Can I talk to you after class?"

I nod, doing my best to avoid appearing freaked out at the request, and return to my seat next to Emma. What the heck could Professor Hale want to talk to me about? I didn't bomb the presentation. At least I don't think I did.

She thanks us for our presentations and dismisses us. The room fills with the rustle of winter coats and bags, accompanied by laughter and murmured voices as everyone files out. A couple of

177

students walk to the front. I glance back at my delusion. Without even looking at me, he leaves with everyone else.

Disappointment stumbles through me that my delusion couldn't even smile at me like the real Marcus would—if he were talking to me. Great, even my delusions are ignoring me.

"Why was Marcus here?" Emma pushes herself out of her seat and picks her bag off the floor. "I thought you guys broke up."

"You saw him?" I squeak. "You saw Marcus?"

"Yeah." The word is drawn out, almost a question. "Didn't you see him? You looked right at him."

"I thought I was imagining him," I mumble and shove my binder into my knapsack. I want to race after him, to see why he was here, but I can't. Professor Hale is waiting to talk to me.

Emma sits back down. "Amber, he must still care about you. I don't understand any more than you do what's up with him, but he wouldn't have been here if he didn't. He knew your presentation was today."

"I know, but it doesn't matter. If he doesn't want to talk to me, and clearly he doesn't, there's nothing I can do."

Emma shakes her head and stands again. "For someone who's so smart, sometimes you're pretty dense. You've sent him texts and left messages, right?"

"And he never responded to them."

"When was the last time you tried talking to him face-to-face?" When I don't answer, she continues, "That's what I thought. If you love him, Amber, you need to talk to him and find out what's going on. You two are great together. Don't let him walk away."

I stand and she hugs me. Then I walk down the steps to the front. As I approach Professor Hale, the two students talking to her walk off, leaving me alone with her. Emma has left for her next class.

"That was a great presentation, Amber. Both your research and arguments were impressive, as was your delivery. You had everyone hanging on to your every word." She smiles. It's a comforting smile, like chicken noodle soup when you're suffering from a cold. "And I don't believe for a second the lies circulating about you. No one can give a speech like that without having been impacted the way you obviously have been. Have you given any thought to a career working with children and teens who are victims of crime?"

"I'm not sure what I want to do yet. I only know that I want to help victims find a way to move on." Like I've been trying to move on.

"Well, if you're interested, I know of a summer internship that you're the perfect candidate for. It's nothing heavy. Considering what you've been through, it could be a while before you'll be ready to deal with anything too emotional, but it's a great place to gain experience, and I know you'll have a lot to give the kids."

"I would love that." The lightness I felt during my presentation comes back for an encore.

"Good. Why don't you come to my office tomorrow, and I'll give you the application. And I'll be more than happy to be a reference for you."

I smile and thank her for thinking of me.

As soon as I exit the classroom, I dodge past students and run to the engineering building. Emma's right. I need to talk to Marcus. Enough with his stupid silent treatment. I want to know what's going on with him. And if the relationship really is over, he owes me the closure I deserve.

MARCUS

Amber scans the room and her gaze settles on me as the girl in front of me leans over. She stares for several seconds, blinks, and at the sound of her name, turns to her professor.

The woman talks quietly to her. Amber nods and returns to her seat.

The professor thanks the class for their presentations and dismisses them. The room fills with laughter and talking as everyone packs up to leave. Two students walk down the steps to the front.

I glance toward the door and then at Amber. The dark circles under her eyes warn me she's had as much sleep as I've had. I can't tell if they're due to her presentation, which I knew she was dreading, the harassment Jordan told me about yesterday, or because we're no longer together.

I clench my fingernails into my palms. All my life I've been given the fucked-up end of the stick. I finally get something good in my life and it gets fucked up, too—and hurts the girl I love.

I leave the room without looking back at her. Coming here was a mistake. I'm supposed to pretend she has never been part of my life, but damned if I can do that. I needed to see her one last time. I was hoping she wouldn't notice me. The last thing I wanted was to make this harder on her than it's already been. Chase has been updating me, thanks to Jordan, on what's going on with Amber and the upcoming trial. Jordan has no idea he's been passing the info on to me. She can't know, or else she'll tell Amber that I still care about her—and that's the last thing Amber's mother wants.

I head to the engineering building. I don't have class for another hour, so I don't exactly rush. Normally, I'd be studying in the library, usually with Amber, but ever since her mom visited me, I'm having a harder time focusing on my studies. Even math is a chore. Maybe it's because I can't focus on the subject without thinking of the lame math jokes I used to tell Amber, and how she laughed whenever I did. Every time I do my homework, the beautiful sound of her laughter plays in my head. It's the only time I'll hear her laugh again, and that hurts worse than my gunshot wound ever did.

I yank open the door to the engineering building and enter. A few people are walking around the main entrance, but most students are already in their next class. Unsure where to go next, I stand here like an idiot.

"Marcus?" Amber says softly behind me.

I close my eyes, searching for the strength to face her. I didn't think she would come after me. Or maybe I just hoped she wouldn't.

I release a long exhalation. It doesn't numb the urge to envelop her in my arms and smell her strawberry-scented hair. It doesn't numb the urge to kiss her long and hard. It doesn't improve my current situation or how I feel.

I open my eyes and turn to her.

Up close, the circles under her eyes are even more pronounced, and her clothes hang off her slim body in a way they didn't use to. The psychopath and I both did this to her. I can't tell, though, if the weight loss is the result of her not eating much, or if she's punishing herself again in the gym, or all of the above. She hasn't been there when I work out, but that's because I changed the time when I go to the gym so I don't risk bumping into her.

I try to formulate something to say, but nothing comes to mind. I'm afraid if I open my mouth, the truth will tumble out. I'm not the only one unsure what to say. Amber watches me, her eyes searching my face for any clues as to my asshole behavior.

"I loved your presentation," I say, finally finding my voice. She had originally planned to do it on a different topic, so I was surprised when she started talking about how children trust the very adults who let them down.

"Thanks. I didn't realize you were there until the end."

"I wasn't sure if you wanted me there, but I wouldn't have missed it for anything." Shit, that was a stupid thing to say. It's not how you would respond if you're pretending the last four months never happened.

"Even though you had a class then?" She knows I live for numbers and equations, but I needed to see for myself that she's okay. I know how difficult it is for her to talk in front of an audience. More so now that everyone is more interested in her sex life than what she has to say.

Five guys exit the elevator, talking about the hockey game last night. They spot us and it's not hard to guess what they're thinking. *Fuck.* The way their eyes strip the clothes off Amber's body makes me want to slam my fist into their faces. It's the same burning need that's been building inside me ever since Jordan told me the truth.

I place myself between them and Amber.

" 'Sup, Reid?" Owen asks. Of the five of them, he has the worst reputation when it comes to girls. Even worse than mine.

"Not much."

He nods at Amber, eyeing her with the same predatory look lions get prior to going in for the kill. "And how about you? What's up?"

Even though I shouldn't, I slip her hand into mine, making it clear she's with me. I doubt this will get back to her mom, so I'm safe on that front. I'm more concerned about what Amber will think. I'm giving her false hope, but hell if I'm letting Owen think he can harass her any time he sees her. I've asked Chase to watch out for her whenever possible, but that will only go so far. He's not with her all the time, and it's not like he's her boyfriend or pretending to be her boyfriend.

A tall, wiry guy smacks Owen's arm. "C'mon, we've got work to do." While he might have checked Amber out to begin with, it's obvious he's not into her the same way Owen is. She's a beautiful girl he appreciates, but she's nothing more than that to him. His mouth moves into an apologetic smile.

With the exception of Owen, the guys walk off. He doesn't seem to have realized they've left. He's still eyeing her. "If you're looking for a real man, give me a call, sweetheart. I can make you come screaming faster than this dickwad and the other one ever did."

I release Amber's hand and step forward, closing the distance between me and the jerkoff. "Come near her again and you'll be eating your dick for lunch."

"Is there a problem, gentlemen?"

At the familiar faint southern drawl, Owen's face pales. I whip around to find Professor Hopkins watching the three of us, his gaze steady, challenging. Rumor has it he once served with the Navy SEALs. If his physique is anything to go by, he still follows their training regime even though he's in his fifties.

"No, sir," Owen and I say. I shift on my feet.

"Good. I trust I'll see you both in class this afternoon?"

"Yes, sir." Owen practically stands to attention. I nod.

Owen stalks off after his friends.

"While I don't appreciate your language, Mr. Reid," Hopkins says, "I appreciate it even less when a man fails to treat a woman with respect." He smiles at Amber and strolls toward the stairs.

"Sorry about Owen," I say. "I'm sure there're a few women in my program ready to file sexual harassment complaints against him, if they haven't already."

"He's not the first." She shrugs. "I'm getting used to it."

She might act as if it's no big deal, but she's hurting. The strain of it all is too much. Until those damn letters, she rarely had to deal with comments like that—I mean other than from me when I first met her. But even I was nothing compared to Owen.

"I should go." I struggle to come up with an excuse as to where I need to be. All I can focus on is the beautiful girl in front of me who has my heart and always will.

"What's going on, Marcus?" Her words are hesitant, curious but afraid at the same time. "I told you the video didn't matter to me. I understand your reasons for doing it. I mean, unless you got tired of me because I don't get off on being beaten or tied up and never will." Her voice cracks.

I'm not sure which hurts more: that she couldn't tell from all the time we've been together that the man in the video couldn't possibly be me, or she believes I would treat her so callously and dump her, since I'm supposedly into S&M and she isn't.

"It's not that. The video isn't what it looks like. It wasn't all me. The S-and-M stuff wasn't me. I told your mom and the cops. They're investigating where it came from."

Her eyebrows scrunch together. "My mom? When did you talk to my mom?"

Fuck.

"I've gotta go," I deadpan. "I have to meet up with Chase to work on an assignment." I start to back away.

Amber grabs my arm. "This is about my mom, isn't it? What did she say to you?" I flinch at the bitterness in her tone.

"It has nothing to do with your mom, Amber. The decision was all mine." And then I go for where it will hurt the most but will give her a chance to move on. "I got tired of having sex with only one girl. That's not who I am." The last part of me clinging on to the hope that I wasn't the worthless piece of crap Frank believed me to be crumbles away with my last words, the aftermath hidden by the indifference in my tone.

Without giving her a chance to reply, I storm from the building. The last image of her now burned in my brain is the same pained expression the psychopath must have witnessed when he held her captive and tortured her.

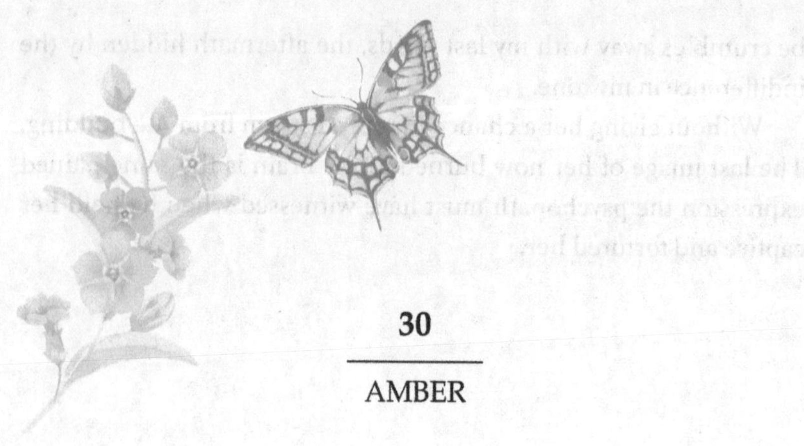

30

AMBER

I press the buzzer for Marcus's apartment. Chase's car is in the parking lot. Marcus's isn't. He still has classes for another hour.

"Yes?" Chase says through the static.

"It's me, Amber. I've come for Smoky."

"Oh. Okay." There's no missing the disappointment in his voice, although he should have known this was coming. I would have picked Smoky up sooner, but part of me had hoped Marcus had been too busy with classes to respond to my messages and texts, and the rumors about our breakup weren't true. But after I talked to Marcus an hour ago, I realized I've only been deluding myself.

The main entrance unlocks, and I pull the door open. The building brings up too many memories, most of them happy. All cause me pain. The sooner I leave, the better. Naturally, the elevator has other plans. I have to wait longer than normal before it finally arrives. And then it takes even longer to creep up to Marcus's floor.

They say when you're in a life-or-death situation, you flash back to the highlights of your life. I'm not sure how true that is. I just know I'm flashing back to all the hot make-out sessions Marcus and

I had while in the elevator, and this isn't even a life-or-death situation. It only feels like I'm dying.

I walk to the guys' apartment and knock on the door, bracing myself for a new flood of memories.

Chase opens the door, wearing jeans and a dark-gray T-shirt. "Hey." He moves aside to let me in. I haven't seen him since Marcus's video went viral. He doesn't resemble my ex-boyfriend. I'm not talking about how Marcus has black hair and Chase's hair is dark blond. Chase doesn't look like he's been pulling all-nighters for the past week. Marcus appears as though he has slept as much as I have. His nightmares must be getting worse. It's obviously not because he's struggling with our breakup. Unlike me, he's already moved on. Maybe even with Tammara.

That thought is a baseball bat to the chest. I'm amazed I can even get air into my lungs with how much it hurts. I avert my gaze, afraid Chase will see the effect the breakup is having on me. He can't know how much I'm dying. He can't know how I'm the same empty shell that cuddled with Smoky when we were held prisoner. I need to be brave.

"Smoky," I call out. Tears distort my voice. Not only did I lose the guy I love, the guy who I once thought loved me, I'm losing Smoky, too. I'm taking him to Grandma's, which means I'll barely see him. While he was living with Chase and Marcus, I saw him at least several times a week.

"No matter what you might think, Amber, Marcus still loves you."

Hearing those words, the lie, opens something in my chest and the sob building since Marcus told me he was tired of having sex with only one girl breaks free. The last thing I want is for Chase to see me this way, but I've long since learned I don't always get what I want.

Chase gathers me in his arms and lets me cry on his shoulder. I can't stop. Everything is fueling the tears. Marcus turning his back on me, losing Smoky, losing Michael and Trent, Paul and what he did to me, the media, the harassment because of the letters and the video, the exhaustion I've been battling forever. Everything crashes in on me and threatens to take me down.

Chase doesn't say anything, not even to give me false hope. He tightens his hold on me and doesn't let go.

I have no idea how long I've been crying for—maybe a few minutes, maybe a few hours—when Smoky rubs up against my leg. He always knows when I need comforting and when I'm afraid.

I pull away from Chase and pick up the gray furball. He purrs in my arms as I cuddle him. "Hey, boy. You ready to see Grandma?"

"You don't have to take Smoky," Chase says. "You can still visit him here."

I shake my head. "No, no I can't. I know Marcus is dating again." I don't have to clarify what I mean. We both know the only dating Marcus did prior to me involved one-night stands. "I can't bear the thought of seeing him. It'll hurt too much." My voice cracks once more, hinting it's time to leave before I have another breakdown.

"Look, Amber, I don't know what Marcus told you, but not everything is what it seems to be."

I give him a sad smile. *All right, you believe that if it makes you feel better.*

Chase helps me gather Smoky's stuff. I leave the things he bought Smoky, like the carpeted tree, in case they get another cat. Once Smoky is settled in his carrier and my car has been loaded with his supplies, I say bye to Chase. He gives me another hug. It's not the last time I'll see him. Marcus and I might have broken up, but that won't change his and Jordan's friendship. And maybe one day I'll be able to see him without my heart aching at the memory of who his best friend is.

The weather is better than the last time I drove to Crossfields. I talk to Smoky the entire way but avoid the subject of Marcus and why Smoky couldn't stay with the guys anymore. I drop him off with Grandma and spend an hour there before heading to Mom's.

While Marcus has made it clear he's ready to move on, I need to know how much influence Mom had on that decision.

I park in the driveway and let myself in. The familiar smell of spicy chicken casserole greets me. It's not enough to kick-start my appetite.

Mom steps out of the kitchen. "I didn't know you were coming today." She frowns. "Is everything all right?" She looks me over, and her frown deepens. I'm wearing Trent's old hoodie again. I've been wearing it a lot since Marcus's video surfaced. Trent's scent has long since vanished, but the soft fabric still comforts me.

"I had to take Smoky back to Grandma's house."

She doesn't act surprised by the news. Not a good sign. "Let me make you something to eat. You must be hungry."

"I'm not. And I can't stay long. I just want to know what you said to Marcus."

"What do you mean?" She has switched into lawyer mode. I recognize it in her calm voice and the way she holds herself.

"You know exactly what I mean," I snap. I'm tired and I don't have time for her defense-lawyer games. "Marcus's sex video goes viral, and suddenly he's not talking to me."

"And why would you believe it has anything to do with me?"

I clench my teeth. I'm surprised they don't fracture from the force. "Because he told me he wasn't the only guy in the video. Someone set him up to make it look like he's into S-and-M. He told you and the cops. When exactly did he tell you that?"

"I don't remember." Her voice lacks all hint of remorse for what she did. It lacks all hint of emotion. It's like she's an actor, reading her lines for the first time.

"Like hell you don't. You're an excellent lawyer because of your attention to detail. I wouldn't be surprised if you know the exact time and date you spoke to him."

"Amber, you think you're in love with him, but he's all wrong for you. You can do much better." Her voice remains even. I want to scream at her. I want to ask her if she feels *anything*. I don't, though.

I know she's capable of feeling. That's why she had to block it with alcohol last year. She was feeling too much for her to function normally.

"You're wrong, Mom. Marcus was perfect for me. You know why? Because he understands what I've been through."

Mom shakes her head. This time when she speaks, her voice is full of emotion. "That's not true. I understand what you've been through."

"You can't possibly understand," I scream. "You think you do. But until you've been tortured and raped, you have no idea." She only understands what it's like to lose someone she loves.

Mom steps closer. "You're right. But that doesn't mean Marcus understands you any better than I do. He was shot, yes, but it's not the same."

I let out a bitter laugh. "That's where you're wrong. Marcus wasn't just shot by his stepfather. Marcus and his brother suffered years of physical abuse at the hands of the man. And then when Marcus was thirteen, his stepfather sexually assaulted him and raped his fifteen-year-old brother in front of him, and he couldn't do anything to stop it. That monster killed Marcus's brother last summer after Ryan tried to save Marcus from being raped by his stepfather, when he held him at gunpoint." I sniff back the angry tears. "You might not believe Marcus is the right man for me, but I can tell you, there isn't anyone who is more right for me than Marcus."

I leave her there standing, her mouth open in shock, and storm out the front door. I hadn't meant to tell her about Marcus's past. I was so angry at her for what she did, and how she felt that he's not good enough for me, the truth kind of came out.

I climb into my car and reverse out of the driveway before Mom has a chance to come after me. I don't want to give her the opportunity to feed me any more excuses as to why she believes she did the right thing. It doesn't matter anyway. Whatever she said to him was enough for him to see I'm not worth the effort.

Biting my lip hard to keep from crying, I head to the one place I visited a lot last summer. The cemetery.

The parking lot is empty other than a few cars near the entrance. I pull on my winter coat and trudge past snow-covered graves until I end up at Trent's. Then I crumple to the ground and start sobbing, much like I did when I was with Chase. The cold temperature of the snow and the air is nothing compared to the chill growing inside me. I don't say anything. There's nothing I *can* say. It's not like I can ask my dead boyfriend for advice.

I'm not sure how long I've been crying when an arm wraps around my hunched shoulders. I startle, half thinking it belongs to Trent. I sit up to discover the arm doesn't belong to my dead boyfriend. It belongs to Mom.

"I figured you might come here." Her gaze is fixed on Trent's gravestone. "And I'm sorry. I had no idea Marcus had gone through any of that." She doesn't say anything else, and I interpret it to mean it wouldn't have made a difference. She still doesn't see him as an equal to me, not like I do.

"He was in juvie because he was caught stealing DVDs," I explain. It's obvious she holds his stint in juvie against him. He and I might no longer be together, but I want her to see how wrong she is about him. "He was going to sell them so he and his brother could buy food. Up till then, his mom and stepfather couldn't be bothered to make sure there was enough food for their sons. But that's not who Marcus is now. He's been working hard so he could have a better future than the one he had growing up. He's nothing like them. I wish you could have seen how amazing he is."

Mom looks away, toward where Michael is buried. "The sex video showed his poor judgment, and it jeopardized his scholarship. I gave him a choice, Amber. You or his future as an engineer. You might not have liked the fallout, but I did it to protect you."

I vaguely hear the last few words as the part before it plays in repeat mode: *I gave him a choice, Amber. You or his future as an engineer.*

I understand why he chose the route he took, but it doesn't stop the voice in my head from pointing out one painful fact—he didn't try to fight for me. He didn't fight to keep me in his life.

"You're wrong about him," I snap and push myself to my feet. "I can't believe you gave him that ultimatum. Marcus was there for me when you weren't. He has worked hard to turn his life around, and you try to cut him down because of what? Because you think you know what is best for me? Well, news flash, Mom. You don't."

I storm off, not caring to hear any more of her excuses. I need space from her before either of us says something we can't take back.

31

MARCUS

"**M**arcus Reid." Professor Keegan steps up to my desk and riffles through the test papers in his hand. He pulls a booklet from the pile and passes it to me. "I expected a lot more from you than this."

I got a fucking D. Fucking brilliant.

I knew I'd been struggling since Amber's mom threatened to have my scholarship terminated, but I had expected to do a lot better than this. Shit, I need to pull my act together or else I've lost Amber for nothing.

I drive home, vaguely aware of what I'm doing. The sun is shining, the sky is blue, but none of that improves my mood.

I park next to Chase's car and trudge to my apartment. I'm not in the mood to see him right now, but if I plan to pull up my grades, I need to do some serious-ass studying. I don't have time to drive aimlessly around like I've been doing lately.

I enter the apartment. Smoky isn't on his carpeted tree and he isn't on the recliner, his other favorite hangout. He isn't on the couch, either, but Chase is, with a beer in hand and the same distraught expression he had when he found the contract from

Amber's mom in my room. Guess I'm not the only one having a crappy day.

For a moment, I consider grabbing a beer and joining him, but I've been drinking way too much lately, which partly explains my quiz mark. I can't keep doing that. I'm not Frank.

"Crappy day, huh?" I walk past my bedroom. Smoky also isn't in there, and for the first time since I arrived home, panic inches its way in. "Where's Smoky?"

Chase doesn't even look at me. "Where the hell do you think he is?" he snaps.

I flinch at his tone. Guess I deserved that. "She didn't have to take him. She could've still visited him here." I'm not a therapist, but even I can see the difference in Amber when she's with him. Cuddling him relaxes her in ways I can't. She won't be able to do that very often if she took him to her grandmother's home. And with everything going on, she needs what Smoky can do for her more than ever before.

Chase pushes himself off the couch and stalks over to me. He stops inches from my face, nostrils flaring. "Why the fuck does she think you're screwing around again?"

Shit.

"Are you?" He steps away from me, disgust leaking from his pores. "Are you back to screwing girls like you used to? Are you back to screwing Tammara again?"

"Hell, no. I love Amber. She's the only girl I want to be with." The force of my tone would be enough to put a dent in the living room wall if my words were solid. "But she needs to move on with her life, and she needs to do that without me in it. That's what her mom wants." Never mind what Amber and I want.

"I get that. I hate it but I get it. But what I don't get is why she thinks you're screwing around again."

Everything inside of me—the strength I got from Amber, the hope, the anger at what I've been forced to do—drains away. My head and shoulders slump forward. "Because I told her I was." I close my eyes and see her pained expression in my head. "I screwed up and mentioned that I told her mom it wasn't all me in the video. I didn't want Amber to figure out the real reason I broke up with her. So I lied." I reopen my eyes. "I told her I was bored with having sex with only one girl."

Chase glares at me. I step back. He'll never forgive me for what I did. No more than I'll forgive myself for putting the pain on her face.

"So, what?" he asks. "You thought she'd be okay after you dropped that bombshell on her? You thought she'd be okay after you told her you never loved her after all? 'Cause I can tell you now, Marcus, that was a shit-headed stunt you pulled. She was barely holding on before with the trial, the lies, and the harassment. You destroyed her."

He pushes past me and grabs his coat. "Hope you can live with yourself after that, 'cause I sure the hell can't." He leaves, slamming the door behind him.

I stare at it, unable to move, unable to think, unable to breathe. I haven't felt this helpless since the night I saw Frank rape Ryan. I have no idea how to fix the damage I've caused. The one thing I can do, should do, is the one thing I'm forbidden to do—talk to Amber.

32

AMBER

Sitting on my bed, I bounce the back of my head against the wall. The cracks in my heart deepen, threatening to sever chunks of it, like the face of an eroding cliff.

I want to scream and I want to kick, but I also want to hide from the knowing glances. Everyone's positive they know exactly what happened between Paul and me—because of the letters and Marcus's video. Now Paul is the innocent one, not me. And to prove my theory correct, I've even received "fan" mail claiming I'm a whore.

I touch the worst of the scars on my back, beneath my lotus tattoo. The scar aches at the memory of Marcus kissing it. It aches at the memory of how strong and beautiful I feel when his lips press on the raised scar. It aches at the memory of being loved by him. My entire body aches at the memory of being loved by him.

It's been three weeks since the video surfaced, a week since we officially broke up, but the images of Marcus and the girl are all I see in my head, again and again and again. And they don't contain themselves to when I'm studying or sitting in class. The images haunt my nightmares, too. Only in my dreams, I watch them have sex while Paul is whipping me.

I press my palms against my eyes, as if that will erase the images in my brain. As if that will erase the pain in my chest from knowing Marcus walked away from what we had because of my mother, and because what we had wasn't enough to fight for.

A knock at the door intrudes on my pity party.

"Come in," I call out, not having the desire or energy to climb off my bed to open the door.

It opens and Jordan enters carrying a beach bag. "You know what you need?" She drops the bag at the end of my bed.

My head flops back against the wall. "A time machine, so none of last year happened." I'd warn my seventeen-year-old self not to accept the volunteer position at the animal shelter. I'd warn her to listen to her mom and accept the internship with the law office.

If I had done what Mom wanted me to do, none of last year would have happened. Trent and Michael would be alive. Trent and I might still be a couple. And what Marcus did with that girl would have nothing to do with me, since he and I would never have met to begin with.

Jordan chuckles at my comment. "Not a time machine," she says. "You need to go out into the world of the living again."

"I go out."

"I'm not talking about classes. Or the gym. I'm talking about going out with your friends."

"I'm not in a going-out mood. Besides, I need to study." I pick up the psychology textbook lying next to me, which I had planned to read when I first climbed on my bed three hours ago. It's still closed.

"You need to do this, Amber. I promise you won't regret it."

I hug the book. "Maybe another night." A night that isn't Valentine's Day. The last thing I want to see are happy couples in love.

Jordan tugs on my arm and pulls me up. I don't bother fighting it. I'm not going to win even if I try, and something tells me she's not in this alone. Emma will be here soon to help drag me out.

"Where're we going?" I ask as Jordan searches through her bag.

"To see a movie." She straightens, holding several wigs.

The door opens again and Emma strides into the room. "Good, she convinced you to come with us." She flashes Jordan a big grin, which Jordan has no trouble returning. Glad they're so happy, considering how miserable I feel.

"I'm not sure about this," I say.

"That's what you think now, but you'll change your mind once you see the movie."

"What movie?"

"The animated one with talking dragons. It seems cute." Translation: There's no chance of romance.

"Don't you have a date with Liam?" I ask.

"We went out last night for dinner, and I'll see him after the movie."

I eye the wigs in Jordan's hand. I recognize the one I borrowed from Shannon. "I get why I need the wig, but why you two?"

They exchange glances, and Emma sighs. "Ever since the video of Marcus surfaced, and you've gone into hiding, the media's been getting on my case, asking about you and Marcus and Trent—as has everyone else. I'm sick of it."

That's when I get it. Tonight isn't only about my going out and having a good time. Emma needs it, too.

"And what about you?" I take the black wig from Jordan.

She picks up the long blond wig and waves it. "I've always wanted to see what it's like to be blond."

I narrow my eyes. "You sure we're not going dancing?"

"Positive," she says.

Even though we're only going to dinner and a movie, that doesn't stop us from dressing up. I can't help it. Maybe it's my alter ego, Nikki, speaking, but I want to wear something other than jeans and a hoodie. I slip on my black sweater dress and thick tights. Emma helps me with my makeup to give me the same smoldering look as before.

By the time we're finished, I'm beginning to think that maybe we should hit Nightshade for a night of dancing and forgetting. Except that's where Marcus and I first kissed. Not the best place to go if I want to forget him.

After the movie, we return to Jordan's car. While the other two check their voice mail, I turn my phone on and discover someone left a message. I don't recognize the number. My heart sinks lower and slams into my stomach. But what did I expect? That Marcus would give up his future for me? Not when he's worked so hard to get this far. Not when he's worked so hard to give himself a new life.

I listen to the message, needing the temporary distraction.

"Hi, Amber. It's Lily Cummings. I got your letter and would love to talk to you. Please call me when you have the chance." I save the message and hang up. Emma's still talking on her phone, her back to me. Jordan finishes her call.

"So, are we going to the dorm now?" I ask.

"Nope." Jordan slips her phone into her purse. "We've got one more stop to make first."

33

MARCUS

"Where're we going?" I ask Chase as he drives along the wintry streets.

"Nightshade," he says matter-of-factly. "If you're gonna beat yourself up over everything, we might as well have fun at the same time."

I'd much rather go home, but since it's obvious Chase wants to go clubbing, and he's driving, there's not much I can do. I'm just glad he didn't permanently turn his back on me after I lied to Amber that I had moved on with other girls. He didn't return to the apartment for three days. It took him that long to get over what I'd done.

He might have gotten over it, but I haven't forgiven myself for how much I hurt her.

Fortunately, the bartender who didn't card me last time, the one Amber is positive has a thing for me, is working and has no issues serving me and Chase beers without checking our IDs. I give him a big tip, even though I'm sure he'll take it the wrong way. I don't care, as long as this isn't the last beer for the night.

I turn and spot the place where I first kissed Amber. The memory of the kiss and not having her in my arms is a knee to the

200

gut. I gulp my beer, attempting to numb the memory. When I realize that's not possible, I tell Chase to give me a second and return to the bar.

"I'll have a double Jack Daniels straight."

The bartender gives me an understanding smile. "Tough day, huh?"

Tough day, week, month, year. "Possibly."

He pours the drink. "For what it's worth, you looked hot in the video."

"Yeah, um, well, thanks. I guess."

He laughs as I pay for the drink. "I'm not hitting on you, if that's what you're worried about. For starters, I'm not into things getting rough, not like you obviously are. And two, it's obvious you're as straight as they come." He turns to the two girls approaching the bar and flips on his flirting charm.

Relieved he knows where I stand and isn't put off by that, I grab my glass and beer bottle and join Chase at a table with two guys from our engineering classes.

"Hey, if it isn't the porn star," Max says in a tone implying more awe than anything else.

Much like his friend, Pete, a skinny, zit-faced guy who turns a brilliant shade of red whenever a girl talks to him in class. "Dude, you're so lucky."

"How so?" I mutter.

"Now that you're famous, girls won't be able to keep themselves out of your pants."

"Great, if that's what I wanted. But it isn't." I've already had that. It's overrated compared to being with someone who loves you and gets you.

"Really? Last year you went through half the girls on campus, getting it on with them. The hot girls that is." Max glances at Pete for confirmation. Pete nods.

"That was last year. I have a girlfriend now." Had a girlfriend. As her mom pointed out when the video went viral, Amber's better off without me. A comment I'd rather not share with these guys. "And I didn't make the video."

"Looked like you."

"Only some of it was me."

"So, what? The rest was a body double?" The way Pete says it, you'd think he was talking to a Hollywood director.

"Pretty much." At least that's the theory Chase and I have going. It's too convenient that the girl happened to have footage of a guy who resembles me when the picture is slightly blurry. The question is, why did she do it?

I told the cops that it wasn't me in all the frames, but I'm not sure they believed me. And even if they do, it's too late for me and Amber. The public has condemned us for things we never did.

"Okay, guys, let it go. We didn't come here to talk about it. We came here for some fun." Chase scans the area and spins out of his chair to stand. "And it starts now."

He joins two girls standing near the dance floor. They're pretty, and last year I'd have been over there in an instant and talked my way into one of their beds. Now they just remind me how much I miss Amber, even though she looks nothing like them.

Chase talks to the short brunette. She giggles and follows him onto the dance floor. It doesn't take long before she's all over him, trying to keep up with his moves. I have no idea when my best friend began resembling a dancer from an MTV video. Too bad the girl doesn't. She's definitely not Jordan. Now that girl can dance.

The brunette's friend watches them for a few minutes, then glances in my direction. She's pretty, blond, with a tight bod and large breasts squeezed into her tank top. I swear I hear the guys nearby pant at the way she moves her hips as she sashays in this direction.

I look away and chug back my Daniels.

"Oh, shit! She's coming over," Pete says.

"Down boy," Max replies. "She's not coming over to see you. She's coming to see *him*."

I study my empty glass. The beer and the Daniels weren't enough to stir up a buzz. Just as I'm contemplating getting a refill on both and getting seriously shit-faced, a warm fingertip traces across the bottom half of my tattoo. The rest is hidden under the sleeve of my T-shirt.

"I love hearing the story behind why someone selects a specific design over another." Her tone is the one art lovers use when discussing a painting. The tension in my muscles releases slightly.

"There's a story, but it's not one I'm willing to share."

"Too bad. I'm Sharon, by the way."

"Marcus."

"You wanna dance?"

I shake my head. "I'm not much in the mood for dancing." I glance at Chase and the girl he's dancing with. She's all over him, as in, "I want this to go much further than a dance. I want to have your babies." He's smiling, but it's clear to only me that he's not smiling *at* her. His body might be on the dance floor but his mind is elsewhere.

Sharon's fingers skim their way down my arm. "I can get you in the mood." Gone is the art-lover tone, easily replaced with the I-want-to-screw-your-brains-out one.

I subtly inch my arm away. "Thanks, but no thanks."

"He has a girlfriend." Pete's face reddens and he becomes interested in the table, rubbing his finger over a water stain.

I don't bother to correct him, since I was the one who told him the lie to begin with. Plus, he's given me an out.

"You do?" She doesn't seem surprised or disappointed or even resigned. "I'm guessing since it's Valentine's Day and you're here looking all moody with an empty glass and beer bottle, you're having girlfriend issues."

I lift an eyebrow. "Or maybe I'm looking all moody with an empty glass and beer bottle because she's not here and I wish she were."

"If you're not having girlfriend issues, then why isn't she here?"

"She's with her sick grandmother." Or more likely, Amber's in her dorm, hiding from all the staring and whispering, thanks to something stupid I did last year as a way to deal with my brother's death.

I stand. "Now, if you'll excuse me, as you've pointed out, I have an empty glass and beer bottle"—I pick them up—"and I plan to rectify that." I'd tell her if she wants so badly to dance, she should ask Pete or Max. But since both are good guys, I don't want to risk her shooting them down.

Heading to the bar, I glimpse Chase struggling to remove the arms of Sharon's friend from around his neck. It's not a slow song, but she's determined to kiss him. I buy him a beer, plus one for myself and another Daniels.

Sharon's not at the table when I return, but both Pete and Max are. They eye the drinks in my hands as I place the beers on the table. I move one over to Chase's spot so they realize the drinks aren't all mine.

"You must really miss your girlfriend." Pete nods at the beer.

I finish the contents of my glass. "I do."

"So why aren't you with her?"

"I already explained why. She's with her sick grandmother."

He shakes his head. "If that's true, you wouldn't have been moody for the last few weeks. Everyone on campus knows about the video, which means so does your girlfriend. And I'm guessing your video is damaging the case against the sick shithead who kidnapped her."

The corner of my lips curls up. Not by much, though. "Are you sure you're an electrical engineering student and not a would-be lawyer?"

"And you're avoiding the question, which means I'm right." The taste of victory tints his tone.

Pete, Max, and I are busy talking when Chase returns soon after, minus the girl, his hair damp with sweat. The guys excuse themselves to get more drinks.

Without saying a word, Chase grabs the beer bottle I bought him while he was dancing and lifts it to his mouth. "Thanks, man."

"You should just kiss her. Then she'll know what she's missing out on."

"Except I wasn't into her. I mean she—"

"I'm talking about Jordan." I finish off my Daniels.

"Yeah, well, I'm not too interested in having her boyfriend smash my head in."

"Hey, it's just a thought. But it sure beats dancing with girls you wish were Jordan."

"Says the guy whose love life is all screwed up." He toasts me with his bottle.

I wince. "And maybe it's because my love life *is* all fucked up that I can give advice."

I expect Chase to give me a hard time or something. I don't expect him to say, "Oh, shit," while looking over my shoulder. I turn to see what the problem is.

Tammara is near the dance floor with a few of her friends. The roaming spotlights ignite the fiery color of her hair. Her green eyes burrow into me, stripping me naked in a way that will never happen for real. Those days are long gone.

Without saying anything to her friends, she walks over.

"You want another drink?" Chase asks. He doesn't wait for a reply. He heads for the bar. I haven't told him what Tammara did to Amber and me. If I had, he wouldn't be putting distance between himself and his least favorite person. He'd stay to protect my virtue.

Tammara slides up to me, holding a fruity drink, and sits in Chase's seat. She studies the dance floor. The tension between us vibrates like the loud beat of the bass.

I toss back some beer, relieved Chase is getting me another one. I'll need it. "What do you want, Tammara?"

"I never realized you were into the kinky stuff." She's still watching the dance floor.

"Don't believe everything you see or hear."

Her gaze snaps to me. "What's that supposed to mean?"

"It means exactly that. I had nothing to do with the video."

"So you're telling me you have an identical twin who's a porn star?" Her cutting tone suggests she believes that possibility as much as I do, even though at some level I wish it were true. It would make things a lot simpler. "He can't be too impressed that you're getting all the credit."

"There is no twin." *Unless there's something Mom hasn't told me, but I doubt it.* "Only a slightly blurry video shot in a dimly lit room, with parts that were definitely me. But most of it wasn't."

"You're saying it's fake?"

"That's exactly what I'm saying. Too bad no one believes me."

"Including your girlfriend." There's no delight or scorn or mocking in her voice. More like sympathy.

I shrug. I have no idea why I'm telling Tammara this, other than the alcohol buzz is finally kicking in and my thoughts aren't all that interested in shutting up. Even to the woman who caused Amber and me so much trouble.

"Is it true what the police said about your stepfather?" she asks. "That he molested you and your brother?"

I startle at the question. The news mentioned it a few times after Frank was arrested for shooting me, but it was dropped shortly after when the cops couldn't prove anything. Neither my name nor Ryan's was mentioned at any point. And since Frank has a different last name than us, the media had no issue reporting it. I'm surprised Tammara figured it out.

"Yeah, it's true."

"That's why you were upset when I lied about my sister's fiancé and about...about what happened after that?" She doesn't have to say it. She's referring to the roofie she slipped me to get photos of her kissing me, so Amber would think Tammara and I were back together.

"I would have been upset either way."

"I can see why you love Amber. You understand each other."

She stands and hugs me. Despite my natural instinct to pull away from any woman who isn't Amber, I return the hug. "I hope things work out for you both." She gives me a sad smile and leaves, passing Chase as she makes her way over to her friends. Neither acknowledges the other.

Grinning, Chase puts a glass down in front of me.

"What's this?" I ask, eyeing the clear liquid.

"I believe it's commonly known as water."

I frown. "I thought you were getting me a drink."

He chuckles. "The last I heard, people actually drink this stuff."

"But I wanted a beer." Great, now I'm a pouting two-year-old.

"I figure you'll thank me tomorrow when you're not suffering from a shitty hangover."

He's probably right.

"Anyway," he adds, "I'm ready to bail."

That makes two of us. I weave after him through the dense crowd of sweaty, drunk bodies and out into the cold. The slap of the icy wind against my face sobers me up a little.

I expected Chase to drive us home. He doesn't. He drives to a hotel and pulls up to the entrance. "Here"—he passes me a key card—"go upstairs to room three-seventy-seven."

I open my mouth to ask what the hell's going on.

He grins. "Just go. You'll understand when you get there."

I do as I'm told and take the elevator to the third floor. As I walk to the room, I spot a girl with chin-length black hair and purple streaks sliding her key card into the slot a few doors ahead of me.

"Kitten?"

34

AMBER

"**K**itten?"

I turn to find Marcus standing a few feet away. "Wh-what are you doing here?" I whisper. The vision of him with the girl in the video is still etched in my brain. Along with it, the memory of the conversation with my mother.

"Chase brought me here." He looks at me with a mix of awe and disbelief, his words not much louder than a murmur. "And let me guess. Jordan's responsible for you being here."

"Jordan and Emma," I somehow manage to say despite the shock and pain of seeing him. Though deep down I'm not surprised. Why else would my two best friends bring me here? I told them what had happened between Marcus and my mom, and the deal she made with him in order to keep us apart. They understood why he had made the choice he did, but they also weren't happy that he didn't fight to stay with me.

Still holding the key card, my hand drops away from the slot. "I should go." I'm not sure how I'll get back to the dorm, but I'm not sticking around for whatever my friends have planned.

Marcus reaches for my arm. Even with a coat on, a tingling warmth spreads through me at his touch. His fingers caress my face, and I fight the urge to lean into his hand. I close my eyes, hiding the tears at seeing him here and at the memory of everything we've been through. Both the good and the bad.

"Please don't go," he whispers. I reopen my eyes and a tear escapes. He brushes it away with his thumb. "I'm sorry about everything. I'm sorry about hurting you, and I'm sorry about lying to you. I should never have told you I was tired of having sex with only one girl. That wasn't true. I wasn't tired of having sex with only you. And I haven't been seeing anyone else. You are the only person I could possibly want to be with."

Chase told me nothing was what it seemed. Until now, I hadn't realized it also meant what Marcus had told me about moving on with other girls. But it makes sense now. He knew I would guess the truth once I found out my mom had talked to him. He did the only thing he could think of to push me away, like Mom had wanted him to do.

"I know about the deal my mom made with you to keep you away from me. And I understand why you made the choice you did." *But that doesn't mean it didn't break my heart*, I want to add, but I turn away instead.

"Why don't we go into the room, and we can talk about it. If you want me to leave afterward, I will. If you want me to permanently stay away, I'll do that too. I just want to make you happy."

That's what I want, too. To be happy. Happy and free of this ever-growing nightmare.

I can only nod, not ready to give up on us, but uncertain if I want to risk my fragile heart again. It can only take so much abuse from Marcus and everyone else.

Using his key card, Marcus opens the door and we enter the room.

The sweet smell of roses assaults me and I stagger a step in reverse. Marcus flips on the light and curses. Hundreds of red, pink, and white rose petals cover the bed. Emma must have placed them there. Chase and Jordan witnessed me have a flashback last term when Jordan received roses from her boyfriend. She might be studying for her psych degree, but she would never purposefully do anything that could initiate a flashback. Not when she's witnessed what they do to me.

"C'mon, let's get outta here." Marcus takes hold of my shoulders and tries to steer me from the room.

I shake him off. "No. I can't keep freaking every time I see roses. My therapist started exposure therapy to help me deal with what happened. Consider this homework."

Marcus looks at me like I've gone crazy, and maybe I have. So far I've been taking baby steps with success. This is going to be a large leap. But Paul has already stolen so much from me. My mom has inadvertently stolen so much from me. I need something back of my own. Something I once used to love—and something I still love.

Even though I don't know what will ultimately happen between Marcus and me, I thread my fingers with his and pull him to the bed. He glances at it, uncertain what to do. That much is clear.

I cup his face with my hand and brush my lips against his. "You hurt me. I know you were trying to help, but you, more than anyone, know how it feels to be manipulated. That's what you did to me. You didn't even try to fight for me. I get why you did that, and we are going to talk about it. But right now, I want to make love to you. On the petals. Every time I see roses, I want to think about you and how you make me feel."

Hope shines in his eyes. This obviously wasn't what he was expecting, not after the video, not after keeping away from me for so long, not after choosing his future as an engineer over me. But he didn't participate in the video to hurt me. He did it out of grief for his brother's death. And I can't be too angry at him for being an idiot and listening to my mom. She can be very persuasive.

Focusing on Marcus, I gently pull on his lower lip with my teeth. The rose petal smell is still here, but unlike before, in the cold damp basement, the smell is different. It's sweeter, softer, filled with hope instead of death. And the sweet scent combined with Marcus's spicy one intensifies the feeling of hope.

Kissing his slightly parted mouth, I slide my fingers under the edge of his T-shirt. He moves his hands to my hips but doesn't make an attempt to do more than that. He's letting me lead the way, though from the way his fingers are tensing, it's taking a mountain of restraint.

I guide his T-shirt up, caressing the soft skin covering the hard ridges of his abs. His thumbs stroke the side of my breasts.

My hands continue moving up until my thumbs brush his nipple. Marcus sucks in a sharp breath, and I smile at the power I have over him. It's the same power he has over me.

His hands leave my hips and he removes his T-shirt. It falls to the floor somewhere near our feet. "Your turn," he murmurs, his breath fanning my lips.

I step away, remove a boot, and toss it toward the door. Grinning inwardly, I remove the second boot and also toss it at the door, then wrap my arms around his neck.

His gaze travels over my body. "I thought you were going to take off your dress."

"You only removed one item. I removed both boots. Which means I'm one ahead of you." I lean in, whisper against his ear, "Your turn," and run the tip of my tongue along the outside of it. Marcus groans.

He sits down hard on the bed, squashing a pile of petals, and removes a military boot. And then the second one. Now it's my turn to groan. We have the same number of clothes on. I'm going to lose this game and be naked before he is.

And he knows it. His sexy, one-sided smile tells me as much. "What's it gonna be next, Kitten?"

Without moving from the bed, he watches me run my fingertips along the outside of my thighs. He licks his lips, his eyes dark with longing. Not much different from mine, I suspect.

No matter what happened in the past, no matter how many

girls there were prior to me, the guy I love so deeply it almost hurts is not the guy he used to be. The man in front of me is the one I want inside me, making me feel normal, making me feel alive.

My hands continue up the sides of my legs until they reach the waistband of my tights. The skirt of my sweater dress barely covers anything as it rests near the tops of my thighs. With a ragged breath that has more to do with anticipation than nerves, I pull the tights down, exposing scars I'm no longer self-conscious about, at least not around Marcus.

I toss the tights at him. He stares at my legs as if they're the most beautiful things he's seen. He never looked at the girl in the video the same way. Never looked at her like nothing else exists. The intensity of his gaze causes my black satin panties to grow damp, and a small moan escapes my lips. I can't believe how little it takes for my body to react this way, but I shouldn't be surprised. Every caress, every kiss, every hot word he says has my nerves on super charge. It doesn't require much to push me closer to the edge.

"I want your jeans next." I take in the muscles on his arms, shoulders, chest, stomach. Anatomy class was never this hot.

He shakes his head slowly, the smile deepening. "Sorry, Kitten, you don't get to decide what comes off next. I do." The way he says *comes*, with his smooth, sexy voice, almost has me coming without him touching me.

Marcus tugs off a sock and adds it to the growing pile of clothes. Lifting his eyebrow, he sends me a look. "Your turn."

"But you only took off one sock," I protest.

"That's one item."

"But you took off both boots as one go."

"That's 'cause you did. I can take off both socks, but then you have to remove two items. Fair is fair." He winks at me.

I wrap my fingers around the edge of my dress and inch it up. At Marcus's expression of wonderment and lust, a subtle thrill trembles through me. I feel sexier than ever. I continue lifting the dress until I peel it off over my head, taking my wig off at the same time.

They drop to the floor, leaving me in nothing but the satin bra and underwear. I shake out my hair and catch sight of it in the mirror. I've got a major case of sex hair going on.

"Oh, God," Marcus murmurs. I expect him to remove his other sock, but he doesn't. He drinks me in, the hardness in his jeans becoming more distinct.

His gaze remains on me as he reaches down and rips off a sock. Forgetting the rules of our game, he undoes his jeans and strips them off. Now I'm the one wearing the most clothing...if you can call a bra and panties clothing.

As I reach for the hooks at the back of my bra, Marcus takes a step closer. "Don't." His voice is rough, thick. "I'll do it."

My hands drop away to be replaced by Marcus's. His warm fingers brush my skin and he slides the straps off my shoulders, his gaze never leaving mine. With deft fingers, he unhooks my bra and pulls it away, our previous game long since forgotten.

His body presses into mine, and I can feel how much he wants me. Before I can take my turn, his lips find mine and he reverses me the short distance to the bed.

He eases me down so I'm lying on a cloud of rose petals. I breathe in their scent, and gasp softly when Marcus's tongue finds my nipple, creating new memories. I arch in reply and run my fingers through his soft black hair.

His tongue circles my nipple, pushing me closer and closer to the edge. And just when I think I can take no more, his tongue traces its way to my other nipple and starts the sweet torment again.

I'm about to run my fingers across the expanse of his chest, when he backs up and his tongue paints a dizzying path down my stomach. It swirls in my belly button, setting off an explosion of fireworks. It gives me a taste of what's to come....

Marcus's fingers slide under the waistband of my underwear and he begins to slip them over my hips. He sits up so he's kneeling beside my legs and guides the satin along my skin until the panties are around my ankles. They end up with the rest of the clothes.

"I wanna try something different this time," he says, studying my face. "Let me know if you want me to stop, okay?"

I nod, unable to vocalize my thoughts even if I wanted to.

He gently guides my knees apart and plants feathery kisses on the inside of my thigh, first by my knee. Then he moves inch by slow inch along my skin, testing to make sure I'm all right.

The sweet smell of roses caresses me as Marcus's tongue finds the spot with the power to finally send me over the edge. All I can think about is if I fall, this is the perfect way to go.

Marcus's tongue teases me, offers promises of what's to come as he swirls and strokes the ache between my legs. I've never done this before. Never realized it could be this good.

Moaning, I reach for his head and wrap my fingers in the soft strands. *Oh. God.* Everything he's doing to me and everything about him is proving to be too much, but as I'm about to take the plunge, he pulls back.

He moves up the length of my body and his lips find mine. The taste of him startles me, because it's my taste and...and it's not so bad.

With a recently discovered confidence, I wrap my hand around the base of him and ease my way to the tip, lovingly tormenting him as I go.

Knowing I'm pushing him to the edge gives me the same power I've enjoyed since the first time we made love. Marcus is all about making sure I'm in control, that I'm comfortable with everything we do. He shifts his body and in one easy move he's in, ready to push us both over the edge. It doesn't take us long to get there, first me then him. I cry out as my body clenches him hard, and he does the same.

He withdraws, but instead of curling up with me like I expect, he gathers an armful of crushed rose petals. "I'll be right back."

He heads for the bathroom. Seconds later, the sound of running water sparks my curiosity. Marcus usually doesn't shower right after we make love. We usually lie in bed first and have a shower together.

I scoot off the bed and throw back the covers, sending the petals everywhere. Silently, I thank Emma for the roses and the new memories. While I'm at it, I thank Chase and Jordan for manipulating Marcus and me back together again.

I want him in my life.

I need him in my life.

Marcus returns a few minutes later. The water is no longer running, but his hair isn't wet like it would be if he'd been showering. Without a word, he takes my hand and leads me into the bathroom.

He's been busy. The Jacuzzi tub is filled with water and rose petals float on top. He pulls me to the tub. "Happy Valentine's Day," he whispers.

"Happy Valentine's Day," I whisper back.

"And we're good, right?" His teeth bite into his lower lip, a gesture I rarely see him do. "When we leave this hotel tomorrow, you're my girlfriend, again, right?"

"Yes, I'm your girlfriend again if you promise me one thing."

"What's that?"

"You're honest with me next time. You're not going to do what you think is best for me without talking to me first. And you're not going to let my mom persuade you to keep away from me."

He chuckles. "I thought you said only one thing."

"Okay, three things. Do you promise?"

"I do. I promise you all of that, and I promise I won't hurt you again." He kisses me deeply, his relief that we're together again bleeding into my heart. Then he steps into the Jacuzzi, sinks into the water, and gestures for me to join him.

I step in. The hot water swirls around my legs, sending petals crashing into me. I smile at everything he's done since we entered the bedroom, and how he's helped me avoid a flashback. With the smile on my face, I settle between his legs and lean back against him.

"Can we stay here and not leave the room until the trial is over?" I ask softly, half meaning it.

Marcus kisses the top of my head. "I have no problem with that. Better yet, how about we never leave the room again."

I could definitely live with that option. "Deal."

35

MARCUS

The following Monday, Emma and Liam are deep in conversation when Amber and I approach them in the Sports and Fitness Center. Emma is leaning back against the wall. Liam has her caged, his palms on either side of her head.

Emma spots us and says something to him. He drops his hands away from the wall and turns around. Both smile at us. Their curiosity at what Amber wants to talk about is stamped on their faces.

Saturday morning in the hotel, after we talked about the deal I had made with Amber's mom—which I've already told her mother I won't be accepting—we talked about Ryan's gravestone. Or rather, we talked about an idea Amber dreamed up to raise money for it.

Even though classes are finished for the day, the building is busy with athletes and people wanting to use the fitness facilities. We find a quiet spot where no one can overhear us.

"So what's up?" Liam asks.

"We're hoping you can help us with a fundraiser we want to do," Amber explains.

"What kind of fundraiser?"

"We want to organize a basketball tournament. Something entertaining. I thought maybe we could get players from the different teams to participate, and everyone wears a costume. The more cumbersome the better."

"The money will partly go toward my brother's gravestone." They already know why I was tutoring Amber. I have some money saved but nowhere near enough. "The rest will go to the Chicago Little Heroes Center. It's an organization that helps kids who've dealt with sexual and physical abuse." I wasn't sure about Amber's plan at first, until I realized how much she wants to do it, needs to do it. It's like her ray of hope in all the darkness that currently shadows her.

Liam and Emma exchange looks and nod. "I can think of a few players on the women's team who would love to help out," Emma says.

Liam checks his watch and asks Emma if she can round up some of her teammates. "Give us five minutes," he tells us. They jog toward the team locker rooms.

He returns a few minutes later without Emma and waves for us to join him. He leads us to a small classroom. At least twenty individuals from the various athletic teams are sitting at the desks, chatting. Half appear as though they were in the middle of a workout when they were dragged here. Their clothes are damp with sweat.

Emma's standing at the front of the room and waves for us to join her. There's a murmur of voices as people recognize Amber. "As Liam already explained, our friends want to tell you about an event they're planning that we thought you might be interested in participating in. Amber?" She nods at her best friend.

Amber's eyes widen and she glances back at me. I nod for her to go on. It was her idea. I want her to get the credit for it, and after watching her presentation, I know she can do this.

"H-hi. Thanks for coming. Marcus"—she points at me—"and I

are planning a fundraiser. First, we want to raise money for a grave-stone for Marcus's brother." She inhales deeply, her fingertips tapping her thigh. She catches herself and curls her fingers to her palms without clenching them. I'm probably the only one who notices.

She looks at me and I nod for her to continue, knowing what she's going to say, knowing what we agreed to share with the group.

"Ryan and Marcus spent most of their childhood being physically abused by their stepfather," she explains. "Ryan was a hero who protected his brother at all costs, but was recently killed by the very man who was supposed to...to love them, not harm them." Her words falter. "No one ever knew what they were going through. Just like it is for so many kids who are victims of abuse. These kids, society's most vulnerable victims, often don't know where to turn. Their trust has been shattered and they need the love and support of those who can help them through the trauma. This is why we want to donate part of the proceeds to the Chicago Little Heroes Center. They help our youngest victims on their long road to recovery."

It's like during the presentation in class. She starts off unsure of herself and the power of her words, but then something clicks inside her and her passion and confidence builds. As she continues explaining her plan, the change in her seems to be felt by everyone in the room. They're all leaning forward in their seats, interested in what she has to say, thinking about those children she described. The children who feel lost and abandoned.

And like during her presentation, when she moved the class to near tears, I have to turn and blink away my own tears from the memory of what Ryan and I endured—and what Amber endured.

"What we're looking for are volunteers who can help make this event happen," she says. "And we're especially interested in athletes, whether you can play basketball or not. You don't have to decide now, but if you could let Emma or Liam know in the next few days, that would be great. Thanks." She glances at me. "Is there anything you want to add?"

You mean other than I'm terribly turned-on from watching you talk? "No, that's everything for now."

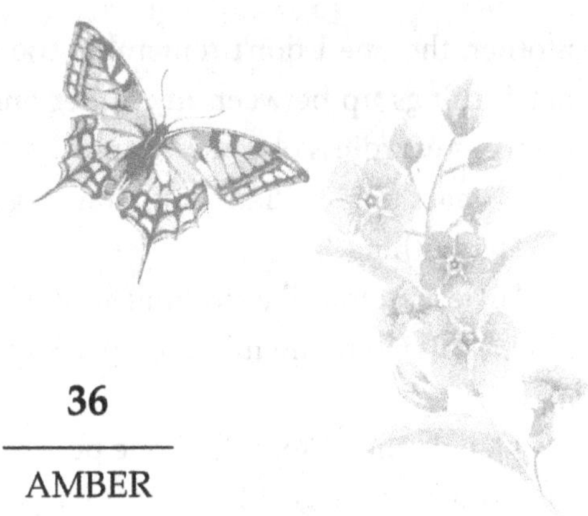

36

AMBER

As I head toward the bedroom door, to hang out in the common area with Jordan, my cell phone plays the latest Pushing Limits song. I glance at the number and recognize it. Part of me doesn't want to answer, but the other part realizes I can't keep escaping this. I've spent my life wanting answers and now I'll finally get them.

"Hello?" I say into the phone.

"Hello, Amber, it's Lily. I wanted to see if you've made a decision yet."

I don't respond at first, the arguments wrestling in my head over the past few days start up again.

"Your father wants to be there for you," she continues, as if sensing the reason for my silence.

"I'm not ready yet. He abandoned his family. The last thing I need to deal with is him as well as the trial. Please understand."

She sighs. "All right."

I hang up and stare at the phone for a minute as if that can take everything back. I should never have contacted her after my father sent me the letter. But at the time, I had no idea she would want to reconnect me with him. Though what did I expect? She's my grandmother, the one I don't remember too well. Of course she'll try to patch things up between my father and me if that's what the jerk wants—regardless of what *I* want.

"What's up?" Brittany says, startling me out of my anger fest.

"It's nothing."

"Doesn't look like nothing to me." She shrugs. "I don't know. Maybe talking to me might help. It's not like I'm not gonna try and fix you."

I laugh once. "You're the one person I can trust *not* to try."

"And I won't go blabbing your secrets. I've got plenty of my own."

She's got a point there. "I told you that my father walked out on my family. Well, he sent me a letter a few weeks ago. I ignored it at first, but I guess I wanted to find out why he abandoned us. I thought my grandmother, his mother, might know. Michael and Trent left me." I swallow back the pain at their names and how I still feel their loss every day. "I was scared that losing every man I've ever loved would become my life—and my future with Marcus." And it almost was, thanks to Mom.

"That's crazy. Your brother and old boyfriend didn't leave you like your father did. They were murdered."

I cringe.

"Sorry, but it's true."

"I know, and maybe that's why I changed my mind after my grandmother left me the voice message. I don't want to talk about him anymore. I need to trust Marcus, and trust he'll be here for me, and that he won't do what my father did." And that he won't make the same mistake as before and not fight for me. Though after the long talk we had at the hotel over a week ago, I do trust he won't do that again. Next time, he will fight to keep me in his life.

She tilts her head to the side, but not in a way that tells me she's analyzing me. "Does he know about your father?"

"Yes, but he doesn't know about the letter or that my grandmother's been trying to contact me. No one knows, including my mom. And I want to keep it that way." I give her a pointed look.

"Okay, got it, but what are you gonna do about him? Pretend he doesn't exist?"

I reach out and my hand pauses on the doorknob. "Why not? He's been doing that to my family for years. He only wants to see me for the same reason everyone is suddenly interested in me. He's seen my story on the news."

The news is on TV when Jordan and I join the small group of poli-sci students in the common room. None of these guys are the ones who verbally harassed me. Those guys avoid me now after the university threatened to expel them.

"Chicago Police are warning the public to watch out for a thirty-to-forty-year-old male who is impersonating a police officer," the male anchor reports. *"He has been pulling motorists over and robbing them at gunpoint. The vehicle is reported to be a white four-door sedan. If you are pulled over and have any doubts about your safety, call nine-one-one and the dispatcher will confirm if it's safe."*

There's a murmur of reactions from people in the room, ranging from outrage to stunned silence.

A voice inside my head whispers that I should tell them the other danger. The danger they're clueless about. The danger the cops kept from the media when it came to my kidnapping. A stalker could cause a slow leak in your tire and follow you, hoping you'll be stranded in a secluded area so he can attack and possibly kill you.

I wish I could warn them, but unlike the people who've been spreading lies about me and about Marcus, I'm required to keep quiet about the very thing that could save lives.

At least until the case against Paul is over.

"...you may remember two months ago we reported that students at Lake Wood High School were planning to raise money so they could paint murals inside a local children's emergency shelter." The reporter is on location. Behind her is a cheery wall-sized painting of a rainbow and an assortment of animals. It's the same woman who tried to get

an interview from me the other day, when I was playing basketball with Emma. The reporter who told me about the sex video starring Marcus.

The screen flashes to two teenage girls, not much younger than me, smiling nervously at the camera. Behind them is the rest of the mural, showing Noah's Ark and more happy animals.

"I was doing a school project about the shelter and the director gave me a tour," the shorter girl explains. *"I love murals and how they can make a huge difference. After I explained my vision for the walls, the director told me she loved the idea, but the shelter didn't have money for a project like that. Thanks to the support of our school—including the teachers, administration and students—my friends and I were able to organize a bake sale, and we raised enough money to paint murals on every wall."*

"The outpouring of support from the surrounding community when they heard about what we were doing helped too," the taller girl says, a little too fast. *"Once they found out about the bake sale, we had all kinds of offers to help, including money for paint and supplies. And many of the people who showed up to buy the baked goods weren't from the school."*

The reporter then shows the viewers around the building, but I don't see beyond the first two rooms. Telling Jordan I'll be right back, I scramble off the couch and head to my room. I know what I have to do. What I should have done when Marcus and I first started planning the charity event.

I just hope I'm not too late.

37

———

MARCUS

I stare at the fucking math problem, but the numbers that usually come easily are nothing but a mess. I can't concentrate as memories of the night with Amber roll around in my head. Thank God my grades have improved now that we're together again, or I'd be in serious trouble.

From the other room, voices on the news permeate the thin wall. I try not to listen to if they are talking about Amber or me. My assignment is due tomorrow and the problem isn't going to solve itself. And it definitely won't be finished if I keep thinking about Amber—naked or not.

As I'm contemplating having a cold shower so I can focus on my math, Chase calls from the living room, "Hey, Marcus, come here quick! You have to see this."

Figuring he's talking about something on the news, I get my ass into the other room as fast as humanly possible. He wouldn't be calling me if it weren't something important about Amber or me. But all I see is Tammara on the screen, and then the picture flicks back to the male anchor. He moves on to another story.

My insides crumble like stone statues during an earthquake. "What the fuck did she do?"

"She might have just saved your ass."

My gaze darts from the TV to him. "What do you mean?"

"She told the reporter you were never into S-and-M. She said she was into it, but you refused to do it. She gave you an out when it comes to what the girl with the bogus video is claiming."

Hopefully he's right, and it doesn't end up costing Tammara. I can't imagine her straight-laced father will be too thrilled with what she did, not when it's a black smudge against him and the family values he supports. Then again, she was tired of how her family determines who she can and cannot date. Hence her obsession about me and my bad-boy image. Maybe this is her way of breaking free and gaining control of her own life.

I call Amber from my room and ask if she's heard the news.

"I just got off the phone with my mom." Her words are hurried, her excitement unmistakable. "What Tammara is claiming supports your story that you're not the one in the video because you've never engaged in S-and-M." She pauses. "Is she really into that stuff?"

"Not as far as I know."

"Well, for her sake I hope no one treats her like they've been treating me," Amber says.

I hope so, too. No matter what Tammara did to us in the fall, no one deserves what Amber's been through due to those damn forged letters.

"Speaking of the news..." Amber continues. "The station got back to me regarding the basketball fundraiser, and they're interested in talking to us about it. I was thinking of asking Liam if he would be the spokesperson. He'd be good at it."

"When are you gonna ask him?"

"He, Emma, and I are getting together in about twenty to play some hoops. I'll ask him then."

"I'll be right over." I conveniently ignore that I have to finish my math assignment. But hell if I'm missing out on playing with those guys.

I GO FOR THE SHOT. LIAM DODGES PAST AMBER'S BLOCK AND JUMPS for the ball. He misses and the ball swooshes through the hoop for the winning basket.

Not caring that I'm dripping with sweat, not that she's much better, Amber jumps up and hugs me. Her legs wrap around my hips. It's amazing how the girl can still smell of strawberries even after the workout we just had.

She gives me a quick kiss. If it weren't for where we're standing, I'd carry her into the shower, soap her up, and make mind-numbing love to her.

Amber slides down and my body cries foul. Half the time I swear she doesn't realize she's a tease, but based on her smile, I can tell this isn't one of them.

With my hand on Amber's lower back, I high-five Liam, then Emma. I've missed playing at this level. As good as Alejandro is, it's not quite the same playing with him and the other teens at the youth center. Regret bites me that I never got to play in my senior year of high school because I had to work a part-time job. It was the only way Ryan and I could escape the hell we had endured for so long.

Like Amber, I missed my chance to be recruited by a university and win an athletic scholarship. But the freedom I gained was worth all the sacrifices I made to survive. For Ryan and me to survive.

"So, I contacted Channel Four about our charity basketball game," Amber explains, "and they're excited to interview us about it. You know, to get the word out so attendance will be greater than if we just promote it around campus."

"That's a great idea," Liam says, being the marketing major that he is.

Amber smiles, and I wish it was directed at me. "I'm glad you feel that way. We'd like you to be our spokesperson."

Liam passes the ball to me. "Why me? I mean, it's not that I'm not interested. But this charity is your baby, and I think Marcus should be the spokesperson."

I shake my head. "You have the people skills. You're definitely the right person."

"Yes, but I'm not the one who's been hurt like the kids the charity is helping." He looks at Emma, and she nods. "I know you haven't gone public about what your stepfather did to you and your brother, but I think you should. You're not alone, but I bet it felt like you were at the time, right?"

Shit.

Amber wraps her hand around mine and gently squeezes it. I nod, any words I might say in agreement too chickenshit to reveal themselves. Ryan and I did feel like we were alone. That no one could possibly know what we were going through.

"How did you know?" she asks softly, though I'm not too surprised he figured it out, given that Tammara did the same.

"When he was shot," he explains, "the news reported that a twenty-year-old had been shot by his stepfather. Later they reported that the stepfather had been accused of sexually assaulting his sons when they were teens."

"We didn't piece it together," Emma says, "until Amber told us about her idea for the charity event. I bet there're kids who feel the same way. If you do this, you're letting those kids know they aren't alone and that someone does care. You do this, and you'll bring light to an issue people like to pretend doesn't exist."

Liam reads my mind. "No one's going to think bad of you because of what happened. What happened wasn't your fault."

Amber places her hand on my cheek, forcing me to look at her. "They're right, Marcus. You need to do this." She doesn't say the rest, but I can see it in her eyes. This will help me move forward. It will help me finally separate myself from what Frank did to me and help me become whole again.

I'm just not sure I can.

38

AMBER

I stride to where Jordan is waiting inside, near the main dorm doors. A group of five or six freshmen cling to each other by the wall, their faces streaked with tears.

"What's going on?" I ask Jordan, nodding at the girls.

"One of their friends was raped by a guy she was going out with. She fought back, but he snapped, and now she's in the hospital."

"I-is she going to be okay? Physically, I mean."

Jordan glances at the girls. "From what I've heard, she's in pretty bad shape."

The girls hug, seeking each other's strength. I'm still thinking about that as Jordan and I head for the gym. Emma and my other friends tried to be there for me after what happened with Paul. I turned my back on them because I didn't know how to cope, and I was punishing myself with the guilt of knowing Michael and Trent's deaths were my fault. My friends were eventually able to move on, but Emma was left to struggle as she came to terms with her brother's death and what happened to me and how I had changed.

I keep thinking about this while I run hard on the treadmill. While sitting in class. While eating lunch. And by the time I see the girls again after dinner, on the other side of the cafeteria, my idea has fully taken shape.

I tell Jordan and Emma that I'll catch up with them, and I walk over to the girls' table. "I'm sorry about your friend." I sit on an empty seat at the end.

They look at me, a glimpse of recognition on a couple of their faces. They don't say anything, though. And what is there to say? "Thank you" doesn't sound right, even if it's what most people say. Out of politeness.

"I was wondering…" I gulp, trying to loosen the words stuck in my throat. My plan seemed like a great idea while I was thinking about it all day, but now that I have to share it with them, my usual fear of speaking in front of a crowd hits. "I was thinking of organizing a candlelight vigil. For your friend and for other girls on campus who have been sexually assaulted. And for their friends and families." Once the first words are free, the rest come naturally, like they've been waiting patiently this past year for their turn. "It would be a private event. So no media. But you could videotape it if you want to show your friend. Then she'll know how many people care about her and about others who've gone through the same thing."

The petite girl in the seat next to mine studies me, her head cocked to the side as if she's attempting to peel off my layers and figure out what's inside. I try not to squirm in my seat, and she eventually nods to herself. "You really were raped, weren't you?" Her gaze remains locked on me.

I nod. "You're right. I was kidnapped and I was raped. Several times." And unlike when I first told Marcus that sex with Paul had been consensual, that I had agreed to have sex with him so he wouldn't force himself on me, I now know it's not true. It's still rape when you agree to have sex with someone who will otherwise brutalize you. That's self-preservation. That's not consensual.

The freshman and her friends exchange glances. "When would it be?" she asks.

"We could do it Sunday night at seven in the baseball diamond on campus."

The girls nod their agreement and say they'll spread the word.

"But make it clear we don't want any publicity about the event. So no posters or anything." The last thing I want is for this to become about Paul and me and the trial, which is what will happen if the media shows up. "And only tell those people you trust will be supportive or who have been sexually violated. We don't want this to become a rally screaming for justice against those who've hurt us and those we love. It's about sharing our strength and support." What I want to avoid is some misguided idiots showing up, claiming that most girls ask to be raped because of what they wear, or some other like-minded belief.

TWO DAYS LATER, WITH MARCUS BY MY SIDE, WE WALK TO THE baseball diamond. It's still early. The vigil won't start for another ten minutes, but I wanted to be here before anyone else.

As we get closer, it's obvious we're not here soon enough. A small group is already gathering. The field is too thick with snow to do the vigil there, but the path is at least clear.

"Hi, are you here for the vigil to support all those impacted by sexual crimes?" A few girls are holding candles, and while I assume there isn't another vigil planned for the same time and location, I figured I should ask anyway.

"Yes," a woman in her midthirties says. "I'm Olivia." She holds out her hand to me. "I was raped while I was a student here."

I shake her hand. "Hi, I'm Amber. I'm the one who organized this. How did you hear about it?"

Next to her, a girl my age peers curiously at me.

The woman puts her arm around the girl's shoulders. "My niece told me."

"And some of my friends told me. They're gonna be here soon."

I introduce them to Marcus. The younger girl blushes when he smiles at her, but I can tell they haven't met before. It's not the usual reaction he gets from girls he has slept with.

"Are you the girl they keep talking about on the news?" a girl with a striped knitted hat and matching mitts asks.

"Yes, I am."

A few girls whisper to each other, no doubt like everyone else, discussing whether the rumors are true or not. Their attention then turns to Marcus.

"Did you really star in that porn video?"

"I'm the idiot who trusted the wrong girl and she turned my drunken actions against me. But no, I never starred in the video. The credit goes to the guy who pretended to be me for part of it."

"The woman who posted it will be facing criminal charges," I add. That was the one thing my mom reassured me about. The police are attempting to locate her. She didn't post the video under her real name, and Marcus can't remember it.

"Why did she post it?" Olivia asks.

I shrug. "We don't know. She never approached either of us for money to keep it quiet. And she used a weird login, which means she wasn't looking for her fifteen minutes of fame."

"Why didn't either of you tell the media this?" Striped Hat inquires.

"I've been asked not to say anything. The DA's office is handling it."

"But you haven't even defended your own innocence in light of the allegations," Olivia points out as more people join us.

Marcus places his hand on my lower back and I lean into it.

"I doubt it would make a difference if I tried. People believe what they want to believe, no matter what I tell them. Some are more than willing to turn my brutalization into their own form of entertainment. I'd rather talk about how dangerous stalking is and what I wish I had done to avoid it. But all the reporters want to hear about are the latest sensationalized headlines. They don't care about me as a person. I'm simply a ratings draw to them."

There are a few cries of outrage. Emma, Jordan, Brittany, Chase, and Liam join the group. They're silent, but deep down I'm sure they are agreeing with everyone.

"But none of it matters since that's not why we're here," I say as the group continues to grow to more than twenty people. "We're here to remember those individuals who have been affected in some way by a sex-related crime, whether as a survivor, friend, family member, or loved one."

Marcus hands out candles to those individuals who don't have one. I light mine and use the flame to light Emma's. She lights Liam's, and one by one the candles are lit.

And then we stand here ignoring the cold, honoring a minute of silence before we talk among ourselves and get to know each other's stories. I'm not sure if this is what one does during a candle-light vigil, but no one seems to care. We're just happy to share our pain with others and gain each other's strength.

If the weather were warmer, we would have stayed out longer. But as it is, winter in Chicago isn't the most outdoor vigil-friendly season. Thirty-or-so minutes later, the last participant has left, leaving me alone with Marcus and Olivia and her niece. Emma and Liam are off to the side, waiting for us.

I thank Olivia for coming. I'm about to leave when she says, "Amber, do you know who I am?"

I study her for a moment and shake my head. She seems kind of familiar, but it's hard to tell since she's bundled up in winter clothing.

"I have a daytime talk show on Channel Four. *The Olivia Wilson Show.*"

My entire body clenches, and I throw her niece a hurt look of betrayal. At least that's the look I'm aiming for. But then, I can't blame her. The "no media" message probably got lost somewhere along the way, though knowing this doesn't do much to help unclench my muscles.

"What you said earlier makes sense," Olivia says. "If you're interested, I would love to have you on the show to talk about stalking."

I open my mouth to protest, but she cuts me off. "You won't have to talk about your case or what happened to you specifically. But like you said, there are things you wish you had known back then that might have changed what happened."

I can't argue against that, but there is one thing I can do to show her I'm the wrong person for what she has planned. "I'm not good when it comes to public speaking."

"You looked pretty good to me." She smiles like a proud parent.

"She's right," Emma pipes in, moving closer. "You rocked your psych presentation. You can do this."

Marcus leans in, his breath brushing my ear. "What you did tonight, Amber, was amazing." His voice is low. Only I can hear him. "I'm so proud of you, and I know you can do this." He straightens and I immediately miss the closeness.

"All right." I inwardly cringe. Mom told me not to talk to the media. But this is important. It could save lives.

What's more important than that?

39

AMBER

Heat claws at the air, at my exposed skin, and singes the edges of what's left of my hope. Smoke reaches into my lungs, igniting another round of coughing as I fight for what little oxygen remains in the room, my prison. My eyes burn, but the tears in them aren't enough to extinguish the heat as a plaintive meow rips at my heart. I tighten my hold on Smoky, my kitten, my only source of comfort.

My only friend.

With Smoky sheltered against my chest, I bang my fist on the heavy closed door, again and again and again. "Please, Paul!" Don't leave me here to die. I've lasted this long. Two weeks, five days, by my guestimation.

"I'll do anything you say." The last part comes out as a spluttered whisper, barely noticeable over the crackling flames engulfing the room. Please don't let me die.

But something tells me it's already too late as the words "Don't worry, Amber. You and I were meant to be together. Forever and ever" ring like funeral bells in my brain. He doesn't plan for either of us to escape. He had it planned all along. My murder. His suicide.

A voice yells outside the door, but it's too muffled for me to make out the words.

I slam my palm on the warm wood. "Help me!" The words scrape past my raw throat. Words I've been taught are only for the weak.

Shame doesn't have time to consume me. A loud cracking noise followed by a splintering crash and hissing, as the ceiling caves in, drowns out my screams.

"AMBER." SOMEONE SHAKES ME. "AMBER, YOU'RE HAVING A nightmare. It's not real." Brittany's voice slowly sinks in, and I open my eyes. It's the same dream I've been having for the past week. Prior to that, it was a dream I'd managed to avoid.

I curl myself in a tight ball and whisper, "Sorry."

She glances at the alarm clock. "I needed to get up anyway and review for my exam."

That's a lie. She doesn't have to review. She knows the info cold.

I push myself up and check the clock. 5:30 a.m. Marcus won't be at the gym yet; it will be another hour before he shows up. Which means I can push myself super hard and he'll never know.

And I need to push myself hard.

Today's the interview. On live TV.

Fifteen minutes later I enter the gym. Not too surprisingly, there are only a handful of people here. I secure a spot on the treadmill and increase the speed from a walk to a jog to a run. My feet pound against the fast-moving belt. *I can do it. I can do it. I can do it.*

I can talk in front of a live audience without freaking out.

I repeat the thought to myself a dozen more times, pushing myself harder as I do. My shorts and T-shirt cling to my sweaty body, but I keep going. I have to. It's the only way I can survive this.

I run until the treadmill console warns me I've been on the equipment for the maximum time allowed: thirty minutes. A quick glance around tells me no one will care if I keep going. Eight other treadmills are unoccupied.

I adjust the incline and push myself harder. At five minutes before I've officially run an hour, I stumble. I passed runner's high a while ago, and I'm sprinting toward crash and burn.

Someone reaches across the console and slows the treadmill. "Didn't we agree you weren't going to punish yourself anymore with exercise?" Marcus frowns.

He's right. Guilt and embarrassment stagger through me. "I wasn't punishing myself."

"Nice try. But I'm not buying it."

I glare at him. "I'm sorry—I had a nightmare this morning that left me screaming." *And apparently bitchy.* "And I'm going on TV in front of a live audience. And the trial begins next week. And I'm sorry if it's making me a little stressed and I need to burn off some of my nervousness."

If my edginess surprises him, he doesn't show it. His frown smooths and he brushes a wayward strand of hair out of my face, tucking it behind my ear. "It's going to be okay, Amber. I'll be there for you during the interview and during the trial. I just wish I could be there for you when you have nightmares."

I know it's true. It's killing him that he can't help me with them. I can see it on his face.

I nod, and after downing water from the water fountain, I join him on the weight floor. My legs have been rubberized and don't want to cooperate. I do my best, though, to keep Marcus from guessing the truth. He lost it on me before Christmas for pushing myself too hard. I don't need an encore.

We work out for the next forty minutes, with me taking things easier this time; then we get ready to hit the TV station. Marcus drives us, which is just as well. I'm too fidgety. I'd cause an accident for sure if I got behind the wheel and managed to turn the engine on.

"Why aren't you even nervous?" I ask, taking in his cool exterior. I'm not the only one going on the show. After we told Olivia about the fundraiser we're doing, she invited Marcus to join us.

He glances briefly at me. "Would it make you feel better if I told you I'm nervous?"

"Yes." Who am I kidding? This guy stood up to Carlos, the leader of a gang in Marcus's old neighborhood. And even when Carlos's men attacked him, Marcus kept his cool. I guess being reckless also means being fearless.

"Well, I am."

I'm positive my eyes are as round as the steering wheel. "Seriously?"

He nods, his attention still on the road. "I've been thinking about what Liam said, you know, about me going public with what happened to me and Ryan. I was awake all night thinking about it."

Now that I study him more closely, I notice the faint shadows under his eyes, which nearly match mine. Mine are a shade or two darker, but that's nothing new.

I settle my hand on his thigh and stroke my thumb against the soft denim. "You don't have to do it if you don't want to, Marcus."

He places his hand on mine and interlaces our fingers. "But I do have to do it, and I want to. What Liam said made sense." He gently squeezes my fingers. "Plus, your life has been splashed on the front page of every newspaper. The least I can do is admit what happened to me. I might not be allowed to say Frank's name, but I can at least tell mine and Ryan's story." He cringes. Not because he's going to reveal what his stepfather did to him, but because he's going public with what happened to Ryan as well. The story he swore to his dying brother he would never tell.

But if Ryan is watching from heaven, I'm positive he'll be proud of his brother. Marcus is turning his horrifying childhood into something good. Something that will benefit other kids like him.

Ryan can't fault him for that.

We arrive at the studio on time and are hurried to the makeup station for a quick touch-up. Much to Marcus's chagrin. I laugh at his expression, but he can't complain. Neither of us is coated with makeup like Olivia. No wonder I didn't recognize her when I first met her at the vigil. She looked younger, more natural than she does now.

"You ready?" she asks, smiling. There's something reassuring about her smile. It's as if the tap to my emotions has been turned on to a fast drip, draining away some of the tension.

I smile back and nod. I can do this.

We're directed to the green room, where we wait until it's our turn.

The production assistant, a girl a few years older than me, fetches us after ten minutes. "It's time." Her tone is a mix of cheery and excited.

She leads us along the hallway, chatting as she goes, and flashes appreciative glances at Marcus. He doesn't notice. His focus is straight ahead, hands fisted.

I wrap my hand around his and give it a light squeeze, like he gave me in his car. We're in this together and I'm proud of what he's about to do. Of what we're both about to do.

While the show is paused for a commercial break, the production assistant shows us to the couch and the sound person descends on us. He connects a tiny microphone to Marcus's shirt and one to my blouse. Then he asks us each a question before walking away.

Olivia gives us the same reassuring smile as earlier. "You two will be great."

A bald man tells her we're on in five and counts down with his fingers....Four. Three. Two.

And we're on.

"Welcome back." Olivia's long blond hair glows under the hot stage lights. "I'd like to welcome our next guests, Amber Scott and Marcus Reid."

A moment of panic slams into me. What if this is all a lie and she's planning to ask us questions about the trial and all the controversy bubbling around us like boiling lava?

My heart jumps up, eager to scramble its way out of my throat and out of the studio.

But then I remember what's at stake if she does. After Olivia contacted me to confirm the show, I talked to my mom, the DA, and my lawyer, Sheryl. We discussed the benefit of my doing the show and how to make sure I wasn't jeopardizing the case. In the end, Sheryl gave Olivia a contract to sign, outlining the questions that were acceptable to ask. In turn, Olivia gave me her questions ahead of time so that I'd be more comfortable during the interview. If only the defense would do that for the trial.

"As many of you are aware, Amber was stalked and kidnapped while in her senior year of high school. Because her alleged kidnapper's case is going to trial soon, we won't be discussing details about her ordeal last year. Amber will be sharing tips to keep you and your family safe. Things she had to learn the hard way. Contrary to what many people believe, stalking isn't exclusive to Hollywood. Isn't that right, Amber?"

Without looking too obvious about it, I rub my hands against the soft fabric of the couch, conscious not to start tapping my fingers on my thigh. "That's right. It's estimated six million people each year will be stalked. This number includes those individuals involved in relationships that have turned abusive, either now or in the past."

The more Olivia and I talk, the more relaxed I become. She's living up to her promise, and everyone in the audience is listening to me as if I'm telling them the winning numbers to next week's lottery. Some women nod, as if they know what I'm talking about, as if they too have been stalked in one capacity or another. No one's judging me. All they want is to learn how to protect themselves and their loved ones.

"Thank you, Amber." Olivia's smile tells me I did well. I rocked my first television interview.

She then changes the topic to the one Marcus has been dreading most. "Amber, you and Marcus have been organizing a special basketball tournament at UIC. Can you tell us more about it?"

I subtly brush Marcus's hand with mine. He releases an equally subtle long breath, which does nothing to ease his nerves. Tension rolls off him like a thick fog off the lake, but I suspect I'm the only one who notices. Everyone else just sees a hot guy.

"While I was a kid"—his voice is smooth, unaffected—"my brother and I were victims of domestic abuse. Our stepfather used to hit us. We felt we had nowhere to turn, so we kept silent. In our teens the abuse continued, but things grew worse. He...he sexually assaulted me and raped my older brother." A collective gasp rises from the audience.

I glance at Olivia. The reassuring smile has vanished, to be replaced with the same look of horror everyone else wears.

"Again, we told no one," Marcus continues. "We were afraid we would be put in the system and separated. We couldn't handle that. My brother died last year trying to protect me from our stepfather. Amber and I started organizing the fundraiser so I could buy my brother the gravestone he deserves—instead of the small place marker currently indicating where he's buried—and also so we could donate proceeds to the Chicago Little Heroes Center."

"What is the CLHC?" Olivia inquires, not missing a beat.

"They help kids who are at risk of being sexually abused, and kids who have been abused and are now struggling to cope."

Olivia asks questions about the event, all which Marcus easily answers.

"Is it correct to assume your stepfather is currently serving time?"

Marcus shakes his head. "Unfortunately not. Because it happened a long time ago, the cops can't prove anything. I know there are other victims who have been sexually abused by my step-father, but none are willing to step forward. And without that, he could remain free, and won't be listed as a sexual offender."

"Why do you think no one else will come forward?"

"They're scared. Ryan and I"—his Adam's apple slides uneasily up, then down—"Ryan and I didn't tell anyone because we were afraid of what others would think of us if the truth came out. We were ashamed. This is the same fear that keeps other boys from coming forward. But it's also this fear and shame that lets my stepfather continue to hurt others." The pain and guilt etched on his face causes tears to well in my eyes.

And I'm not alone. A number of women in the audience brush away the tears from their cheeks.

This time when I touch his hand, the gesture isn't subtle. I thread my fingers with his and hold on tight.

Olivia clears her throat. She's a professional, but it's obvious his words have had an impact on her like they have on everyone else. "It takes strong individuals to do what you two are doing in the face of everything you've gone through. I hope it inspires other victims to find their voice and get help." She turns to the camera. "We'll return in a moment after our sponsors' messages."

"And we're off," the bald man announces. The sound guy rushes to remove the microphones from our clothing.

"That was an amazing thing you did, Marcus," Olivia says. We stand and she hugs us both.

As Marcus and I head to the exit, a woman stops us to talk to Marcus. I pull my phone from my purse. I'm curious what she wants to talk about, but I should text Jordan and Emma to let them know we survived, even though I'm positive they skipped their classes to see the show.

While she asks him about how to spot signs of sexual abuse, I check my messages.

Amber, I need to talk to you. Pls.

40

MARCUS

I shove my way through the crowded food court, accidentally bumping shoulders with someone as I pass. He yells at me but I ignore him.

Jordan and Chase are sitting in our usual spot, laughing and eating lunch. I drop onto the seat across from Jordan. "Have you seen Amber?"

"Not since she left yesterday. Why? What's wrong?"

"She left?" And why am I only hearing about it now?

Jordan frowns. "I thought you knew."

I grunt. "Apparently not. Where did she go?"

"She didn't say. She came back after you guys were on the show and said she had to go away for a few days. She probably had to go home since the trial's next week."

"Did you try calling her?" Chase recoils at my glare that says *of course I did, dumbass.* "O-kay. I take it that's a yes."

"I haven't seen her since I dropped her off at her dorm after the interview," I explain. She was acting a little off, but nothing that screamed she was upset. I figured she was coming off her adrenaline rush after the show. I asked her if she was okay, and she said she was fine. *And then abruptly changed the topic.*

"Maybe you should call her mom and see if she's there?" Jordan helps herself to Chase's fries.

I cringe. "It might be better if you do it. Her mom still isn't a fan of mine." I'm hoping with time things will improve between us, once I'm able to prove I am the right guy for her daughter.

Now it's Jordan's turn to cringe. "I guess not." She takes out her phone and makes a call. "Hi, is Amber there? This is her friend Jordan." Silence. "Oh...okay." More silence. "Thanks." She hangs up. "According to her mom, Amber's here."

Chase and I exchange glances. "I don't like this." The urge to race out of here and find her builds like steam in an overheated radiator. Except where the hell do I start searching?

"Maybe she needed a break from everything and went off somewhere."

"But why not tell me? And why not tell Jordan where she's going?"

"Because she knows you'll go chasing after her," Chase points out, and he's right. "The girl's on the verge of cracking. You haven't known her all that long, Marcus. This could be her way of dealing with things when they get too out of control."

That's more me than Amber. The Amber I know may hide from the world when she's upset, but she doesn't completely disappear. "I'd feel better if I knew where she is. What if something's wrong?"

All I can think about is how Paul kidnapped her and she was missing for eight hours before her brother's body and Amber's abandoned car were found. Eight hours before anyone thought to look for her. By then it was too late.

My phone buzzes and I check to see who sent me a text. Amber. Relief slams into me. At least she's alive.

> Amber: I'm fine, Marcus. Just needed to do
> something. Will be back soon.

All kinds of horrible scenarios kick around in my head about what could have happened to her.

                    Me: How do I know this is you?

I know I'm being paranoid. The chances of her being kidnapped again are low, but it doesn't stop me from worrying.

    Amber: How do you tell that you are in the
    hands of the Mathematical Mafia?

                    Me: I don't know.

I do know. I was the one who told her the joke.

    Amber: They make you an offer you can't
    understand.

I smile even though I miss her more than anything, and I send her a text to tell her that. Then I add:

                    Me: Can you tell me where you are?

    Amber: No. You need 2 trust me. I just need
    a little time while I sort some stuff out.

                    Me: About us?

    Amber: About me.

    Amber: Love U. XOX

                    Me: Love U 2

My phone rings. It's not Amber. "Hello?"

"Hello, this is Anthony Emerson with Emerson Power Sport Management. Is this Marcus Reid?"

"Yes?"

"I represent Eric Walters, the center for the Chicago Bulls. He asked me to arrange a meeting with you. Today if possible."

"What for?" Not that I wouldn't kill for a chance to meet him, but why the heck would he want to meet me?

"He didn't say, other than it's important."

We set up a time for later this afternoon, at a coffee shop near the United Center. When I arrive, I spot Eric sitting at the corner booth. At six foot seven and wearing an orange T-shirt, he's hard to miss. Several high school seniors are standing around the table, chatting with him. He seems more than happy to talk with them. Since he already has a coffee, I place my order with the barista.

While I wait, I watch him interact with the teens. He has an easygoing manner that's a complete contrast to how he is on the court. During a game he's fierce and a force you don't want to get on the wrong side of.

Once my coffee's ready, I join him and his fan club. "Hi, Eric. I'm Marcus Reid."

He gestures for me to join him, and I slide into the opposite side of the booth. Apparently sensing we want to be left to talk in private, the teens wander off and sit at another table not far from us. But far enough away so they can't overhear our conversation.

Eric leans forward, his elbows on the table. "You're probably wondering why I want to chat with you." His tone is friendly, but there's something beneath the surface I sense he's holding back.

"You could say that."

Other patrons watch us with an open curiosity. Eric appears oblivious to all of this as he sips his coffee. "I saw you admit the truth on the daytime talk show about how your stepfather had molested you and your brother. That took guts."

I laugh but it sounds forced. "I don't know about that. I was pretty freaked out about admitting it. But I knew I needed to be honest about why I'm doing the fundraiser."

"To me that took guts." He sips his coffee again and glances around the room. For some reason he suddenly seems slightly nervous as he scans the place.

"I just figured it was time people stop hiding from the truth. It's a bigger problem than most people want to believe. And I want to give kids the voice they don't often have. You know what I mean?"

He nods, and the sadness rolling off him shoves against me. "While I was in high school, the person I was supposed to trust the most, my coach, started touching me. I never told anyone. Like you said on the show, I was too ashamed to tell the truth." He takes a long gulp of his coffee. I'm too speechless to utter anything. This was the last thing I expected him to tell me. He was the last person I expected to know how I feel.

"I've spoken with several of my teammates," he says, "and they're interested in helping you and your girlfriend with the charity event. Whatever you need, we want to help. Also, I plan to end my silence about what my coach did to me. He's dead, so I can't press charges even if I wanted to. You did a brave thing, Marcus, and I want to do the same. I want kids to know that they shouldn't feel ashamed for telling the truth."

"D-do you think you could talk to a friend of mine? He's fourteen, and I'm positive my stepfather hurt him. But he won't admit to it, and I'm worried about him."

"And you're hoping by talking to me he might change his mind?"

I nod, silently praying Eric will say yes. "He's a huge fan of you and the Bulls. And right now he's the only person I know for sure who was victimized by my stepfather. If I can get him to tell the cops the truth, maybe my stepfather will finally be found guilty."

Eric smiles. The movement is small, nothing like the smiles I've seen from him when his team wins. But there's also an air of determination about it. "I can't make any promises that talking to me will change anything, but I can at least try."

THE NEXT AFTERNOON, I DRIVE ALEJANDRO TO THE UNITED CENTER. Matt also comes with us. Juan managed to get himself stuck in detention. A fact Alejandro is still chuckling over.

The team is finishing up practice when we arrive, and Eric introduces us to several players.

"That's a great thing you're doing with the charity." Daniel Rodriguez slaps my back. "Lookin' forward to it."

"Yeah, man, that was a brave thing you did admitting what the asshat did to you," Rhys Peterson adds.

Alejandro's mouth drops open and he glances at me, confused. He has no idea what I said on the show. He doesn't watch it, and neither does his mom. She works full-time.

"Let me have a shower first," Eric says, "then we can chat."

As soon as Eric disappears, Alejandro turns on me, eyes narrowed. "What the hell's going on? Since when do you know the players?"

"Amber and I have been planning a charity event at the university. We were on a daytime talk show the other day and explained about the event and about what happened to me. Eric heard about it and wants to participate. So do some of the other players."

"And that's why you're here?" Alejandro asks, tone notably impressed, his earlier suspicion appeased—for now.

"More or less, yes."

While we wait for Eric, Alejandro and Matt ask all kinds of questions about the event. By the time Eric reappears from the locker room, they're up to speed on everything there is to know about what Amber and I have planned.

"Here, this is for you guys." Eric hands each boy what appears to be a rolled-up poster. "All the guys signed it."

"Wow, thanks!" Alejandro unrolls his. As promised, the guys have signed it and at the top it says "*To Alejandro*."

"This is great. Thanks," Matt responds in that shy way of his.

Eric studies him for a second or two. "So I guess you heard what Marcus said on *The Olivia Wilson Show* the other day?" The question is directed at both boys.

"He just told us," Matt says.

"What he did took guts. I admire him for putting himself out like that when it wasn't an easy choice to make. It's not a choice I made when my coach began touching me. I should have. I wish I had. But I didn't."

Alejandro narrows his eyes at me again, and I inwardly flinch at the string of Spanish cusses no doubt running through his head, along with the word "traitor."

It's the opposite look of what Matt is wearing. "Y-you were touched?" he whispers. But his expression is not one of horror, as I would expect. It's one of relief and understanding.

A cold sensation snakes through my veins. Not only was I right about there being other victims, Matt was one of them. *Fuck. Fuck. Fuck.* This is one time I wish I'd been wrong. It was bad enough knowing there was another victim—Alejandro. But realizing that my suspicions were correct and he wasn't the only one burns deep. Guilt and pain claw their way through me once more. No wonder he and Alejandro—the two guys who I thought had nothing in common—were friends. They felt they only had each other to turn to for support.

They didn't realize how wrong they were.

"How do you even know Frank?" I glance between the two boys.

"He was doing odd jobs at the center," Matt says. "Whenever Dave needed him. But then he started hanging out there more regularly."

"When was that?"

"In the fall." While I was busy with school. After Ryan's death.

Alejandro glares at his friend, then turns to Eric, arms folded across his chest. "But you're okay," he stubbornly points out, "even if you never told anyone the truth."

Eric shakes his head. "I was a mess. I began abusing drugs and alcohol. If it hadn't been for a school counselor who reached out, I might be dead by now. And one of my friends is dead because of what happened." At the boys' gasps he continues. "I wasn't the coach's only victim. My best friend was also on the team. He couldn't deal with it and committed suicide."

"Well, Marcus isn't messed up," Alejandro says. Anything to avoid the real issue.

"I was and I still am. If it weren't for Amber, I'd be a bigger mess. I was on a path to destruction, not letting anyone get too close. Taking risks I shouldn't have. But I'm now growing stronger every day thanks to her." But I can't rely on her alone to get me there. She was right all along. I do need help, and Alejandro needs to realize it, too. "It's why the charity event is important to me." It's a way to fully let go of my guilt about Ryan, like Amber's been pushing for me to do.

Matt's gaze drops to the wooden floor. "I wanted to tell someone what your stepfather was doing to me, but he threatened to kill me if I did." His eyes move to mine. "I came close to killing myself once, but Alejandro talked me out of it." He swaps looks with his friend, then peers back up at me. Tears fill his eyes but somehow refuse to spill. "I want your stepfather to pay for what he did."

"So do I," I whisper. *So do I.*

41

AMBER

I stand awkwardly in the doorway as the gray-haired woman hugs me. Hard. Apparently I didn't get my height from her side of the family. She barely comes up to my chest.

Lily, my grandmother, the one I vaguely remember, pulls away and brushes the tears streaming down her face. A familiar numbness crowds the periphery. I'm not sure I'm ready for this "happy" reunion.

"Come on in." Smiling, she gestures for me to enter the small cottage-style house. "You look like your brother."

"Y-you've seen Michael?"

Her smile vanishes and a new round of tears fills her eyes. "Yes, before he was…" She swallows and a familiar pain flickers on her face. "Right before he was killed, he came here searching for your father. He was going to tell you the truth."

"He never said anything. All I knew about that weekend was he had something important to tell me." I wrap my arms around me in a weak attempt to keep myself together. "He was killed before he could tell me what it was."

"So you never knew," she says, more to herself than to me.

She leads me into the house, to a small living room. It reminds me of Grandma's place, but Lily has porcelain thimbles grouped all over the room.

I study one collection on the tiny shelves attached to the wall. Each thimble contains a different state flag, plus there's one with the U.S. flag on it. The cluster of thimbles on the next display has kittens on each one, including a kitten that reminds me of Smoky. My heart tightens at how much I miss him.

I tear my gaze away from the thimble and sit on the faded flowery couch near the window.

Lily sits next to me. "I'm glad you came, Amber. I've missed you so much, but your pigheaded father decided it was better if I didn't contact you anymore after he…after he left your family."

A ping of pain bites me, and I hate my father even more for what he did. He not only abandoned us, he hurt his own mom, too. What kind of jerk does that?

"I never agreed with his reasons for leaving his family," she says. "And I especially didn't approve that he kept his reasons a secret. He had cancer, but it didn't give him the right to hurt you and your brother and your mother."

I feel my eyebrows pinch together. "Cancer? Mom never told me he had cancer."

"She didn't know. He had bladder cancer. He figured it would be easier on everyone if he left without a real explanation. He thought he was dying and didn't want to put you all through that. So he ran away." Bitterness fills her tone, and she sighs long and hard. "I thought his father and I raised him better than that, but apparently we hadn't."

I'm not even sure how I feel about this. My father didn't leave because he no longer loved me. He left because he didn't want to cause us pain. But why would he assume abandoning his family would cause us less pain than watching him die?

Something occurs to me. "You said Michael managed to locate our father. Does that mean he didn't die?"

She visibly cringes, no doubt having an idea of what I'm thinking. "He went into remission."

My fingers tap-tap-tap my thigh. "So what? He didn't die, but he still couldn't be bothered to return home and be a father again?" I can barely get the word *father* out.

"He'd been gone for so long, he knew it was too late to repair the damage. He was positive your mom wouldn't want him back. She's a strong woman who had no use for someone like him. At least that's how he felt. He paid her child support without fail, I made sure of it, but he never told her the truth."

"Why does he want to talk to me now? And why does he think I would even want to talk to him?" I immediately regret my harsh voice. It's not Lily's fault he abandoned us.

She takes hold of my hands, her skin feathery soft. "He's been watching the news, and what you're going through has kept him fighting to hold on a little longer." Her gaze flicks to the window and the vast white emptiness outside. In the distance, the glow from a pair of headlights, like pale eyes, comes into view and slowly moves closer through the falling snow.

"The cancer returned, but this time he hasn't been able to beat it." Her voice cracks at the last part. "He's been fighting to stay alive long enough to see how the trial ends. He wants to make sure justice is served and Mr. Carlson goes to prison for what he did to you and Michael."

She tucks my hair behind my ear, lingering for a moment. Her fingers drop away. "Despite what he did, Amber, he loves you. He was never quite the same after he left you and your family. While the cancer might not have physically killed him the first time, a large chunk of him did die. All he wants is to say good-bye to you before he dies. But he also understands if you don't want to see him. We both do."

I remove my hands from hers and run them over my face, wishing the simple act could erase the truth and the lies that have plagued me for years. That continue to plague me.

All this time I had believed he left because I was unlovable. Trent stormed out the day he was murdered because we had an argument over my fears that he would walk out on me one day, like my father had. But Trent wasn't my father. He would never have done what my father did. Trent was better than that.

And so is Marcus.

"I'm not sure I can." My voice is little more than a whisper.

"That's all right. But why don't you stay here for a day or two? I haven't seen you in over thirteen years and I've got some catching up to do. What are you studying at university? I remember when you were five you wanted to be a veterinarian. Are you still pursuing it?"

I explain to her about my career goal and what caused the change from my original one. And the more we talk, the more at ease I become. To the point of agreeing to stay for a few days, especially since my father isn't here. He's staying at a palliative care center.

We talk about everything. About my childhood. About what happened last spring and about everything that has happened since. Lily asks plenty of questions and listens. She's especially interested in hearing more about Marcus. The real Marcus. She doesn't believe the lies about his supposed porn-star alter ego. She sees him as the guy who's turning a negative past into a positive future for so many kids.

It's not until the following evening that I finally decide to see my father. While I might not agree with what he did when he first learned he had cancer, at least I can say good-bye to him.

I promise Lily I'll visit her as often as I can, then drive to the hospice.

During the spring and summer the small garden is probably beautiful, welcoming to all who visit. Now it's lonely, forgotten, filled with nothing more than snow and dead plants.

Unable to move, I sit in the car, staring at the building.

I close my eyes and remember the good days when my father

was part of my life. The times when he took me to get ice cream. The times he took us camping and tried to catch fish. And the times I was scared of the weather and he was there for me—back before I had reason to be scared of storms.

I can do this. I've got to do this. For both of us.

I inhale deeply and climb out of my car. My fingers tap-tap-tap my thigh as I walk. I don't bother to stop them.

Inside the building, it's brighter and decorated to add warmth and sunshine for the patients' final days. I approach the front desk and tell the nurse my father's name and that I'm his daughter. Lily phoned ahead to tell them I was coming.

The nurse leads me to his room and tells me how my father's day has been. Rough, from the sounds of it. And she tells me it's a good thing I came when I did. She's not sure if he'll last another night.

It's hard to believe the stranger behind the door is related to me. Even more so when the nurse opens the door and lets me in.

On the bed is a frail-looking man who's nothing like the father I remember. That man was tall and strong with sandy-blond hair. This man is not much more than a stick, and any hair he used to have has long since disappeared.

"Amber?" he whispers, the sound of it a dry, dying autumn leaf.

I nod, unable to put together a simple word let alone a full sentence.

"Let me see you."

I step closer to the bed. My legs keep moving; the rest of me begs them to turn around and run. Fast. And never return.

"You're as beautiful as I always imagined you'd be." He smiles, but not without a lot of effort.

Silence.

"I'm sorry about everything you've been going through, Amber. I should have been there to protect you." He coughs. "And if it weren't for me, Michael would be alive."

Guilt must run in the family. This is no different from how I felt until recently. "How do you figure that?"

"Your brother tracked me down last winter. We had been... slowly repairing our relationship. The weekend he was killed, he had gone back to...Crossfields to bring you here to see me. He wanted to give you and me the same chance he and I had. I should have talked him out of it. Told him...to wait"—he coughs again—"until the term was over. I knew he was busy with classes. When I didn't hear from you, I was hoping Michael hadn't had a chance to tell you. I was hoping you didn't hate me for what I did to you, to Michael, to your mom."

I should say something but what? All I can do is stand, battling a chaos of emotions—anger, pain, sorrow being the forerunners. My vision blurs, and I blink it clear.

"I wanted you to know I never stopped loving you," he says. "I was a coward, an idiot, and I'm sorry I hurt you, but I never stopped loving you."

His tears crumple the final part of the barrier I've kept erected for so long. I could continue hating him for as long as I live, but that's not who I am. And when it comes down to it, he's not the one who tried to destroy me. He's not the man who deserves my hate.

"I'm scared." My voice trembles. I'm not talking about my father, and I'm not sure why I'm even telling him this. But the fear of what I'll be facing next week seeps through my cells like a cancer consuming my body, like his cancer is consuming his. "I'm so scared."

He pats his bed and I sit. "I know you're scared, Amber. And you have every right to be. But you need to have faith in the system. You need to have faith in your mother." He smiles, and I can tell from that simple move he still loves her. "Your mother is brilliant. I've watched her career, and I know she hasn't left you flailing. I can guarantee she's working harder for you than she has for any of her clients, and that's saying a lot. The woman has always been a workaholic."

"But she's not the DA."

He lets out a small laugh, which turns into a coughing fit. It takes a minute or two, and a sip of water, until he's able to talk again. "She might not be the DA, but I can guarantee she's been working alongside, making sure nothing slips through the cracks. There's a reason she's always been the lawyer you want on your side. You need to have faith in her. She won't let you down."

I think about all the things Mom's done for me lately when it comes to the trial. She's been the liaison person between the DA and me, making sure I know everything that's going on. She's pushed to make sure no piece of evidence goes unexplored. She's pushed to have another handwriting expert analyze the letters, the results still pending. She even visited a few times last week, helping me prep for what I'm about to face.

"I know," I whisper. And I do. Things still aren't perfect between us, but Mom would never let me down. Not now. Not when she has so many reasons for wanting Paul locked away forever. For Trent. For Michael. For me. "I know," I repeat. Unlike his voice, mine isn't weak and dying. It's a tiny seed poking from the soil, ready to leave its world of darkness, ready to begin a new life of hope and forgiveness. I won't let the monster win.

"I have something for you." Dad lifts his hand. The effort proves to be too much and the movement is slow and shaky. He points to a wooden box on the bedside table.

I pick it up and run my fingers along the delicate snowdrop-flower carvings covering the lid.

"Open it," he murmurs.

I do, and I discover a pile of envelopes, the top one addressed to me. A single elastic band holds them together.

I remove the pile from the box and slip the elastic off. The other envelopes are addressed to either Michael or me. Some are post-marked. The majority aren't.

"Once I beat the cancer, I tried writing to you and your brother. The letters were always returned unopened. So I continued to write to you, but I never sent them. I figured you didn't want anything to do with me."

"I didn't know." Once again, Mom was trying to protect me, even if I didn't need protecting. What I needed was to know that my father loved me, and that I wasn't the reason he had left.

A small silver medallion with a clover etched in it rests on the bottom of the box. I pick it up.

"You gave me that. I took it with me and it brought me luck. It extended my life. It brought you and Michael back to me, no matter how briefly." He coughs, this time worse than before. "It meant everything to me. I want you to have it."

I remember giving it to him. Grandma helped me pick it. I thought it would make Dad the luckiest person alive. Considering everything he's been through, maybe I was wrong. But then, the medallion didn't cause him to make bad choices. That was one hundred percent him.

"Thank you." My vision clouds again as I slide the medallion into my front jeans pocket. I will the tears away, not wanting my father to see them. He needs me to be strong, not a sobbing mess.

He coughs and I can see how much this—our conversation—is costing him. "I should go and let you rest," I say, a piece of my heart splintering.

He shakes his head, the movement barely perceptible. "I'm fine." A smile ghosts his lips. "More than fine."

My fingertips beg to tap my thigh, but instead I wrap them around his hand. His fragile, paperlike skin clings loosely to what is nothing more than a bag of bones. I want to pull my hand away but I don't.

"I've watched you on the news and I saw you on *The Olivia Wilson Show*." His voice grows weaker with each word. "I wish I had a tenth of your courage. I'm sorry I haven't been there for you...I love you, Amber. I love the beautiful, strong young woman you've become."

He closes his eyes, and a moment or two later drifts off to sleep.

I curl up in the armchair near the window and read the letters my father had sent Michael and me. The ones sent to me are sealed. Michael's have been opened, the tops of the envelopes ripped jagged. And for the first time since entering the room, I let the tears fall. Would things have been much different if he hadn't left us? Mom wouldn't have become an alcoholic, but would things have been any different for me?

Paul's father left him when he was a child. It was the one thing that had connected Paul and me at some level. We talked about it when we worked together. If my father hadn't left me, would Paul still have targeted me? Was that one connection the difference between the girl I used to be and the girl I was forced to become? The girl who is stronger than before. The girl who has found a new meaning in her life.

The girl who will never be what she once was, because of the choices other people made.

I watch my father's slow, even breaths for the longest time. He made mistakes, but Paul's obsession with me wasn't one of them, nor was the stalking and kidnapping. That was all Paul.

I uncurl from the chair and kiss my father's cheek. "I love you."

During the night, while I sleep in the chair, my father dies.

Standing on the porch steps of the hospice, I remove a letter from the box. It was the last one he wrote to me. The last one I read. I put the box and my purse down and rip the letter in two. I keep ripping until I can't make the pieces any smaller, then smiling, I toss them into the wind—and watch them dance and tumble and be free. Free like my father, now that he has finally found peace, and free like me now that I finally know the truth.

42

MARCUS

I pull up to the hospice an hour after getting Amber's call. She didn't say much when I talked to her, other than where she was and that she was okay. Except...she sounded anything but okay.

She sounded broken.

I wasn't sure if she'd stay put when I told her I was on my way, but I also didn't expect to find her sitting on the porch steps, in the cold. I sit next to her and gather her shivering body in my arms. Since my car will be a lot warmer than hers, I stand and lead her to it. She still hasn't said anything. As it is, I have no idea why she's hanging out at the hospice.

Once she's settled and the heater is going full force, I ask the question burning inside me for the past two days, when I discovered she had left, and no one knew where she'd gone. "What's going on, Amber?"

She doesn't say anything, but the shivering at least slows.

"I've been going crazy worrying about you." Frustration flares, but it's muted with the relief that she's safe. "You didn't even tell me you were leaving. I had to find out about it from Jordan." I watch a snowplow drive past, clearing the street. "I thought you trusted me enough that we could be honest with each other."

When I turn back to Amber, her gaze is fixed on the hospice. I open my mouth to ask why she's here, but she starts talking before I can get the words out.

"For years I feared falling in love only for the guy I loved to leave me. My father walked out on my mom. I was afraid the same thing would happen to me. That fear was there with Trent, which is why he never fully had my heart. A small part of it was locked away."

This is nothing I don't already know. It's the one thing keeping a slight wall up between us. Not a full wall. But a wall to part of her heart. I've been chipping away at it for weeks, but all the fucking media craziness has kept me from completely knocking it down.

Amber sighs. "My father contacted me a few weeks ago. He wanted to make amends for what he did. I didn't want to see him. I've been hurting for so long, I wanted him to hurt, too." She nods at the building. "He died last night of cancer."

"I'm sorry." I don't know if I am or not, considering how much he hurt her, but it's the right thing to say because she does seem to be sorry that he's dead.

"I realize now," she says without acknowledging my words, "I was wrong all this time. My father was scared when he left us. He thought he was dying of cancer and didn't want his family to be there for him. He thought it would be better to go it alone."

A smile curves onto her face. Not a big one. But at this point, I'll take whatever I can get.

"In the beginning you kept the truth from me about what happened to you and Ryan. And you had every right to do that." I open my mouth to explain, but she places her finger against my lips. "Don't worry. I get why you had to. I kept things from you, too."

Her gaze averts for a heartbeat before she looks back up at me. Her brown eyes are full of warmth and longing. Not longing for sex. Longing for something deeper, something from the bottom of our souls. "But when I discovered the truth, you didn't push me away. You let me in. You let me love you, scars and all. You're not my father. You never will be."

And with those simple words, the rest of her wall crumbles. "I'm sorry I didn't tell you I was going away. It's not that I don't trust you. I do. More than you can ever imagine. But until I knew why my father was so desperate to talk to me, I didn't want to tell you. I wasn't planning to tell my mom or Emma or Jordan, either. I needed to face my demons. On my own." She smiles. This time it's bright and full of life, the sun burning away the last of the morning fog.

I lean over and kiss her cool lips, thanking the powers of the universe, once again, for bringing us together.

43

AMBER

Mom hands me a glass of chocolate milk and sits next to me on the couch. The midafternoon sunlight reflecting off the snow casts soft shadows on the living room wall.

When Michael and I were little and were upset with each other, she would sit us at the kitchen table, serve us a glass of chocolate milk, and get us to talk out the problem. Although back then, it was only Michael and me who had the milk.

I tighten my hold on the glass as if that will send me back in time so I can see my brother again. So that I can appreciate him more, knowing that his life will be cut short.

"I'm not sure where to begin." Mom takes a sip of her milk, and her mouth slips into a satisfied smile. "I forgot how good this stuff tastes."

The corners of my own mouth twitch. "Since when do you drink chocolate milk?"

Her smile widens. "After you and your brother resolved your battles over a glass of chocolate milk, you would go to bed, and that's when I got to sneak some." She sets her glass down on the coffee table. "I'm not sure where to start: Marcus or your father."

My muscles tense, and I have to push down the desire to walk out the front door. When she called this morning and told me she needed to talk to me, I'd thought she meant about the upcoming court case. I was willing to meet her for that. "You didn't ask me to come 'cause you want to talk about the case?"

"We can discuss it if you want. *After* we talk about Marcus and your father and how I failed you in every possible way when I tried to protect you from getting hurt and making the same mistakes I did."

"What mistakes are those?"

She leans back on the couch. I don't. I twist around to face her, but that's as close to relaxing as I can get.

This isn't the mother I remember growing up with after my father left us. That woman would turn the point she was making into a court case, standing on her feet and making eye contact with each juror.

"I loved your father very much. When he left us with no explanation, it nearly destroyed me. I had no idea what I'd done wrong, because he didn't tell me anything. So I thought he was intimidated by my success as a lawyer and couldn't handle it anymore. I believed that was why he left me. I never wanted another man to make me feel like I had to be less than I am in order to be loved, so I never dated after that. I didn't trust myself not to repeat the same mistake.

"I wanted to prevent the same thing from happening to you, Amber. I didn't say anything when it came to Trent because you two were friends long before you started dating. Plus, I had been so wrapped up in work, I was the last person to realize you two were together as more than just friends."

She picks up her glass but doesn't drink from it. She just stares at the contents. "I didn't know your father had cancer. Either time. And when he began sending you the letters, I didn't want him to break your heart again. Once was enough. I was a defense lawyer, so I slotted him in with the sort of man who does bad things regardless of whom it hurts. I imagined your father had turned into one of those men and was only contacting you because he wanted something from you. Not love, but money or information or something along those lines."

Her gaze lifts to mine, and the pain I see in them is a twisted knife to the heart. "I was going to throw away the letters he sent you and your brother, but I wanted your father to believe that neither of you wished to have anything to do with him. So I sent them back to him unopened, hoping he would leave you alone. Eventually, he stopped sending them, and I thought I'd been right all along. I thought I had done the right thing.

"I took the distrust that resulted from your father's actions, from his inability to tell me the truth, and turned it on Marcus. I never really gave him a chance, even from the beginning. But when the 'porn video' of him surfaced, all I could think about was the defense clients who claim they're innocent when they're far from it. I forgot the basic fundamentals of a fair trial: innocent until proven guilty. I wanted him out of your life before he could hurt you like your father hurt us both. I was wrong, and I'm sorry, Amber. Marcus wasn't the one who hurt you. That was all on me.

"I don't blame you if you can't forgive me for everything I did. I convinced myself I was protecting you, especially after I was unable to protect you from Paul Carlson. But you're no longer my little girl. You're a woman. An intelligent woman. It's about time I treat you that way." She takes a long sip of her milk, her cue that it is my turn to speak.

I release a soft breath, the earlier tension in my muscles already drained during her confession. "I wish Dad had told us the truth from the beginning. You weren't the only one who made mistakes because of his actions. I loved Trent, but I never fully let him in as much as he deserved. A small part of me expected him to walk out of my life the way Dad had. And it was no different with Marcus. Up until I talked to Dad the day he died, I kept expecting Marcus to decide he'd had enough of me because I was broken. I kept expecting him to dump me because I wasn't enough for him."

Mom cringes. "And I didn't help the situation any."

I shake my head, the movement barely visible. "No, you didn't. But even then, he proved to me repeatedly that he loves me and that I mean everything to him. He's a better man than Dad was, and I hope you give him a chance. *Really* give him a chance, because I don't see him leaving my life any time soon."

She smiles, and there's no doubt in my heart the action is genuine. "I can do that."

I smile in return. "Thank you. And I do forgive you. I understand now why you acted that way." I place my half-empty glass of milk on the coffee table and hug her. I'll soon be facing my worst nightmare from last year in court, but at least things are better between my mother and me.

44

AMBER

Paul looks nothing like I remember. Gone is the disheveled guy who haunts my nightmares. Gone is the twenty-five-year-old who wore casual shirts and jeans when he volunteered at the animal shelter. Gone is the sweet guy I trusted with my friendship.

The Paul sitting next to his lawyer is nothing like those versions. This version is dressed in a suit and his light-brown hair has been trimmed short. If this were any other situation, I might have thought he was possibly another lawyer waiting for his client to enter the courtroom.

Except I know better.

This is the same thought I've had since I first saw him during the opening arguments, and during everything up till now. But I can't help but compare this man to the one I once knew as my friend.

"Amber." The DA pulls my attention away from Paul. But even though my gaze is not directed on him, I can feel his eyes fixated on me. Searching for my weaknesses. Searching for the best way to break me.

I can barely breathe. I'm trapped in the basement all over again.

Waiting. Praying. Knowing it's going to end soon. Knowing I'll die when that moment comes.

My hands start shaking. *I can do this. I just have to survive all the questioning.*

Now if only I can convince myself of that.

I glance at the people sitting behind the DA's table. My mother, Grandma, Marcus, Emma, Liam, Jordan, Chase, and Brittany are all watching. Grandma Lily isn't here, but she phoned me this morning to let me know that she's thinking about me and to remind me that she loves me.

Emma looks like she's going to be sick, and I hate that she has to be here. She never met Paul, but she's a witness for the DA They want to throw a shadow of a doubt that Paul and I were involved in anything beyond friendship, contrary to what the rumors claim. Melissa, my former teammate, is listed as a witness for the defense.

I shake my head at how far she's willing to take the lie. Doesn't she realize she could go to jail for perjury?

"Amber," the DA repeats, "on the night you had a flat tire, in your words, please tell the court what happened."

I dig my fingernails into my legs, willing myself not to break down. Not here. Not now. I swallow past the basketball-sized lump in my throat and glance once more at Marcus. He gives me a reassuring smile, telling me I can do it. He knows I can.

"I had basketball practice that evening at my high school. Once it was over, I drove home. But on my way I had a flat tire and had to pull over. It was dark and raining, and I had no idea how to change the tire, so I called my brother, Michael. He said he would be right there. While I was waiting, a midsized blue car parked behind me. Paul got out and asked me what happened. I told him I had a flat tire, and he offered to fix it. He returned to his car, and that's when Michael showed up. He parked his car in front of mine."

My stomach clenches at what comes next. I fight the urge to be sick. "He asked me who the other car belonged to, and I told him. Paul was still in his car when Michael opened my trunk and removed the spare tire." I squeeze my eyes shut. "Paul finally got out of the car again when Michael started changing the tire. He walked behind Michael and raised his arm. I didn't have a chance to warn my brother before Paul shot him in the back."

I flinch at the sound of the gunshot in my head. "He shot him again." My voice cracks. "And again. And again." I open my eyes and the tears I was holding back flood my face. "Michael slumped to the ground, and I ran to him. Screaming. I didn't know what to do and I didn't know why Paul shot him. He didn't even know my brother."

"Then what happened?" the DA asks, her tone full of sympathy.

"I kept telling Michael to hold on, help was on the way, even though I knew it wasn't. My cell phone was in the car and I was too scared to leave him alone with Paul. I begged Paul to call nine-one-one, but he didn't move. I stood up to get my phone and something hard hit me from behind. That's all I remember." I start sobbing. I can't stop.

I cover my face with my hands and let my heart break as I watch in my head the image of Michael bleeding to death—and know there's nothing I can do to stop it.

A loud hammering, which is not much louder than my heartbeat, intrudes on my pain. The judge says something about a ten-minute recess while the witness pulls herself together, but I don't know if I can. This is only the beginning of the trial. This is only the beginning of my having to recount my story and each of its painful memories. And right now, all I want to do is curl up and die. Like I came close to doing so many times as Paul's prisoner.

Everyone, including Paul, leaves the courtroom, and I'm vaguely aware that the DA is talking to me. I think about the lotus tattoo on my back and the charm Marcus gave me, and how the flower symbolizes strength and rebirth. I lived through hell, but I survived. And it made me stronger. Strong enough to make sure Paul is locked away forever.

I breathe in deeply and accept the glass of water the DA's assistant hands me.

"Do you think you can continue?" the DA asks as I take a sip of water.

I nod. "I'm sorry. I'll do better. I swear."

A crack reveals itself in her hard demeanor and she manages a small smile. "You're doing fine, Amber, given the circumstances. No one expects this to be easy for you. You've been through so much. Just hold on for as long as you can, okay? It's my job to make sure Mr. Carlson pays for all his crimes against you, your brother, and your boyfriend." She rests her hand on my arm, and I absorb any extra strength she's willing to share.

Everyone returns to the courtroom. My family, friends, and Marcus all throw me worried glances, poorly disguised by their you're-doing-well masks. I nod at them, then pretend no one else in the room exists, other than the judge, lawyers, and Paul. And I'd be happier if I could pretend he's not in his seat, watching me with the empty expression on his face.

Behind him is a woman a few years older than me, with the same light-coppery-brown hair as Paul. She's studying me, a mix of emotions on her face, none of which I can get a firm grip on.

I tear my gaze from the woman who has done nothing but destroy me with her lies about the love letters I never wrote. Unlike the ones Paul sent me, which were printed from a computer, her fake ones were handwritten and will be included into evidence, unless the FBI gets back to the DA soon. Mom was able to pull in a few favors, and now they have the one major piece of evidence the case pivots around.

I'm not the one on trial. Paul is. I didn't do anything wrong. I repeat the words several times in my head while toying with the lotus flower charm on my bracelet.

"Amber." The defense lawyer's voice is smooth as if he's on my side. But I know better.

I've spent over an hour answering the DA's questions about

everything that happened to me during the time I was held captive. I couldn't even look at the spectators or the jurors, humiliation burning on my face. Now it's the defense's turn to cross-examine me.

"You claim you didn't write the letters to Mr. Carlson in which you professed your love and suggested what sexual acts you wanted him to perform on you."

"That's right." Exhaustion sits heavy on me. I fight to keep it from creeping into my voice.

"Then why does the police expert claim your handwriting and that of the letter is a match?"

"He made a mistake. I didn't write those letters. I've never written a love letter. Ever."

"Not even to a boyfriend?"

"Not even to a boyfriend," I say firmly.

"So, if you didn't write them, who did?"

I shrug. "I don't know. Maybe Paul's sister, since she was the one who supposedly found them."

He nods, but it's not to agree with me. He's pretending to be thoughtful. "The police expert compared her writing with that of the letters, and they were not a match. That means you're the only person who could have written them."

"Your Honor," the DA says, "does Mr. Bischoff have a question for the witness?"

The judge looks sternly at the defense. "Your question, Mr. Bischoff?"

The asshole nods. "According to you, Miss Scott, Mr. Carlson whipped your back. Is that correct?"

"You saw the pictures." After I was found, the ER physicians took tons of photos of my body from all angles. I've seen the ones of my back. The skin was raw, sliced open, bleeding, and showed signs of infection. Marcus and Emma didn't see them, but they could tell from the jurors' expressions the pictures were bad.

"I did, and I'm sorry my client didn't have the clear mind to take you to the hospital after the sexual act you wanted him to perform on you went awry."

"Objection!" The DA stands abruptly. "The pictures clearly show signs of physical abuse inflicted on Miss Scott, not a sexual act she willingly partook in."

"Approach the bench." The judge's tone warrants no argument.

They do as instructed, leaving everyone in the courtroom to wonder what the heck's going on. I can't believe the asshole lawyer is trying to make it sound like I wanted Paul to abuse me. How Mom managed to sleep at night when she was a defense lawyer is beyond me. No wonder she started drinking after I was brutalized, knowing Paul was the type of person she often claimed was innocent, the type she often defended.

The lawyers walk away from the judge after a heated discussion.

"Miss Scott," the man I'm beginning to hate with everything inside me says, "according to the medical report from the ER physician on duty, there were no internal or external signs indicative of rape. Photos entered as evidence also fail to show signs of rape. Is it true you were not raped and all sexual intercourse between you and Mr. Carlson was consensual?"

"Objection!"

"Overruled," the judge says, "but I'm warning you, Mr. Bischoff, to proceed with caution."

I swallow back the memories but can't stop the tears. I brush my hand against my cheek. "By the time Paul had decided to stop punishing me for not talking to him and refusing to eat, I barely had enough will to live, let alone fight him off. And I knew if I tried to fight him, I'd lose. He would rape me and he would kill Smoky."

"Smoky being the kitten Mr. Carlson gave you because you had always wanted a pet?"

"Yes."

The asshole lawyer puffs out his chest. "So Mr. Carlson gifted you a kitten and you had consensual sex. That doesn't sound like the makings of a murderer as you want the court to believe."

I look at Mom and remember what Dad said, that she'll never let me down. And I can't let her down. I need to fight. Fight and show everyone there's a reason I survived. A reason Paul is on trial.

"I never said the sex was consensual. Not in the sense that most people here would describe it," I respond, finally finding my voice, like when I presented in class, like when I talked at the candlelight vigil, and like when I spoke on live TV. "I knew if I didn't do what he wanted, he would kill me. That doesn't make it consensual. That makes it self-preservation." I sit straighter, gaze locked on the asshole lawyer, staring him into a million pieces.

"I wanted to live and the only way I could do that was to be a 'willing' "—I finger-quote the last word—"partner. Please do not take it to mean I wanted to have sex with him. I didn't. I wanted to live and return to my family. Show me in what law book it says that's a crime. Show me, Mr. Bischoff, the law book where it says it's against the law to have sex in order to stay alive, because if you don't, the man will kill you." My voice grows stronger with each word, each sentence.

"Show me where it says I'm not a victim because I had sex to stay alive. And just so you know, because you want the intimate details of my sex life with Paul, I cried while I was having sex with him. I cried when he was done and left me numb on the bed. I cried when I was positive I couldn't do it anymore.

"Maybe this is how women respond when they have sex with you, but I assure you, Mr. Bischoff, this is not the response of a female who is enjoying the act."

Asshole Lawyer turns a brilliant shade of red, but the majority of the people nod their approval.

I expect the judge to strike the gravel and call me in contempt, but all he says is, "Mr. Bischoff, do you have any more questions for the witness?"

"Yes, Your Honor, I do." He turns to me. "If you wanted him to stop, then why didn't you use your safe word? If you had used it, he would have known the sexual fantasy was over and he would have stopped."

Mom had prepared me for this question; otherwise, I'd have no idea what he's talking about. "I didn't have a safe word because I never consented to any sexual role-play."

"It's in the letters you wrote to Mr. Carlson."

My heart stops beating and all the blood drains to my feet. "The letters I didn't write," I counter.

Asshole Lawyer smirks. He knows I'm screwed. Whoever forged the letters included a safe word. If I claim I used it, the abuse will be considered criminal instead of a sexual role-play, and therefore Paul raped me. But it means I have to lie and admit to writing the letters. "I don't have any more questions." He walks back to his seat.

The euphoria from besting him at his game vanishes, and I return to my friends and family.

Marcus leans over and whispers, "You did great, Kitten." He threads his fingers with mine, and his warm hand reminds me I'm not alone. No matter what the outcome, he'll be there for me.

My chest tightens. Even if Paul gets a reduced sentence and is eventually free to stalk me again, Marcus will be there for me. And then both our lives will be at risk.

The police officer who was on duty when Trent's wrecked car was found is called to testify. He's listed as a witness for the defense.

"What did you find when you approached the vehicle?" Asshole Lawyer asks.

"There was a teenage boy trapped in the mangled wreck. He was unresponsive when I checked him. He died en route to the hospital."

Struggling to hold back a sob, I tighten my hold on Marcus's hand, to the point I'm positive I'm crushing his bones. He doesn't try to loosen my grip.

"Did you find anything else? Like evidence that Mr. Carlson was responsible for causing the accident?"

"No. There was nothing in the car other than Trent Kincaid and a dead crow. It was believed to have been hit by the vehicle when it lost control, and the crow wound up inside when the windshield shattered. Its neck was broken."

The prison door opens and a crow flies in. I have no idea which one of us is more scared.

It swoops around, looking for a place to escape. Its squawks and cries for help are deafening. As much as I want to, I can't block out the sound. My arms are handcuffed to the wall.

I start screaming for it to stop. I just want it to stop. Someone, please make it stop.

Paul enters the room. "Don't worry, Amber. I won't let it hurt you. Just like I didn't let Trent continue to hurt you."

"What are you talking about?" I scream.

He doesn't answer. He grabs the bird as it flies close to him. It frantically beats its wings in a mad attempt to escape, but it fails and Paul snaps its neck. In that simple move, he says more than words could say.

I scream once more, but this time I can't stop.

45

MARCUS

Amber pulls her knees to her chest, becoming as small as possible. She's staring ahead, but I have a feeling she doesn't see the short wall separating us from the DA.

Then her arms start flailing, knocking away an invisible foe, her eyes wild.

"It's okay, Amber," I tell her. "You're safe." I keep repeating it as her mom and I duck, narrowly escaping being hit in the face by Amber's hands. But my words have no impact; she begins screaming.

Careful to avoid touching her wrists, I gently grab her arms and continue telling her she's safe. The murmur of curious onlookers builds in intensity.

"What's happening?" Jordan's concerned whisper breaks through the noise. Emma answers her question even though she has no idea either.

The sound is interrupted by the banging of the gavel and the judge calling for order. The loud murmur of voices dies away.

I wrap my arms around Amber's trembling body while I continue trying to comfort her with my words.

She blinks herself to awareness as her screams fade away. The trembling's still there, but it's not as bad as before.

Once she's finally able to talk, she whispers, "I remembered something. I remembered about a crow in my prison. And Paul."

The DA turns to us, and Amber's mom leans forward and tells her what happened. The woman nods, turns to the front, and stands. "Your Honor. We would like to call for a recess. Miss Scott remembers something important to the case. I need a few minutes to talk to her."

The judge looks at Amber. Her face is pale, making the dark circles under her eyes stand out more. "All right. It's getting late. We'll adjourn for the day. You can interview her in my chambers."

The shithead defense doesn't appear too thrilled with the outcome. Behind them, a girl who could easily be the psychopath's sister glances at Amber. For a second I swear the emotion in her eyes flashes to fear. But the change in her was so fast, I can't be sure. She catches me watching her and quickly returns her attention to her brother.

During the trial, my anger has progressed from a simmer to a full-out boil. It's taken a small miracle to keep me from jumping over the wall and pounding on the psychopath. I haven't been able to see his face and his reactions to what Amber's been saying, but my imagination is pretty vivid.

He's led away in handcuffs; his lawyer trails behind. Once he's gone, the DA escorts Amber, her mom, and me into another room.

"Take a seat, please." The DA sits in the chair behind the desk. I sense she'd prefer I wasn't here but has resigned herself to the fact that Amber needs me, like she needs the DA to be on her side.

"Can you tell us what you remember?" the woman asks her.

Amber closes her eyes and grows pale. "I remembered something that happened when the cop mentioned the dead crow." She reopens her eyes, but the color in her cheeks doesn't return.

The DA nods for her to continue.

"Paul released a crow into the prison he kept me in. He told me he wouldn't let the bird hurt me. Just like he hadn't let Trent continue to hurt me. Then he grabbed the freaked-out bird and broke its neck."

"And you've never told anyone this before?" I ask. The DA flashes me a warning glance.

Amber shakes her head. "I'd blocked it out until now." Her gaze takes in each of us in turn. "Do you think it's important?"

"It might be." The DA asks Amber more questions about what happened.

I give a snort of disgust once they've finished. "His fuckhead lawyer is doing a great job making him look innocent because of mental issues," I snap, unable to hold back any longer. I've moved way past full-out boil and have ventured into scorching fire. "The psychopath doesn't need to be in a cozy psych ward. He needs to go to jail. For good."

He needs to be locked away where there's no chance in hell he'll ever be free. Where there's no chance in hell he can hurt Amber again.

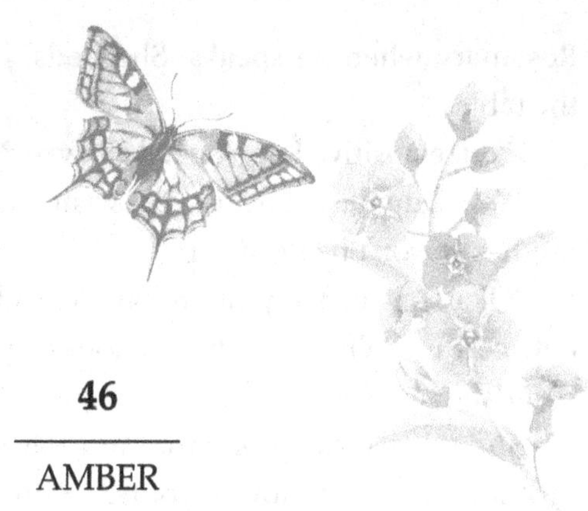

46

AMBER

The interrogation-room walls close in on me. I should be in court, watching the trial. So why are Marcus and I waiting to talk to someone, but the cops won't tell me who it is—or why?

Marcus wasn't invited to join me, but since he refuses to leave my side, the cops caved in to his demands in the end. And although Mom has been assured that I'm not in trouble and don't need a lawyer, Marcus isn't as easily convinced. He doesn't trust cops. I can't say I blame him given everything we've both been through.

The door opens and a detective I recognize enters, followed by Rosemary Carlson, Paul's sister, wearing a waitressing uniform. She's paler than yesterday. Paler and drained. Drained of her life. Drained of her spirit.

The cop pulls out the seat across from me and tells Rosemary to sit. He sits next to her, on the short side of the table.

"Miss Carlson insisted on talking to you, and given what she has to say, I thought you'd be interested in listening. And even though she has declined to have a lawyer here, everything she says will still go on record. Is that understood?" His gaze is directed at

Rosemary when he speaks. She nods, her eyes staring blankly at the table.

"You're positive I don't need a lawyer?" I ask.

"You can have one if you wish, but as I explained to your mother, it won't be necessary."

"Okay." I turn my attention to Paul's sister. Silence stretches between us. When she finally looks up, my eyes are met by her bloodshot ones.

She takes a deep breath. "You have to understand, I love my brothers, like you loved yours." Pain flickers on her face and understanding mists her eyes. She glances down at the table. "After our mom died, Paul gave up everything to care for me and our younger brother. I don't know how we would have survived without him. But then Jacob was diagnosed with cancer. We could barely afford the treatments. I didn't realize at the time we could only afford them because Paul had come off *his* meds. He loved his brother so much, he was willing to risk everything to save him.

"And then Paul disappeared. I had no idea where he had gone, and neither did Jacob. We received the occasional note saying he was okay, but that was it." She wipes away a tear and finally turns her gaze up to mine. "It wasn't until he was arrested for your kidnapping and the murders that I learned where he'd gone. I wanted to contact you and apologize for everything my brother had done, but his lawyer said it would be better for all concerned if I left you alone. I figured he was right. You were recovering in the hospital. The last thing you needed was for me to bring up bad memories."

Her words and pain stun me, but it still doesn't explain the letters I never wrote. I'm about to point that out, but she continues speaking.

"Until two months ago, it looked like Jacob had gone into remission. But then he had a relapse and his new treatment regimen required tougher, more expensive therapy. We couldn't afford it, and I was positive he would die." She lets out a sob that threatens to rip into my heart.

My vision blurs. Part of me wants to touch her hands folded on the table, to let her know I'm sorry...but I hold back. Instead, I grab Marcus's hand resting on my thigh.

I want to ask her about the letters but sense that part of the story is coming. She was found innocent of writing them, though I suspect there's a lot more we don't know. At no point has she asked for the money she desperately needs to save her brother.

"A few weeks ago," she continues, "a reporter approached me. She had found out about me and Jacob while researching a story she wanted to write about Paul. She offered me money to help her. In return, she would pay for Jacob's therapy, and she would pay for a better lawyer for Paul. All I wanted was for my family to be together."

"She wrote the letters?"

Rosemary shakes her head. "No, but she knew someone who could forge them."

"What reporter?" Marcus asks.

"Her name's Angelina Mathews. She works for Channel Four News."

Marcus and I exchange looks and shrug. The name's familiar, but that's all I've got.

The cop removes a page from the file in his hand and places it on the table. It's a mug shot of a woman in her late twenties with long dark brown hair.

"I know her," Marcus says. "She harassed me at the grocery store one day and asked if it was true that we participated in violent forms of sexual activity."

Angelina's been busy. "She tracked me down on campus while I was playing basketball with Emma, and asked what I thought about your sex video. That was before I knew there *was* a sex video."

"She was arrested this morning and her condo was searched.

We now have a suspect for the video." The cop nods at Marcus. "You'll be hearing from us soon on that matter, but according to the suspect, she approached Ms. Mathews with the video. At that point, it was only you and the suspect in the video. Ms. Mathews offered her a much better deal if the suspect participated in the much more elaborate production. The original version wasn't enough for what Ms. Mathews needed. In comparison, it was tame. She was also involved in the editing of the final product."

"But why?" I ask. "Why would she do all of this? It's not like she got anything out of it."

"We're still trying to piece together her motive, but I suspect it's career motivated. She was getting exclusives on the stories because she knew about them first. There will also be an internal investigation since evidence was released to her that should never have been."

He places several pages of lined paper with writing on them in front of me. "Do these look familiar?"

I study them and nod. "They're my sociology notes from last semester."

"They were found in Miss Mathews's condo."

Dizziness washes through me and I tighten my grip on Marcus's hand. "She broke into my dorm room and stole my notes. But why?"

"She needed samples of your handwriting so the letters could be forged. We also found these." He places on the table magazines similar to the ones found in my room when the cops searched it.

"What does this mean now for the trial against Paul?"

"That's for the courts to decide, but I suspect much of Mr. Carlson's defense has been destroyed in light of these new allegations."

My next question is directed at Rosemary. "Why now? Why are you telling the truth now when you could have kept quiet, and your brother might have been given a reduced sentence?" And she wouldn't be in trouble for obstructing the investigation and knowingly providing false information.

"Because you're not the same person Angelina described you as. She lied and manipulated me into believing you had used my brother when you didn't care about him. Yesterday I heard about what you two are doing for the Little Heroes Center with the basketball game.

"And when you started talking about how you had sex with my brother just to stay alive, and then you had the panic attack in court, I knew the lies Angelina had been feeding me couldn't possibly be true. I wanted to believe my brother wasn't capable of what he's been accused of. He's my brother after all. And I love him. I wanted to believe the best about him, but I realized it wasn't enough."

She gives me a sad smile. "I'm sorry for everything my brother did to you, and for what *I* did to you. I don't expect you to ever forgive me, but I wanted you to know that I am sorry."

AFTER A GRUELING, WEEK-LONG TRIAL, AND TWO DAYS OF JURY deliberation, the head juror stands, and I hold my breath, my fingers grasping the life out of Marcus's hand.

"Do you have a verdict for the charges against Paul Carlson?" the judge asks.

"We do. On the charge of aggravated kidnapping of Amber Scott, we the jury find the defendant, Paul Carlson, guilty but mentally ill. On the charge of forced confinement, we find the defendant guilty but mentally ill. On the charge of five counts of rape, we find the defendant guilty but mentally ill. On the charge of the murder of Trent Kincaid, we find the defendant guilty but mentally ill. On the charge of the murder of Michael Scott, we find the defendant guilty..." The juror lists more charges, the majority of which Paul is found guilty.

A sob escapes me as I sit, stunned, absorbing the verdict. Piecing together what this all means. It's only when Marcus hugs me, and tells me I won, that I come to life. Still sobbing, I hug him back; then I hug Mom. I want to hug Emma and her family, too, but the judge has more to say.

My heart goes out to Rosemary and Jacob, especially Jacob. Despite what Paul did, his family doesn't deserve to be hurt the way it was in the end. If it hadn't been for Angelina's greed at advancing her career, regardless of what it cost everyone else, the worst they would be facing would be Paul locked away.

Now, Rosemary faces jail time while her younger brother battles cancer.

No one deserves that.

47

MARCUS

Amber and I watch from the sidelines as Emma waddles down the court in her oversized duck feet, dribbling the ball. The sold-out audience laughs and cheers her on.

As she gets close to the three-point line, she passes the ball to Eric, who is dressed as a fairy princess. In basketball shoes. The women participating in the event argued he should be in heels, but good luck finding those for a six-foot-seven-inch man. Plus, the Chicago Bulls would have been royally pissed if he had fucked up his ankle or knee.

But even without the heels, he looks hilarious as his hooped skirt flips up at the front and reveals his...basketball shorts.

Beside me, Amber is grinning, free of everything weighing her down for the past year, especially after Paul was sentenced to life. He'll never be able to stalk and terrorize her again. She's a different girl now but also the same one I fell in love with. Dressed in an overstuffed bunny costume and floppy ears, she bounces in her seat, cheering. And shit, even in that outfit she's sexy as hell.

Eric catches the pass and makes the shot. Amber jumps around, screaming for her best friend's team. Our team.

I glance at Matt and Alejandro on the bottom bleacher. Like

285

Amber, they're freer than they've been in a while. Thanks to both boys, who found the strength to tell the cops what happened, Frank is currently serving time while he awaits his trial for multiple counts of rape, sexual assault, murder, and attempted murder.

I wrap my arm around Amber's shoulders. She leans into me, letting me fully into her heart. The place I've longed to be ever since I offered to tutor her in math and she told me where to go. I knew even then there was something different about her, something special.

She smiles at me. I cover her mouth with mine.

As I slip my tongue into her mouth and taste her minty breath, the crowd cheers. Without looking, I know someone made a basket, but a small part of me pretends the crowd is cheering for Amber and me, and for how far we've come—both separately and together.

But I'm not going it alone. I finally gave in to Amber's insistence that I need professional help. She was right. I do.

Someone nudges my arm. Reluctantly, I pull away from her.

"We're up." Liam stands. He's dressed in a sexy French maid costume. In sneakers. I'm dressed as a genie. As in *I Dream of Jeannie*. Complete with a pink bikini top stuffed with socks.

We swap places with Eric and Emma. Emma and Liam exchange a quick kiss. Eric and I high-five.

One of my teammates tosses me the ball, and I dribble the length of the court, dodging past the opposition. I pass the ball to a player from the women's soccer team.

She moves the ball closer to the hoop, then fake passes it to Liam before passing it to me. The audience counts down the time. Five seconds left. The score is tied.

I jump up and send the ball flying toward the basket. My shoulder, the one Frank shot over four months ago, aches in protest, but I don't care. It's worth it in light of everything I've been through.

We watch the ball spin in slow motion, and as the buzzer

announces the end of the game, the ball whooshes through the hoop. The crowd cheers and all the players run onto the court.

We all hug or high-five. It doesn't matter which team won. The real winners are the kids who will be helped. The charity game raised both money and awareness of sexual abuse in kids. Having me and Eric step forward helped, too. Now kids know it's okay to break the silence.

The total money raised hasn't been finalized yet. The online silent auction won't close until midnight, but with the ticket sales for the game alone, we've raised way more than we imagined we would in the beginning.

As the players spread out and sign autographs for the fans, members of the media head toward us.

I take hold of Amber's hand. "You ready for this?"

She smiles at me, the confidence in her expression breathtaking. "Absolutely!"

EPILOGUE

AMBER

Spring symbolizes a new beginning, a new rebirth. Maybe that's true. Maybe it isn't. I do know it has brought us the warm weather that welcomes Marcus and me as we make our way through the cemetery.

With the birds chirping like a choir of angels, I tighten my hold on the bouquet of white and red tulips. Marcus leads me to the spot he regularly visits. It's the first time I've been here.

To Ryan's final resting place.

"This is it." The excitement in Marcus's voice is an odd contrast to the place of death and sadness. He hugs me close as we examine the large gravestone's glossy black surface. "Ryan, I'd like to introduce you to the girl I love. Amber, this is Ryan." A bird in a nearby tree tweets in reply.

Marcus smiles as he takes in Ryan's gravestone, the one that brought Marcus and me together. Or rather, the lack of one that brought us together. If Ryan hadn't died, or if his parents hadn't refused to pay for it, Marcus and I would never have gotten together. He would never have had a reason to spend time with me, beyond trying to get me into bed with him, which would never have happened.

The complete opposite of how things are now. Now I miss him when we aren't together, in bed or otherwise.

It's not that I'm incomplete without Marcus, like how Ryan's grave was without the gravestone. But Marcus is my best friend and my lover, the guy who makes me laugh and makes me feel special.

Marcus is my life...and my future.

NOTE FROM AUTHOR

Dear Reader,

The topic of mental illness is dear to me. It's also one that is complex and often misunderstood. It includes a vast array of diagnoses, each facing its own challenges and stigmas.

One of my adult kids deals with mental illness. They have for many years now, ever since they were first diagnosed as a preteen. They take several prescriptions a day in order to function. These drugs aren't cheap and they come with side effects. Some of these side effects impact their quality of life. Like with any medication, it's a balance. You have to weigh the pros and the cons. For my child, the pros outweigh the cons. They chooses to be on the drugs.

Other individuals, though, would rather stop taking their medications than deal with the side effects or the additional costs. The consequences of this can be severe, depending on the individual's diagnosis.

In a perfect world, no one would have to deal with mental illness. And if we did, we wouldn't be burdened with the high cost of the drugs. In its present state, the health care system fails to help those who are most vulnerable. So many people struggle to get help, but there aren't enough resources to handle the current load (which was made worse with the pandemic). Maybe you even know someone in this position—possibly you aren't even aware of it.

For some people, their mental illness is a short-term crisis that will eventually be resolved. For others, it's with them for life. While you might not be able to cure mental illness, you can show compassion and understanding. You can show these individuals love and respect.

Stina

READ ON FOR AN EXCERPT FROM THIS ONE MOMENT

NOLAN

The arena locker room crackled with unspent energy. I grabbed my guitar and strummed a few random chords, experimenting more than anything.

But it wasn't enough.

I'd been edgy for the past hour. Normally it wasn't like this before our band, Pushing Limits, took the stage. Usually I could clear my head of everything that didn't belong there before the show began. Then all that mattered was the music and the fans.

I closed my eyes and pretended the stale air didn't smell like hockey players fresh off the ice after an intensive workout. Instead, the room reminded me of sugar cookies. A room from my distant past.

The random chords transformed into the melody I'd been playing around with for the last two days, after I'd managed to sneak off somewhere quiet.

"Dude, that's really good." Mason drummed along, tapping the beat on his knees.

I stopped playing and cracked open my eyelids, the moment over.

The tattooed drummer draped his arms around the shoulders of the two groupies cuddled up to him. "Hey, why'd you stop?"

"He's right," Jared said, eyes gleaming like those of a pirate who'd just discovered buried treasure. "You've been holding back on me."

I returned the guitar to its case and propped it next to me on the wooden bench running along the wall. "Sorry, that's all I've got so far." Which was a huge amount compared to what I'd written over the past few months. Touring wasn't exactly productive for songwriting.

My phone buzzed in my rear jeans pocket. I removed it and checked who'd texted me. Brandon, my best friend from back home.

Brandon: Call me! It's important.

I ignored the text and shoved the phone back into my pocket. I'd deal with it later, after the show.

Resting my head against the cold concrete wall, I closed my eyes again. Exhaustion sat on the bench beside me, ready to crash the party as the five of us prepared to go onstage. And it wasn't just hanging around me. I'd seen it on the guys' faces for the past few weeks. The next stop on this touring train? An extra-long break with a side order of sleep.

Giggles broke out across from me. I peered through half-closed eyes at Mason and his friends. The blond groupie sitting next to him pushed herself off the stained orange couch and walked over to me, her gaze ripping the plain black T-shirt and jeans off my body.

Not that I was much better.

Her tight Pushing Limits T-shirt, which she'd cut into a tank top, revealed cleavage a guy could easily get lost in. I wouldn't be surprised if Mason had already tried.

"Hi, Tyler. I'm Rachel." She sat next to me and rested her hand on my stomach, just above the waistband of my jeans. My muscles instinctively tightened for a second, then relaxed.

I cocked my head to the side and gave her the lazy grin Mas had dubbed my panty-dropping smile. Hey, whatever worked. "Hi, Rachel. Ready for the show?"

"I'd say," she practically purred. "You're my favorite singer. And guitarist."

I leaned in and murmured against her ear, "Well, thank you."

She sucked in a sharp breath, her fingers curling into my stomach muscles, taut from years of pushing myself to the limit when I worked out. "Wow, you're fit. And hard." The last word came out as a seductive exhale.

Chuckling, I stood. Unlike Mason, I never fucked just before a show. The moment I hit the stage, I was raw energy. Fucking before that would only dull the edge.

I glanced around the room. Mason was busy with the brunette now on his lap. Jared and Aaron were talking to a roadie, Jared flipping a guitar pick between his fingers and across the back of his hand, like he always did just before a show. Kirk was chatting with another groupie who had sweet-talked her way backstage. All the guys were preoccupied, none paying attention to me.

"Maybe I'll see you after the show," I told the blonde. I grabbed my black sports bag from the floor next to my feet and walked to the far end of the bench. Fortunately, she didn't follow me. She returned to the couch, smiling to herself.

I unzipped the bag and removed the laminated photo. The picture was slightly battered between the two plastic sheets, the result of me not having had the foresight to laminate it sooner. Along with my acoustic guitar, which I used for a few songs during the show, I always brought Hailey's picture with me onstage.

A lifeline.

The one nobody knew about.

In it, we were sitting on my bed, both of us seventeen years old. Hailey was holding my guitar on her lap, trying to play it. I was straddling her from behind, repositioning her fingers on the D chord for the tenth time. Hailey was laughing because no matter what she did, the chord always fell flat. That's when my mom had snuck into my room and snapped the photo.

It was the only one I had of Hailey. It was one of the few possessions I'd taken when I escaped my hometown six years ago. Hailey's picture was the only thing that had kept me going all these years.

The dressing room door opened and a roadie entered. He scanned the occupants until his gaze narrowed in on me. "Mr. Remar wants to talk to you."

"Now's not a good time," I told him, slipping the photo into my back jeans pocket.

He shrugged, not having a response, because ultimately it didn't matter if this was a good time or not. If the president of the record label wanted to talk to me, I'd better move my ass and be there five minutes ago. Both the roadie and I knew that.

The guys all made a move for the door. The roadie put his hand up like he was directing traffic. "He only wants to speak with Tyler," he said, referring to me.

I shook my head. "If it has to do with the band, then he needs to talk to all of us."

"You already planning your solo album?" Mason said, laughing.

Jared raised an eyebrow, either echoing Mason's question or silently asking me what this was about. Hell if I knew. Yes, I was the lead singer for Pushing Limits, but the band belonged to both Jared and me. Not only had we created the band five years ago, we'd cowritten half the songs on our debut album. The rest I'd written on my own.

The roadie's sigh was the long impatient sound of someone with a million things to do in the next five minutes. He didn't care either way what we did. He was only the messenger. He'd let Remar chew us out for ignoring the request if that was what we chose to do.

"Can you bring my guitar if I'm not back in time?" I asked Jared, the member of the band least likely to forget my request.

He nodded. Then one corner of his mouth quirked up. "Good luck."

"God, I hope I don't need it."

He patted me sympathetically on the back as I walked out of the room, but he didn't look too disappointed to be missing out on the fun with Remar.

I followed the roadie down the hallway, past the back of the stage. From the sound of it, fans were piling into the arena, screaming and chanting the name of our band as well as the headlining band, Crazy Piper. This was the heart of the building, the love of music pulsating throughout.

Backstage was a rush of people, still preparing for the show. Two bulked-up guys kept a stern eye on things, ever ready for fans trying to sneak backstage. One security guard nodded at me as I walked past, which was more interaction than I was getting from the roadie. He was too busy yapping on his phone about his love life, or lack of, to remember I was with him.

We rode the elevator to the second floor and walked down a surprisingly empty hallway. His cowboy boots clacked against the tile, the sound echoing against the dull brown walls. In contrast to the noisy energy in the dressing room and the arena, here the energy was nonexistent. Sucked away. Forgotten.

If it hadn't been for the roadie talking animatedly on the phone about some lusty brunette he had the hots for, it would've felt like I was being escorted down death row. But while I might've felt like sleeping for all eternity, I suspected that wasn't the reason for my impromptu visit with Remar.

The roadie stopped at a plain black door. The phone in my back pocket buzzed again. I managed to ignore the temptation to check it.

Before I could ask the roadie if this was where I was supposed to meet Remar, he knocked on the door. There was a muffled reply, and the roadie opened the door. He waved me in, then left me to face the three men in the room alone.

Ronald Remar was seated at the opposite end of the long conference table. Two suits, whom I vaguely recognized from our first meeting, flanked him. The tall skinny man had on wire-rimmed glasses, while the dumpy guy looked like he'd been dragged back from his Mexican vacation, where he had taken great pride in getting a bad sunburn. His short white hair was clipped close to his skull and matched Remar's hair perfectly.

The president of the record label waved for me to move closer, but made no indication I should sit.

"You wanted to talk to me?" I didn't know why, but I had a feeling I wouldn't like what he had to tell me. Especially since my bandmates had been excluded from this little get-together.

"That's right, Mr. Kincaid," Remar said, choosing to use my real name instead of my stage moniker. To the rest of the world, including my bandmates, I was Tyler Erickson.

"The label has decided, based on the tour's success and the success of your last two singles, to move up the release date of your next album," Remar explained. "We want to strike while the band is still hot."

I frowned. "How much earlier are we talking about?"

He leaned forward in his chair, elbows on the table, hands interlocked. His silver Rolex gleamed in the overhead light. "We've booked the studio for December twenty-seventh." In four weeks. Three months ahead of schedule. "We've been extremely lucky to land Daniel Maynard, thanks to his recent divorce." A satisfied smile slithered onto Remar's face, as if he personally was responsible for the demise of the producer's marriage. Although I wouldn't have been surprised if he had been. Rumor had it Remar was on wife number five. Presumably he knew a trick or two about wrecking marriages, especially his own. "You do know who Daniel Maynard is, right?"

Just the greatest producer in the United States when it came to rock music. He had produced the albums of some of my favorite bands, and they'd all gone straight to the top of the charts, every fucking time.

I nodded. "I do."

"Good. Then you understand how important this opportunity is for the band. And how important it is that you're ready to record the album come December twenty-seventh. We've managed to book him for a week. Then he won't be available until the following October. Is it correct to assume you'll be ready?" His tone indicated the question was rhetorical. We would be ready or else our contract would be canceled. That was why the two suits were here: to remind me that if the album wasn't ready when the label expected it to be ready, we could say goodbye to the record deal.

"Don't worry. We'll be ready."

"Perfect. Make sure that you are."

I waited for him to say something more, maybe give me a reason why he wanted to talk to only me instead of the entire band. But after a few seconds it became clear I'd been dismissed.

Relieved to escape the chilly regard of everyone in the room and get ready to do what I lived for, I headed for the door.

"And before I forget," Remar said in the tone of someone who was incapable of forgetting, "there's a reporter here from *Rock News*. I granted her a brief interview with you and the band for after your show. Please don't disappoint her."

"No, sir." I hoped she didn't mind interviewing five guys coming down from an adrenaline high. Five guys who tended to forget their filters while coming down from the high, Mason being the worst of us.

And since when did Remar book our interviews? Our publicist was responsible for that, the same way she was responsible for making sure the world knew me only as Tyler Erickson. Although that wasn't an especially tough a job, even with social media. *Thank you, Mom, for being so gung-ho to home-school me.*

Pushing the thought of Remar from my head, because there

was no point in trying to figure out anything to do with the man, I left the room. I respected his decisions. So far they hadn't been wrong. But next time I saw him, I'd make sure he understood I wasn't the boss of the band. It was a democracy. The band and the music weren't just mine. They belonged to each of us, each adding his own vision to the mix.

No sooner had I shut the door behind me than my phone played a classical tune. *What the hell?* I pulled it from my pocket, mentally kicking myself for letting Aaron borrow the phone. Only he would have reprogrammed it to play classical music.

I checked the screen. Brandon. Again. He knew I had a show tonight, so for him to be this desperate to talk to me meant that whatever he had to tell me was damn important.

"What's up?" I asked, half wondering if it would've been better to ignore the call the way I had ignored his texts.

"Shit, Nolan. I've been trying to get hold of you."

"Yeah, got that. Sorry. Had to meet the president of the label for a little powwow." I pressed the elevator down button. "What's such a big deal it couldn't keep?"

"It's Hailey."

My heart slammed against my rib cage at the urgent sound of his voice. What about Hailey?

"She's in a coma."

THIS ONE MOMENT is now available!

ABOUT THE AUTHOR

Born in Brighton England, Stina Lindenblatt has lived in a number of countries, including England, the US, Finland, and Canada. This would explain her mixed up accent. She has a kinesiology degree and a MSc in sports biological sciences.

In addition to writing fiction, she loves photography, and currently lives in Calgary, Canada, with her husband and three kids.

For news about her books, social media sites, and to sign up for her newsletter, check out her website at stinalindenblattauthor.com. Newsletter subscribers will receive several bonus gifts.

9 781990 177439